# THE SECRET IS OUT

GABRIELLE K. CHEVALIER

# Chapter 1

The moon is bright tonight, you can almost see through the woods without any light or cellphone. I usually loved the woods, but tonight was different and I didn't know why. A light dusting of snow rested on all the tree branches, it was almost too beautiful, even though I was completely terrified. The snow on the ground is so cold I can barely feel my feet or even remember how I got myself out here, or why the hell I was out here in the woods to begin with. The wind blew a cold subtle breeze that felt like knives cutting into my cheeks. My arms were wrapped around my body in hopes of creating any kind of warmth as I glanced around me to find any kind of house or light, but there was nothing. Only miles of trees and bushes covered in a thick white blanket of falling snow. I desperately called out to someone for help, I screamed as loud as my freezing throat would let me. To my fear, I was completely alone.

I walked along what seemed like a path between the trees. It was dead silent in these woods, no cars, no horns, complete emptiness. I knew in my mind I needed to keep looking for anything I could find or I was going to freeze to death and die out here and nobody would even know where I was. The skin-piercing breeze calmed itself down. This made it even quieter as I walked through the thick snow. You could only hear my boots impacting the snow, looking behind me was a short trail of tracks I left that was quickly filling with snow. As I turned forward to make sure I was still walking on a path, that's when I saw it. It looked like a man but I was uncertain. It was maybe 30 feet in front of me. I squinted my eyes to make out if it was a bundle of trees crunched together or if this was indeed a human being.

I called out, "Hello?".

The figure stood there not moving a muscle staring at me. I could feel my heart pounding out of my chest, I was in utter fear. What was this thing standing there glaring at me?

I called out again, "Hello? My name is Charlie and I could really use your help.".

Again there was no answer. I swallowed the saliva accumulating in my mouth and kept walking towards the black shadow man who made no movements or sounds. I was convincing my mind that it was a tree but my gut was twisting telling me to get the fuck out of there. As I crept closer I saw it move. I stopped in my tracks and watched it slowly lifting what looked like an arm. It moved so slowly it was unpredictable what it was doing. I stood there staring at it as it raised an arm and started slowly waving at me. Its elbow moving from side to side at a slow pace as it waved at me. At this moment I knew it was a person. A man.

My heart froze, my entire body was dead still. I couldn't get the courage to speak anymore, I just stood there in utter terror staring at this man. I calculated in my head my odds of getting out of these awful woods. My fight or flight response arguing with each other endlessly. It put its arm down very slowly. It began to walk towards me. It was difficult to see but I could hear its footsteps pressing into the thick snow. I was still standing in my tracks not knowing how to respond. Something clicked in my head at that moment telling me I needed to run. As I turned my body away from the shadow man my head was still facing him, I could finally start to make out facial features. He looked dark, not physically but his eyes looked evil. He had a huge grin that stretched from ear to ear as he approached me. He was not blinking, just a cartoon-like smile across his face as he walked towards me like a dark entity that owned the woods.

I spun around and started to run as fast as I could possibly move in the snow. The pain I felt in my freezing feet and weak knees suddenly went away as I sprinted for my life. I couldn't tell where I was running anymore, I needed to get out of there. I felt my foot lock into a root sticking above the ground and I caved onto a frozen river. I felt my face smash into the ice like hitting a block of cement. I could hear heavy breathing, but this was not my breathing. I looked behind me and saw the man still running to get me, he was breathing so deeply it sounded like a smoker trying to run a marathon.

I got back up and kept running across the river towards a giant hill that was free of trees and looked clear. The hill was physically defeating, it was very steep and I had wet, frozen boots on that felt like they weighed a million pounds. I could hear his breathing getting closer and closer to me and I knew he was gaining on me. I reached a part on the hill that looked like snowmobile tracks had crossed up the hill. There was a thin layer of ice covering where the tracks pressed the snow down and my foot slid backward and I fell into the hill catching myself with my hands. I heard the man let out a zombie-like grunt directly behind me as his hand reached out to clench the back of my coat. I turned my body around still laying on the hill so I could fight my way out or die trying. When I flipped over he was gone. Vanished.

I laid there in complete confusion, looking in every direction to see where he went but there was nothing. I couldn't hear any other breathing other than my own. The hill was big and open and had no trees on it and I had a clear view of everything around me even though it was dark. Nobody. Nothing was moving in the wooded area, no noises, nothing. I still laid there terrified and in shock. I could see his tracks in the snow behind mine, but no shadow man. The snow falling from the sky stopped at that moment. It was once again dead silent all around me. I picked myself up off the ground still looking all around me for the man to come back. As I looked down towards where our tracks came from, back towards the river, I could see him. He was standing in the middle of the river alone slowly waving at me with a comical smile across his face. I stood there staring at him in fear as he waved at me in the distance. Then I heard a leery deep voice behind me say,

"I got you now.".

That's when I wake up. My bed covered in sweat and I can't seem to catch my breath. I sat in my bed gathering my thoughts when I heard my mom yell to me from downstairs.

"Charlie get up and get ready for school please!" She yelled.

I emptied my lungs of air with a big breath out and crawled out of bed dreading school. Grade 8 seemed to be difficult for me. Not very many people liked me and I always seemed to over-extend myself to try to fit in with anyone. I had 2 teachers, we would rotate half the day with one and the other half of the day with the other. My teachers also liked to join in bullying some of their students. You could always tell which students were the favourites and which ones were not. The students that had a hard time memorizing pointless, useless facts were immediately deemed unworthy of respect. While the other students that excelled in school work that wouldn't really help them in life, they were treated amazing and never ridiculed in front of the entire class. This made every day a little dreadful for the non-favourites such as myself. Every day was the same routine; wake up, go to school, get yelled at, come home, eat, sleep, repeat. For some students, coming home wasn't exactly a break from the negative atmosphere they endured all day at school. A student like me.

I started to sift through my closet trying to find the perfect outfit, because maybe if I dressed perfectly people would like me more and I wouldn't have to fake it so much. I plucked out a pair of tight jeans and a plain v-neck t-shirt, then started to straighten my hair and put on my makeup. I always wore my hair straight because I was too uncomfortable doing anything else. By this time my sister Elizabeth (we usually call her Liz) and my brother Drew are gone for high school already. My brother's room was right next to mine along with my parents' room and my sister got the cool room downstairs all on her own. My dad was always gone to work before anyone even got up, he worked really hard in a factory that was a 45-minute drive away.

Making my way downstairs I could smell the waffles my mom put in the toaster for me, this was a morning ritual. She was in the bathroom doing her hair as she got ready for work and she asked me the same question every single day;

"Do I look okay today Charlie?" Mom asked.

"Mom you look amazing every day, I don't know why you bother asking anymore when I always have the same answer." I replied.

My mom was stunning and I was always so confused why she was so self-conscious. All the boys at my school thought she was hot as hell and my sister's guy friends all talked about how our mom had it all going on. I ate my waffles and told mom goodbye and left out the front door to wait for my bus to pick me up. The bus to school was always a drag, there was a boy on there that would repeatedly point out my flaws to everyone on the bus and make fun of me, his name was Stephen. My bus pulled up and the big fat bus man opened the door to let me in. I quietly walked to the middle of the bus with my head down, trying not to draw any attention to myself. I sat in my seat with my headphones in and immediately saw Stephen change seats and sit behind me. He smirked at his friends and made a hand motion pointing at me. I could feel my heart start to pound as I knew some sort of embarrassment was coming my way. As I closed my eyes to try to relax, I felt my left headphone get ripped out of my ear. I turned to see what Stephen was going to point out about me today and accepted that this is how today is going to start.

“Look at those giant moles on her face, you could land a rocket ship on those! You could even play connect the dots with how many there are!” Stephen shouted at his friends while most of the bus laughed out loud at me.

I tried to take my headphones back as he pulled them further and further from me. That’s when I felt it, I could feel my throat start to ache and my face got beet red. Then a single tear fell from my eye down my face as I tried my absolute hardest to swallow every ounce of embarrassment I was experiencing.

“Are you crying! Look now the little baby is crying!” Stephen added as he handed me my headphone back.

I turned back into my seat and looked out the window as I cried. I tried to sink my body as low as I could in the seat so the younger kids in the front couldn’t see me and wonder what some of them had to look forward to. These events happened almost every day on the bus to school, and again on the way home.

As we pulled up to school and I raced out of my bus, we all had to line up at the door to go inside. Our teachers were usually standing outside the doors waiting for everyone to line up. We walked through the corridor all in a straight line to our lockers where we got our books and supplies and proceeded to our desks. We had an oral presentation that each student had to do in front of the entire class, we were allowed to present any subject we wanted as long as it was educational and appropriate. I decided to do my presentation about the Emerald Ash Borer, quite a weird subject for me to choose but this is something that hit home to me. I lived on a hobby farm and we had acres of woods, most of our trees were being killed and thinned out by the new invasive bug Emerald Ash Borer. The woods seemed to be the only place I felt comfortable and felt like myself. I had brought into class a piece of a log from home to show during my presentation what the ash borer does to the trees. I was nervous but I felt confident as I really prepared myself for this project. A few kids went up and did their presentations first, the favourites always got good responses from the teachers. The non-favourites however usually got a passive-aggressive comment about how useless they were. I was looking out the window at the sunshine, glancing off into a total zone out when I heard my teacher call out to me.

“Charlie, it’s your turn now.” Mr. Douglas said.

I nervously grabbed my log and walked to the front of the class. Immediately forgetting everything I knew about the Emerald Ash Borer, I began to stutter my way through my presentation. As I looked around the classroom showing everyone the log from home, I could see Mr. Douglas giving me an impatient look and at that moment I knew that he wasn't impressed. I finished up my presentation as best I could and anxiously walked back to my desk. I felt crappy about how it went because I really thought I prepared myself enough and studied the subject, once I was in front of everyone, I tend to forget everything.

Mr. Douglas shouted, "Charlie you forgot your log in the front of the class!".

I raced back up and retrieved the log to bring back home. As I was walking back toward my desk I heard Mr. Douglas add to his original statement;

"Might as well put the log in your chair instead of yourself, nobody would even notice the difference." he said.

Some students began to silently giggle, some could see the shame in my eyes as I sat in my chair because they also endured regular comments like this and knew what it felt like.

The day was finally over and I was on the bus to go home. The bus stopped in front of my house and I was already waiting at the front of the bus to get off quickly. Drew was home by now and I knew this was the fun part of my day. Drew and I were extremely close siblings, we always felt different than my sister. Drew and I had the same biological dad but my sister had a different dad, he wasn't ever around much so my dad raised her as his own. Walking up the driveway I saw Drew wave me over to the chicken coup, we had our regular chores to take care of daily. Even though they were chores I still really enjoyed this, I liked the animals we had and spending time with my brother. We hurried up to feed the chickens, rabbits, horses, and dogs, then we picked up the poop inside the chicken coop and dog pen. We gathered the eggs from the chickens and brought them inside, saving 3 eggs to give to the dogs as treats.

"Come over here Charlie I want to show you this cool trick I learned how to do on the 4 wheeler." Drew said.

We would usually drive the 4 wheelers together in the trails in the woods behind our house every day. Drew would show me how to change gears properly and how to do donuts or jump the hills and try to get any air. I really looked up to Drew, people always thought we were twins except he was a boy and I was a girl with long hair. We would spend the evenings tinkering outside or in the woods, he showed me cool places around where we lived. Elizabeth was quite different, she kept to herself at home or she was usually out with friends. Sometimes it felt like she hated being home with us or spending time with us. Dad was getting home from work while Drew and I were out driving the 4 wheelers around, and he had some repairs to do to the horse stalls. He always filled his days with stuff that needed to be done. Drew and I never approached him because it was difficult to know what kind of mood he was in, sometimes he was edgy and dismissive, sometimes he was silly and funny.

"Supper is ready everyone!' mom yelled from the back deck.

“Yes Christine.” dad replied.

“Robert make sure you take your work boots off before you come in please, I just cleaned this entire house and I don’t want it full of horse poop!” mom said to dad.

I could see dad roll his eyes as me and Drew walked inside to have supper. We all sat down to eat and it felt like we were all a normal family. It was great to have us all together at one table, and mom usually had something really good to eat. It was always shocking mom could make such good food after working all day and barely ever having any time to do fun things. As she approached the table with our dinner, dad looked at her in frustration.

He slammed his fists on the table, “This is what you made? Breakfast for dinner? Are you a joke? You’re that lazy you can’t even make a real meal? You eat breakfast in the morning like a normal person, not at dinner time!” Dad shouted at her.

We kids sat in silence looking down at the food on the table, we all knew what tonight was going to turn into. I peaked my eyes up to get a glimpse of my mom, she sat sunken down into her seat looking defeated, looking exhausted. Mom stood up and threw all the food on the floor and she cried and ran away towards the stairs to go upstairs. Dad got up saying nothing and quietly walked outside slamming the door behind him. We kids were still sitting at the table in silence, looking at each other with uncomfortable looks on our faces. Mom slowly came back to the table, her eyes beet red but no tears in sight. She always had a good way of hiding her crying and making it seem as if everything was okay all the time. She was like the family rock.

“I’m sorry you kids had to see that.” Mom said in a humbling voice as she picked up the broken plates and splattered egg yolks off the floor.

Drew and I got off our chairs to help clean the floor while Liz got the garbage out from under the sink to put the glass shards in. We were all silent and nobody said a word to each other while cleaning, Dad was still doing whatever the hell he was doing outside. We managed to get the entire kitchen cleaned up like nothing ever happened, but I knew after tonight it wasn’t going to look like this. We all knew in the back of our minds this argument with my parents was not over, it never was over. Drew and I grabbed a quick snack and went upstairs to play video games before bed while Liz went in her room and took out her cell phone to call some friends.

“Make sure you pick up your room Elizabeth, I don’t need this fuelling the fire more with Robert.” mom instructed Liz.

“Yes mom I’ll do what I can, I have a school assignment due tomorrow, so I will try my best.” Liz replied.

Liz stayed in her room with the door shut that night, it wasn’t different than any other night. She usually locked herself in her room to sit and talk with her friends on the phone or to do something along those lines. Drew and I decided to call it a night and go to bed, at least maybe we could try to fall asleep while it was quiet downstairs then maybe we wouldn't have to hear anything. I got up off the floor and put my controller on the ground in front of the TV and head to my room. I crawled into my bed hoping I would fall asleep quickly to avoid hearing the anticipated argument that was about to take place downstairs. As I closed my eyes to try to sleep, the yelling below began. I tossed and turned in my bed trying to find an angle that could block the sound, I resorted to putting the pillow over my head as I laid on my side which seemed to work half decent. Then I felt a tap on my shoulder. I turned over as quickly as I could in fright, who the hell would be tapping me on the shoulder right now? It was Drew.

"Fuck sakes Drew you scared me!" I said trying to calm myself down,

"Want to play a game?" Drew replied.

I knew right away what game he was talking about, we often did this when mom and dad fought to help pass the time.

"I'll go first, I bet dad is going to break a chair this time." Drew said.

"That's what I was going to pick! Stealer! I bet dad will break the rest of the dinner plates this time." I replied jokingly.

We sat together at the top of the stairs anxiously waiting to hear what was happening and who would win the bet this time. You could rarely hear mom when they fought, she usually kept silent. It was normally just a series of dad yelling at her with little pauses in between. You could never fully make out what he was saying, it all muffled together in one loud roar. That's when we heard it; the smash, except this time we both looked at each other in confusion as it was a sound we couldn't make out what it was. That was the first time I ever heard mom yell. I could hear her yelling back at him but I couldn't hear fully what she was saying. She was sobbing uncontrollably, it was the worst thing you could hear from your own mother. We could hear footsteps coming towards the stairs and Drew and I rushed back into our beds so we didn't get caught trying to eavesdrop on their arguing. My bed was in the corner of my room facing the door and I usually slept with the door open a crack to let a little bit of light in. Only mom came up the stairs and made her way into her bedroom, I peeped through the crack and saw her sitting on the end of her bed wiping away her tears and putting her hair into a bun. Dad was still downstairs and the house was quiet for the remainder of the night.

# Chapter 2

My phone alarm went off that morning like a pound of bricks to the face. I sat up to the edge of my bed rubbing my face to mentally prepare for the new day. I walked over to click my straightener on and pick my outfit out for the day, tight jeans and a v-neck t-shirt once again. I could smell the waffles cooking already from upstairs in my room, so I rushed to put my makeup on and make my way downstairs. I hopped down the last step and walked past the bathroom and mom wasn't in it. I questioned myself as to what was going on, as our routine seemed to be different today. Elizabeth's door was also still shut which seemed odd as she and Drew were usually gone for school before I got up.

"What's wrong with Liz?" I said to mom walking up to grab my waffles from the toaster.

"She said she wasn't feeling well today and not going to school." Mom replied.

"Can I stay home too?" I said jokingly to mom with a huge smile on my face.

"No sweetheart you have to go to school. Liz has to go to school when you are home ill." mom replied.

"Fine" I replied in a huff. "Are you not going to work today?" I questioned mom.

"No not today, my work gave me a little vacation day today." mom replied.

"Can I please, please, PLEASE stay home mom since you and Liz are?" I patronized.

"Charlie I said no already, you need to go to school." mom replied in frustration.

I took a deep breath out and accepted the fact I had to go to school and walked to the dining room with my plate of waffles. The head chair of the dining table was leaning against the wall broken to bits and all the pieces were grouped together all tucked in the corner. Darn, Drew was right, it was a stupid chair, I thought to myself. I sat at the table to eat my waffles looking outside the back patio door at the woods that stood behind our house. The sun was shining brightly today and not a single breeze pushed the tops of the trees around. It's crazy how a group of trees can be so beautiful.

"This is going to be a good day." I coached to myself.

I walked back into the kitchen and put my plate in the sink and rinsed the rest of the maple syrup off, I quickly threw a bunch of food in a lunch box to bring to school.

"Enjoy your day off!" I said sarcastically to mom.

"Have a good day at school sweetheart, I'll see you when you get home." mom replied.

I opened the door to go outside and wait at the end of the driveway for the bus, still admiring how beautiful this day was. The bus driver pulled up in front of my house and opened the door for me, as I walked on I realized Stephen wasn't on the bus today. Finally, I could have a nice bus ride to school today, and the positive energy lifted me up like a sailboat in the wind. Upon arriving at school we all waited in line for my teachers to come outside to get us at the front door. My afternoon teacher Ms. McNorton came through the door with a new teacher I have never seen before. Mr. Douglas wasn't at school today and this new teacher was his replacement. I was filled with more excitement knowing we had a substitute that day, it seemed as though the odds were in my favour today. Even more positivity came onto me, and I knew today was going to be an amazing day. The time at school flew by, it was a feeling I felt very rarely and I tried to suck it all in as much as I could and enjoy it while it lasted.

The clock was moving fairly quickly today and it was almost time to catch the bus home. The bell rang to dismiss class and I got up and collected my school supplies to make my way to the door.

“Charlie come here please.” Ms. McNorton called out.

“Yes?” I questioned.

“You are not taking the bus today, your mom called and she is waiting for you at the office to drive you home.” she stated.

“Oh, that’s an awesome surprise! Thank you, Ms. McNorton.” I said excitedly walking back towards the door of the classroom.

I put my stuff in my locker and changed into my shoes to go home and made my way to the office. It was really exciting that I didn’t have to take the bus today, today was shaping up to be my definition of a perfect day. I turned the corner and spotted the office. Mom was standing patiently waiting for me beside the waiting room chairs outside the office. When our eyes met I smiled at her and waved, she stood silently looking at me, expressionless. I could tell something was bothering her, her eyes were red and I knew she had been crying.

“What’s wrong mom?” I asked.

Mom looked at me nervously and she grabbed her purse and turned to the door to leave. The secretary was staring at her with high concerns as we left the building.

"Not here Charlie we will talk in the car." Mom replied.

We walked towards Mom's SUV and we got inside.

"So what's up?" I asked anxiously.

"Your father isn't going to be coming home for a while." mom replied.

I sat staring at her in confusion and proceeded to ask more questions.

"Why isn't he coming home? What happened?" I continued to ask.

Mom's head lowered slowly as she put the car in drive to leave the parking lot and small tears began to move slowly down her face. I began to feel stressed, I didn't know what was happening and she looked like she was struggling to even live or hold herself together.

"Mom can you please tell me what happened?" I asked again.

"Me and your dad aren't getting along right now and he's going to stay at Grandma's house for a while." She finally replied.

“Are we allowed to see him?” I questioned.

“We will talk more when we get home.” she replied.

The rest of the car ride was very quiet. I could hear mom swallowing her pain again and I knew she was holding back so much sadness and it was inches from exploding. We pulled into the driveway and parked underneath the big oak tree that stood beside our driveway. We got out and walked across my big old wooden deck towards our front door. Plastic grocery bags full of Dad’s clothes filled the front of the porch, but dad was not in sight. We had a big window facing the front of the house along the deck and you could practically see inside the entire living area. Walking by, I could see Liz and Drew were sitting on the couch quietly waiting for us to come home. We walked into a dead silence, nobody said a word. Drew was looking at me with an expressionless look on his face. Liz sat on the other side of the couch looking at the ground with tears in her eyes. I felt a small rush of annoyance and anger come onto me when I saw her crying. Why did she even care? She was never home and if she was home, she always locked herself in her room to talk to her friends. She never seemed to care about any of us.

Mom sat me down on the couch with my siblings and then she sat on the chair across from us.
She wiped her tears off her face and took a deep breath before speaking.

“Before I begin I want you kids to know nothing is your fault and this is strictly between me and your dad.” mom explained.

"He is going to be staying at Grandma's from now on. Charlie and Drew you will be visiting him two times per week for a few hours at Grandma's house." she added.

"Why isn't Liz going to come too?" I asked.

Mom hesitated and paused briefly. I saw Liz's head peak up to look at mom waiting for her answer. Drew continued to remain silent and seemed uninterested in this conversation, which was weird given what was happening.

"No, she will not be going because Robert isn't her real dad." mom replied.

I could not understand the logic. My dad was the one who raised her since she was 2, just because he wasn't biologically her father that doesn't mean he wasn't her dad.

"She only doesn't want to see him because he doesn't let her party all the time with her friends." I said in anger.

I turned to Drew for some support on the subject but he maintained his quiet emotionless face. I knew he felt the same way about Liz that I did because we spoke about it often how she was the golden child, but why wasn't he supporting me?

Liz silently got up off the couch and walked into her room and shut the door behind her. Drew and I turned to look at mom, she was looking impatient.

“Guys this is between me and your dad and has nothing to do with Liz, and it’s Liz’s decision if she wants to see your dad or not, and that’s none of your concerns. Now go outside and feed the animals please, I will be ordering dinner tonight because no way in hell am I cooking tonight.” mom said.

Drew and I got up off the couch and walked outside toward the chicken coop. Once mom wasn’t around I was dying to ask Drew what he thought of this news we just heard. I could tell by the way he held his head and how obviously uncomfortable he was, that he wanted to avoid talking about it. Periodically through cleaning the chicken coop, I would look up to glance at his face and see if he would initiate any kind of communication. But he just shut down.

We finished our chores and walked together on the path in the woods along the river. He was still so silent.

“We are going this way.” Drew mumbled as he directed me to a smaller path that broke off the bigger one we were already on.

I didn’t reply to him because I didn’t think he wanted me to. The path opened up to the edge of the river where a huge tree fell across the river to make a bridge. Drew hopped closer to the edge of the river and put his feet on the fallen tree. He caught his balance and began to walk across. I immediately followed him, I went to the edge and positioned my feet on the tree, and stood up for balance. We both walked to the center of the fallen tree then Drew crouched down and sat on the tree with his legs hanging off almost touching the water. I sat down next to him not saying a word. We both sat and looked down at the flowing river and felt some sort of peace together. The woods were always a place so sacred to me, my home.

"I think it has everything to do with Liz." said Drew.

I was hesitant to reply and I was surprised he broke the silence. His voice almost sounded foreign because it had been so long since he spoke that day compared to our usual conversations.

"They always fight about Liz, all she wants to do is party and be anywhere but here. Dad hates the lifestyle she lives and he probably left because he was sick of mom supporting that. That's why dad always grounds Liz." I said

Drew sat silently absorbing what I was saying. My brain replayed memories of my sister sneaking out to meet her friends or the wild parties she would go to. Mom always went out of her way to make sure Liz had everything she ever needed. Maybe mom didn't like us because we came from our dad? Maybe she treated Liz better because she missed Liz's biological dad? So many questions raced through my mind all at once and Drew remained silent and aloof. We sat swinging our feet off the fallen tree for another hour or so, talking about what was possibly going to happen now, and why we could only see dad at Grandma's house. We heard a faint yell coming from the house.

"Charlie, Drew, please come back, your dad is on the phone!" mom yelled.

We stood up and slowly walked off the log back onto the edge of the faded path. We both raced each other to the house in excitement to talk to dad. Drew got to the phone first and immediately took the phone into another room. Nobody could hear what was said. I anxiously waited outside the door to have my turn to talk to dad, pacing back and forth and playing with a button on my shirt. After some time, Drew opened the door to hand the phone to me, it felt like forever since I spoke to dad but it was really only that day.

"Hi, dad!" I said excitedly on the phone.

"Hi Charlie, I'm so sorry this is happening to you guys and nothing is your fault." dad responded in a humbling voice.

I knew he was crying as the words could barely make it out of his mouth.

"Me and Grandma are going to be picking you guys up tomorrow after school for a quick visit for an hour or so at Grandma's house. Does that sound okay?" dad added.

“Why do we have to visit at Grandma’s house?” I asked.

“Because we have to.” dad replied trying to shut me out.

“Alright I’ll see you tomorrow I guess, love you.” I said.

“Goodnight Charlie I love you too.” dad replied as he was beginning to cry as he hung up the phone.

I passed the phone back to mom who didn’t say a word and she walked off back into the living room to order dinner.

“Great now we get to go to Grandma’s house.” Drew huffed as he walked up the stairs into his room.

Going to Grandma’s as a child was great, she had 6 kids who all had their own families and children so I had a bunch of cousins to play with whenever we went there. We usually went there every Sunday to swim and have a barbecue with the entire family. I have a lot of good memories with Grandma and Grandpa. She would make us all pick fresh cherries off her cherry tree and she would show us how to bake some pies. Or she would tell us to go pick some veggies out of her huge garden for supper. We often went for sleepovers and we were allowed to stay up one hour past our usual bedtime with a huge bowl of popcorn watching TV. She would take out her big craft box for us all to make stick figure men with acorns as heads, or she would help us color a picture. My Grandpa was a retired police officer and struggled to walk, but he was always joking around or smiling. The only time you heard him get angry was when he was yelling at the TV screen watching golf and someone missed an easy shot.

As I got older I came to learn more about my grandparents, and I learned things were often not as they appeared. Grandma played favourites with her own children and she was very obvious about it. She only had a few favourites, the others she would regularly put down or judge. Dad was one of the non-favourites, he always tried so hard to get on her good side or to make her proud but no matter what she silently hated him. She silently hated a few of her children, and she also silently hated some of her grandchildren that came from her children she hated. When I got a little older it was evident my Grandma didn't like me, my brother, and my sister. A few of my cousins she didn't like as well and she was obvious about it, to us at least. A stranger looking in would see nothing wrong, it was all passive-aggressive comments or snarky jokes she would make to us to silently put us down. When we were little she seemed to treat us all equally, but as we got older she almost became bitter towards some of us. Grandma had a rough upbringing. Her dad left when she was very young and her mother was the queen of narcissism. Her mother eventually left her and her younger sibling for dead in an apartment when they were children, and she never came back. My Grandma cared for her younger sister at the young age of 9. Growing up this way made my Grandma hate the world, she grew in shame and hate and often shared this hate with everyone around her in different ways. She had become the narcissistic mother that her own mother was and she didn't even realize it. Grandpa on the other hand was the complete opposite, he often wondered why his wife Edith hated some of their children, but he wouldn't dare to ask why. He knew where she came from and used it as an excuse as to why she lived her life the way she did. Knowing all this gave me a shock as to why my dad would want to stay there and why we had to visit there.

The food arrived and Drew and I made our way to the dining room to sit and eat, mom had ordered Chinese food. Mom fixed Liz a plate and brought it to her room for her and shut the door behind her. Drew and I ate our food looking at Liz's room with annoyance.

"Guess she gets room service too. Not sure why she's so upset, she hated dad anyways." I said to Drew.

Drew gulped his food down and remained silent once again.

We finished our food, cleaned up, and made our way upstairs to play some video games before bed. We pondered playing either Spyro or Crash Bandicoot, but the choice for the night ended up turning into Guitar Hero once again. We played for a bit when my eyes started to feel groggy and I got up to go to bed.

"Goodnight Drew." I said while walking out of his room.

"Night." Drew replied getting into his bed.

The night passed by very slowly, I felt like I didn't sleep at all. I would toss one way and then immediately feel uncomfortable and toss the other way. I thought about dad, Liz, and mom. How was life going to be for us now?

# Chapter 3

I raced down the stairs that morning anxious to get the day over so Drew and I could see dad tonight. Mom was in the bathroom getting ready for work. I walked by towards the kitchen and noticed Liz was still in her room with the door shut.

“Liz missing school again?” I asked.

“Yes.” mom replied.

I rolled my eyes and headed to the kitchen. Something was weird and something was missing. Mom never asked if she looked good today. She also didn’t put waffles in the toaster for me. Odd I thought but it wasn’t a big deal given the circumstances, I was more pissed off that me and Drew couldn’t miss any school but Liz was allowed to do whatever she wanted it seemed. I scuffed my waffles down and made my way to the door outside.

“Bye mom have a good day.” I said.

“Bye sweetheart hope you have a good day!” mom replied.

My bus pulled up to pick me up and I got on silently. Stephen was patiently waiting to patronize me in the seat behind where I normally sat. He had a stupid smirk on his face as I made my way to my seat. Fuck this shit, I’m sitting somewhere else, I thought to myself. I lifted my head and proceeded to walk right by him not even acknowledging he was there. Stephen could see I wasn’t taking his crap today, he decided “no” wasn’t an acceptable answer. He snuck his foot out in the aisle of the bus right in front of me. My feet caught his foot and I flew forward smashing my face on the ground. This time, nobody laughed, the entire bus went silent. Tears started to stroll down my red face. I got up and kept walking to the back of the bus with my head down. Stephen called it quits for the rest of the ride to school, maybe because he didn’t get a reaction from everyone that time.

I sat in class that day feeling numb to the bone about what was going on at home. It was very hard for me to focus, my head seemed to always turn to the window outside and try to catch a glimpse of a tree or anything green.

“Charlie!” Mr. Douglas shouted at me.

“Yes?” I replied turning my head back to him at the chalkboard.

"Do you know how disrespectful it is to me when I'm trying to teach a lesson and you aren't even listening?" He called out in front of the class.

The classroom got silent, everyone's head turned facing me. Mr. Douglas stood at the front of the class unimpressed waiting for an answer from me.

"Well, are you going to answer my question or sit there lost?" Mr. Douglas added.

"I'm sorry Mr. Douglas, I am having some trouble following today..." I replied with a low tone in my voice.

"You are not going to go very far in life if you keep daydreaming all the time, boys aren't that important! Your brother was the same way when I taught him, useless to teach, always worried about girls." Mr. Douglas said.

I felt a rush of anger come onto me. Nobody talked about Drew that way, not in front of me. The entire class sat in silence patiently waiting for my answer. I stood up very slowly and caught my courage.

"You know what, you're a fucking ass hole!" I shouted back.

I was finished. I knew I was going to be in deep trouble but I couldn't hold it anymore, my brain was exhausted and he kept picking. The jaws of all of my classmates fell to the floor. Mr. Douglas sat at the front of the class in shock, with a mile of anger written all over his face. I kicked my chair back behind me and walked out of class into the bathroom that was right outside the classroom. I wasn't even crying, I was so angry and overwhelmed, how dare he assume I'm thinking about boys? My life was falling to bits, boys were the last thing on my mind. I confided myself within one of the stalls so I could get some privacy. I heard a voice from the other side of the stall, and small feet appeared at the bottom of the stall door in the bathroom.

"Hi, are you okay?" the voice said.

"Yeah I'm okay." I replied opening up the door to the stall.

"I'm Tania, I saw you storm out of your class and come in here, just wanted to make sure you were okay." Tania said.

"Yeah I'm good, daily Mr. Douglas problems." I replied chuckling as I approached the sink to wash my hands.

"I completely understand, he's a joke that one. He's currently cheating on his wife with my aunt, yet he feels he can judge others." she replied laughing.

"I've heard that too, you're right he's a joke!" I said.

She smiled quietly and wrote her number down on a scrap of paper and handed it to me.

"We should hang out sometime, I could tell you so many stories about Mr. Douglas." she asked.

"Absolutely, see you around." I replied.

I left the bathroom and the principal was waiting for me at the door.

"Come with me please Charlie." she said.

I didn't reply and followed her to the office that was at the other end of the school. She instructed me to sit in the waiting room as she called mom. Mom arrived at the school 10 minutes after the outgoing call, she looked very unhappy with me but I didn't care much because Mr. Douglas deserved it. She pointed to the door without saying a word and we exited the school towards the car.

"I am so not happy with you right now it's unbelievable. I expect you to apologize to Mr. Douglas first thing tomorrow." mom said.

I kept my mouth shut because I knew nothing good was going to come out of it at that moment. We pulled into the driveway and she got out of the car slamming the door behind her. We walked into the house and Drew was waiting for me for our visit with dad.

"You guys need to feed the chickens and the dogs before your dad picks you guys up." mom instructed.

We both rushed outside to do our chores quickly. I explained to Drew what happened with Mr. Douglas and he laughed.

"It's about time someone told that prick off!" Drew said laughing.

"Yeah it was exhilarating but mom is crazy pissed at me." I replied.

"She will get over it. I don't understand why we have to do the chores after school today when Liz has been home all day." Drew said.

His support this time felt reassuring, and I was happy I made him proud, even if it was just for a laugh. We quickly finished and hurried back into the house to clean ourselves up because dad would be arriving any minute. I peeked out the bathroom window and saw Grandma's van pull in. We both ran to the door in excitement, Liz sat in her room with the door shut. We both hopped in the back seat of Grandma's van and dad immediately gave us both a sideways hug from the front seat. He began to immediately cry.

"Hi, kids." Grandma said unimpressed.

She seemed annoyed she had to come pick us up or annoyed with the fact this situation was even happening. Once we got to Grandma's house, Drew, dad, and I went in the backyard for some privacy away from Grandma.

"I'm really sorry kids that this is happening." dad said.

"Why is this happening though dad?" I asked.

"Me and your mom have been fighting non-stop and it's really not good this time." dad replied crying.
"Unfortunately for a while, our visits can only be conducted at Grandma's house." dad added.

"But why?" I asked. "It's because of Liz isn't it?" I added.

Dad immediately stopped crying and looked up at me in surprise. Drew remained silent and looked at the grass with the same expressionless look on his face.

"Yes, Liz wants to party and smoke pot with her friends and drink all weekend and I'm not okay with it. She made up a story that I abused her in order to get your mom to kick me out. Now children's aid is involved and we have to have supervised visits." dad replied.

"What abuse?" I asked.

"Unfortunately this is the way it's going to have to be for a while kids. And Liz told your mother I bought her alcohol, and your mother blew up in jealousy and kicked me out. But Grandma agreed to not say anything to anyone if we go out and do things on our own, you kids need to promise you aren't going to tell anyone though. If you tell I'll get into some serious trouble and we won't be able to see each other anymore. It'll be our secret." dad replied.

Drew and I both shook our heads to agree we wouldn't say anything to anyone. We didn't want to be at Grandma's as much as dad didn't want to be. We finished up our short visit with dad and we heard Grandma call us so we can make our way home. It was a long quiet car ride back to mom's house. Drew and I didn't want to leave the car but we knew we had to, watching dad ball his eyes out as we left the car made my stomach drop to the ground. Mom was waiting for us inside the door with a million questions for us, this became regular as our visits went on.

"How did the visit go? Was Grandma there? Did dad say anything to you guys about what happened?" mom asked anxiously.

"No he didn't say anything and the visit went good." Drew replied.

She continued to ask questions and Drew and I kept to our words as we walked to our rooms to go to bed. This routine went on for months with every single visit we had with dad. It was both mentally exhausting and draining, Liz never came out of her room when we were leaving for a visit or coming home from one. Drew and I grew in resentment towards Liz with every visit that took place with dad. Drew began to lash out at mom almost every day. It didn't help that we felt mom took out her anger towards dad on us, and we resented Liz so much for what we thought, basically causing our parents to divorce. I felt Liz wanted to get our parents divorced so mom would maybe want to be with her dad again, we hated her for it. Mom would take Liz out for shopping days or for a lunch just them two and it drove Drew and I crazy how we were so left out. We didn't understand why Liz got such special treatment, what was wrong with us now? With every visit we had with Dad, he would tell us some stories about Liz and what she did behind the scenes, and what mom wanted to hide from us. Some of them were unbelievable and so hard to imagine my sister doing, but dad would never lie to us, his own children. He talked about how Liz would sneak out or lie about where she was, all so she could party with her friends.

We had a visit scheduled with Children's Aid tonight, they would come to our house and talk to all three of us kids individually in regards to our quality of life. They asked a lot about our visits with dad and what we all did during them, it was always a pain when they came around and Drew and I wanted them to screw off already. So many kids go starving or their parents are doing coke in the bathroom, why the hell are they worried about us?

"I'm so done with these stupid visits." mumbled Drew to himself as we were walking down the stairs to sit with the Children's Aid lady.

It was my turn to go first, I liked going first because I could get it over with. We would sit outside on the back deck alone or we would go upstairs in my room to discuss things in private. She asked a lot that day about being at Grandma's house for visits and the sort of things we would do there. She asked what kinds of things we did, and if we felt comfortable telling Grandma and Grandpa anything personal, and if anything happened we could go to them. I understood this but it left me with a lot of questions. The visit went by fast and I was good to go and done with my appointment before I knew it. Then it was Drew's turn. He went into his room for his visit. As I walked downstairs I heard his door open and he stormed out.

"What's wrong Drew?" I asked surprisingly.

"I'm done with these visits, I'm moving to dad's. I'm sick of this place and I'm sick of mom treating Liz like a queen." Drew said angrily.

I stayed silent and moved to the side of the stairs to give him room to storm down beside me. He didn't say anything to mom or anyone and took off outside alone. The Children's Aid lady came downstairs and walked straight to mom in the kitchen. I crept in the doorway but stayed hidden behind the wall to listen.

"He's expressed he wants to live with his father, we don't see this as a problem. His father got a small farm house to rent down the road from Edith's." She said to mom.

"I really don't want him living there." mom replied.

"Unfortunately he's old enough that he can make that decision, and he's a boy so nothing is concerning." she replied.

I quickly turned the corner to sneak out the back door to see Drew. He was standing at the edge of the woods twiddling a stick in his hands, he looked defeated.

"Drew!" I called out walking to him.

He peeked his head up to see me.

"Are you really moving to dad's?" I asked.

"Yes, tomorrow morning." he replied.

My heart sank, he was leaving me here alone. My throat felt like a swollen balloon, I kept blinking fast and looking up to try to hide back the tears that were about to fall down. I had no reply to him, I stood there looking up at the sky trying to process what was about to happen. Mom called us back in the house for dinner, she ordered pizza. It was a quiet dinner, nobody said a word or even looked at each other. Once dinner was done we all hid in our individual rooms for the night. I couldn't sleep, I tossed and turned repeatedly as usual, mom's light was on in her room and the light crept into my room. It was very late, I got up to see what she was doing up at this hour. There she was, sitting on the edge of her bed balling her eyes out. I could tell she was trying to be silent and not wake us up, she looked like her entire world was torn apart. I returned to my bed feeling so sad for mom, my brain was like a tornado. I felt bad for her and I loved her, but I also felt Liz was her number one and Drew and me were dad's number one. I wanted to be at dad's but I didn't want to leave moms, it was such a deep fight.

The next morning Drew already had his entire room packed and ready to go. Drew and I worked together taking load after load downstairs until there was nothing left. Mom stood in the kitchen motionless watching Drew patiently waiting for Dad to arrive to pick him up. She looked empty, but she looked as if she resented Drew for leaving.

"Please can you stay Drew." mom said.

"I'm sorry mom, no..." Drew said without any remorse.

She began to quietly cry to herself just as dad pulled in. Drew took all his bags and belongings outside and began to load them in dads truck. Once everything was in the truck, Drew got in and dad backed out, just like that he was gone. I felt jealous of him. It was just dad and Drew together at the new house, and here it was Liz and mom. I felt like an outcast, the 5th wheel that didn't fit in much anywhere. Things only got worse at moms for me. Liz and mom were always out doing things together and I was left out. Liz would go out with her friends every weekend and try to get into bars underage, and her and mom would go shopping to get her a cute outfit to wear. I felt like I was never a thought to them, I often just walked around the woods by myself or explored near fields. Sometimes I would try to fish in the creek behind our house to try to pass the time. School remained the same for me, everyday being a constant battle to go to school. I hated coming home and having to do all the chores myself now because Drew was gone. Why didn't

Liz have to do chores, she brags to all her friends how shes a "farm girl" but she didn't have to pick up poop or feed the hens. It made me even more angry and irritated towards her and mom.

It was Friday and I'm just getting off the bus, finally done for the weekend. Dealing with Mr. Douglas all week mentally drained me close to the point of burnout each week. It was raining heavily that day, and I was almost soaked just from walking to the house. Mom's car was gone but Liz was home. I walked inside and put my backpack down by the entryway closet. Liz came out of the bathroom with her hair half done and makeup on, it was evident she was going to a bar again that night. It seemed mom just gave her all the freedom she wanted.

"Mom won't be home for a while and she wanted me to tell you to make sure all your chores outside are done before she gets home." Liz said.

"Pfft. And what the hell do you have to do? Nothing?" I snapped at her.

"Yep, I don't have to do anything because I have a stressful life right now because of your dad." she snapped.

I felt a rush of anger come upon me. My fists began to sweat and the blood rushed to my face.

"Oh yeah I forgot you just manipulate shit so you can milk things and get whatever you want from mom out of it, and blame my dad cause he won't let you party all the time." I snapped back.

"Are you for real? Your dad is a fucking joke and caused all of this." she yelled at me.

"Fuck this shit, YOU are the one who caused all this. You are a spoiled little brat that just wants to drink and smoke pot every weekend and your mad dad wanted better for you." I yelled back.

"It's no wonder why you are so hated, you're a stupid fucking loser." she yelled back.

"I'm fucking leaving, I'm so done with you and you thinking you're top shit around here." I said.

I walked away and began to pack my stuff up in garbage bags. I pulled my phone out to call dad, Liz was still yelling at me but I was seeing red and wasn't processing anything coming out of her mouth.

"Dad? I need you to come get me. I'm not living here anymore, Liz is fucking ridiculous." I said to dad on the phone.

"Charlie, I'm not sure you can live with me. I have to call Children's Aid to ask. What's going on there? Is that Liz yelling in the background?" He asked.

"I'm done with this place dad. Come get me." I replied.

"I'll call you back, I'm going to call Children's Aid to ask what to do. Just calm down and go in your room." he replied as he hung up.

I went back into my room and shut the door behind me. Liz swung the door open behind me.

"You're going to move with that loser? I'm calling mom. You're being a fucking drama queen Charlie!" Liz said while trying to empty the boxes I packed, dumping them all over the floor.

I stormed past her to go back downstairs, she followed right behind me. Dad was taking too long to call me back, I can't take this anymore.

"Good tell him to come pick your ass up. Nobody wants you here anyways!" said Liz.

I chuckled, there it was. The information I already knew but I was waiting for someone to admit it. I knew they both didn't want me here, I didn't fit in with their "click", the outcast I knew I was. Once I heard those words, I knew it wasn't me overthinking, I knew that it was real.

"I'm going to bike there." I said.

Liz quickly ran over to where I left my shoes and took them.

“No you are going to wait till mom comes home and shes going to deal with you!” said Liz.

“Give me my fucking shoes.” I said.

She would not give them back to me. She smirked at me while holding my shoes and her cellphone in her other hand. I knew she was not going to give them to me and this would turn into a bigger argument and I would be yelling at her for nothing. I walked outside and got my bike out of the shed. Liz was yelling from the back porch at me as I peddled up the driveway.

“Charlie come back!” She said angrily.

I peddled off down the road towards dads house. It was still pouring rain and I had no shoes on. I didn’t care, I needed to get out of there. Dad’s house was a good 30 minute drive away from where mom lived and I knew I was going to be peddling all the way there, but it didn’t matter to me. I’d rather be out here in the pouring rain peddling, than to be at home getting screamed at by Liz. The hypocrisy and gaslighting from Liz was absurd.

I got to dad’s house completely soaked and with blistered feet. I walked in the back door and dad was standing in the kitchen looking at me in shock.

“Did you bike here?!” dad asked.

“Yes, I couldn't stay there. Liz is everything you’ve ever said. She’s horrible.” I replied.

“I know Charlie, I know she is. Does your mother know you are here?” He asked.

“I don’t know, I haven’t talked to her. I’m not going back.” I said.

“Drew can you come downstairs with some of your pjs, your sister is here soaked.” dad yelled to Drew.

Dads phone rang as Drew was walking down his bedroom stairs to the kitchen.

“It’s Children’s Aid, I’m going to take this.” dad said walking away.

Drew came over and hugged me and handed me the pjs.

“Liz is shitty eh.” he said.

“Absolutely.” I replied.

“Go get yourself dry, everything will be fine now.” Drew said.

Dad came back into the kitchen with me and Drew while tucking his phone back into his pocket.

"Well Charlie you have to go back to your mother's tonight. You can stay here for dinner and for a few hours but your mother is going to pick you up later on. The Children's Aid lady is going to come see you tomorrow to discuss what happened and what our options are." dad explained.

"Alright but I don't care what she has to say anyways, I'm going to live here I can't be around Liz anymore." I replied.

Dad made some chicken stir fry with rice for dinner that night. He wasn't the best cook, but he tried. We all sat together at the table and had a family meal. We all talked and joked about how its been with him and Drew living together. It felt like a normal family, it was something I haven't felt in many years. Once we were done eating, dad took our plates and scraped them in the garbage and placed them in the sink. Things were so much better here, we all talked the same and had the same interests. I felt as though we were all a "click" and I wasn't an outcast anymore.

"I'll wash these up later, your mother will be here soon to pick you up. Are you going to be okay there? Your mother said Liz is gone for the weekend so you don't have to worry about dealing with her." dad said.

"Yeah I'll be okay as long as Liz isn't there. Mom I can handle, Liz I can't stand." I replied.

I saw from the dining room window that mom pulled in. I said goodbye to dad and Drew and walked outside and got in mom's car. She seemed angry at me but she wasn't saying anything. The car was filled with a silent emptiness, it was awkward but I didn't mind. I had nothing to say to her about what happened, she wasn't going to believe me anyways because I knew Liz told her such a bullshit manipulated story like she always does. She finally broke the silence after about 10 minutes.

"So what happened?" she asked.

"Liz was being mean to me, and I snapped." I replied.

"That's not what I heard from Liz, she said you were picking fights with her. Charlie I can't have you causing stuff like this, your sister is going through a really rough time right now." she replied.

I chuckled and shook my head. There was no point in trying to defend myself, she had her mind made up of who was at fault. Liz always had a good way of only mentioning other people's bad actions and leaving out what she did to cause it all. She had a way of making herself the victim of everything, then would cry wolf when drama blew up. I knew I wouldn't be there long anyways, I had the meeting tomorrow to look forward to.

"What are you doing tonight?" She asked.

"Nothing, sitting in my room. Want to watch a movie together maybe?" I asked.

"Not tonight sweet heart, I have stuff to do." she replied.

That was usually the answer I got whenever I asked her to spend time with me. It felt like she never had any time for me but her and Liz seemed to find time to spend together all the time. As much as I liked to act like it didn't bother me, it really did deep down. Maybe it was because me and mom didn't have anything in common. Her and Liz loved shopping, I hated it. I preferred bike rides or walks, mom didn't have time for that.

We pulled into the driveway and I quickly got out and rushed to my room. I would come downstairs periodically to see what mom was doing, she was always sitting on her phone and wouldn't say anything to me. I would grab a snack and rush back upstairs to play video games. Tonight I was playing a game where you can create a house and a family and tell them what to do. I enjoyed this game because it was nice to be able to pretend to have a normal family and a normal life while on the game. It gave me a sense of control of my surroundings. Mom didn't disturb me much that night besides when she came up to say goodnight before she went to bed.

The next day came like a lightning bolt. It was an exciting day for me because I knew I was going to get the go-ahead to move to dad's house. The Children's Aid lady was on her way to our house and I sat patiently waiting for her in the living room looking out the big window. Mom didn't say much to me that morning, more just civil brief conversation. I saw the Children's Aid lady's Jeep pull in and before I knew it she was walking up the deck to come inside. Mom let her in and she stood there looking concerned with her pad and pen in her hands looking at me.

"Hi Charlie, I'm excited to talk to you today." she said.

"You guys can go upstairs in Charlie's room to talk, hopefully, we can resolve this." mom said.

We walked upstairs and got settled in my room. The door was shut and I hoped mom wouldn't hear us.

"So Charlie, tell me what happened last night with your sister." she said.

"You probably aren't going to believe me because mom never does. But Liz was being mean to me, she was the one picking a fight. She always picks fights then cries wolf when the drama blows up. I'm tired of it. She walks around like a princess and mom treats her as such. Me and Drew were always emotionally neglected from mom, I think its because mom is mad at dad or something. I just know it isn't like that at dad's, every time I go there we all act like a normal family. I have more in common with Drew and dad, I like being outside, video games, and hunting. That's all the same stuff they are into. Liz and mom just want to go shopping or worry about what their friends think of them. I feel alone here, and it's been even worse since Drew moved out. Liz kept pushing and pushing then I finally snapped but somehow I'm always the bad guy in these situations. She never has to be accountable for anything but somehow I have to be accountable for my actions and hers put together! It isn't fair. I ended up getting on my bike and peddling to dads house" I explained.

"I do believe you Charlie, always remember that. I got the green light on you moving to your dads but under some conditions. We have to increase our visits to two times per week if you move there. Are you okay with that?" she said.

"I'm fine with that, I just need to not live here anymore." I explained.

"Perfect, we are done here today. I'll submit this report and you are good to go. I will be seeing you Tuesdays and Fridays every week" she explained.

"Thank you so much for this!" I exclaimed.

We both walked out of my room and proceeded downstairs. I quickly called dad to tell him the news and that I will be packing my bags today to move in. He was extremely excited, this made me excited because at least one of my parents wanted me around. He told me about the room him and Drew emptied for me and that I could pick a paint colour out when I get there. I was excited to have a new room and to have it done up the way I like it. Seeing how excited Drew and dad were made me feel very welcome to move there, it made me feel wanted which was something I haven't felt for a long time living at moms. The Children's

Aid lady was finishing up talking with mom, soon enough she was leaving.

“Come here Charlie I want to talk to you.” mom said.

I nervously walked to the kitchen table where mom sat alone with her hands on either side of her face holding her head up. I sat down on the chair beside her. I knew she was disappointed in me, I knew she was hurting, but I didn’t know what else to do. I felt awful living here everyday. I was nervous for what was about to come out of her mouth, but I knew it was a conversation that needed to happen regardless.

“Are you sure you want to move there, I really want you here.” she asked.

“Mom I feel like I fit in there more than here. I love you and I will visit often. I feel like you don’t want me here and I feel like Liz is the princess around here. I’m an outcast and I hate it.” I replied.

She sunk her head even lower towards the table and began to cry. I felt my heart being torn out of me, but I knew what I was doing was for the best for everyone. I scooched my chair closer to hers and put my arms around her. Her tears rolled slowly down her cheeks and fell on her legs soaking into the tops of her jeans. I knew if Liz wasn’t living here Id probably be staying here, but I couldn't take Liz’s crap anymore.

"It's going to be okay mom. I love you so much." I said holding her tight.

"I just feel like I'm losing everyone, my husband, my kids, everyone. And I didn't even do anything wrong." she cried out.

"You aren't losing anyone mom. We all love you, it's just best if I moved to dads. Me and Liz don't get along at all." I explained.

She lifted her head up and dried her tears from her face. The room was silent, you could only hear her sniffles and heavy breathing.

"I'll be alright. You need to call me right away if you aren't comfortable there or if something happens. Right away!" She explained looking at me dead in the eye.

"I will mom." I replied.

She gave me another hug and we both went upstairs to pack the rest of my stuff. I didn't have much, I only needed my clothes and belongings. Dad already had a dresser and bed there for me. I called dad to let him know to come pick me up. We carried all my stuff downstairs and put it by the door. My mind pondered around why she thought I was going to be uncomfortable there, and why didn't she say that to Drew?

"When your dad comes here I want to talk to him privately." mom explained.

I nodded my head and began to put my stuff on the front porch. I turned to look behind me and I saw dad's truck pull in, Drew was in the passenger seat. They both got out and began to put my stuff in the back of the truck. Drew said hi to mom but he mostly shunted her off. He seemed to distance himself from her quite a bit since he moved out.

"Robert could I have a word with you in private please." mom asked dad.

Her voice was aggressive, but monotone. Her eyes piercing through him, and yet dad wouldn't look at her face in return. Almost like he was very uncomfortable around mom. It's probably what happens when people get divorced, it gets awkward.

"Sure Christine." he replied.

They both walked off to the edge of the house. Neither me or Drew could make out what they were saying or talking about. We didn't have much time to take any guesses about their discussion because we had to get my stuff loaded up. Every time I would glance over, it looked like mom was lecturing him and dad sat there quietly. Things seemed different from when they used to argue when they were together. Usually mom sat there quietly and dad was the one being aggressive. Now it was the opposite, dad looked very intimidated and uncomfortable, mom looked aggressive and intimidating. The shift in energy was off to me, maybe dad was sick of the arguing? He walked back over to the truck as we were finishing up.

“We all loaded?” he asked.

“Yeppers!” Drew replied.

“Okay guys I love you so much.” mom said while reaching out to hug me and Drew.

It was the longest hug I had ever received in my life, it felt as though she didn’t want to let go of us. I was going to miss her, but I needed to be away from Liz, she was the only reason I was even moving out. We both said goodbye and kissed her on the cheek and got in dad’s truck. He backed out and honked his horn as we drove off towards his house. Mom stood at the end of her driveway watching us drive off, I could only imaging how heart broken she must have been to walk back into her empty house.

I was excited for this new chapter in my life. I knew it would be easier to live at dad’s where I could be myself and not have to deal with Liz anymore.

# Chapter 4

He was back tonight, the man in black, standing at the foot of my bed staring at me. Why was he here in my new room at dad's. His eyes pierced through me with a dark eerie force of destruction. The room was dark and quiet, the air had a dull musty smell to it, almost as if the house was full of mould. The windows looked dirty, and the walls appears to have black tar and dust all over them. It appeared as though the house was rotting from the inside. I couldn't figure out why I was seeing *him* again. My mother always told me when you have a bad dream, you have the reassurance of never having it again. So why was I dreaming of this same strange scary man in black once again? Was I even dreaming, or was he actually standing there staring at me with that dreadful eerie look on his face.

I laid frozen in my bed, staring at him wondering what he was going to do. I could only hear the sound of my heart thumping repeatedly while I laid in suspense. He stood like a black statue with that same grin from ear to ear, not blinking his eyes. I could feel his thirst for me, but I couldn't figure out if he only wanted to hurt me or if he wanted to kill me. You could see the anger in his eyes, the need to hurt. His eyes so familiar, yet so foreign to me. His arm slowly lifted up to wave at me from the end of the bed. My body was frozen in terror, the goose bumps stood a mile high on the back of my neck. My heart blew repeatedly out of my chest as I held my breath. He waved at me in a puppet-like motion, almost as if someone was controlling his arm for him. His arm and wrist cracked like breaking bones with every wave-like motion he made. He then lengthened his arm out and pointed to my bedroom door. He stood there, once again motionless, pointing towards my bedroom door. I quickly turned my head to see what he was pointing at. My bedroom door was wide open and I could only see the door to my dad's room on the other side. I was confused, what is he trying to show me? When I turned back to look at him, he was gone, vanished. I looked around the room confused as to where he had gone, the room was dead silent and still very dark. I could still feel him there, the suspense, but I couldn't see him anywhere I looked. I then felt his hand grab my head and pull my face to look at the ceiling where he was dangling over top of me. Up close his face looked almost porcelain, like a painted on face you'd see on a clown. His blood filled his eyes as he yelled to me angrily.

"GET OUT!" He yelled in a demonic voice.

His eyes were fuelled with blood and hate. His voice echoed in my head, bouncing from one ear to the other. Why did he want me to get out? Why doe he haunt me? Maybe this house was haunted, but it didn't explain why I saw him before when I was living at moms. Maybe I'm haunted?

I snapped awake, covered in sweat again. I sat up in bed catching my breath and trying to stabilize myself from seeing him again in my dreams. I found it very weird I was seeing him, as things were much different for me in life at this point. I've been living at dads for roughly 6 months and things have been a dream. It is the closest I've ever gotten to a normal life. I hadn't seen the man in black since mom's house right before things started to get really sour there. I started high school and things were much different school-wise too, for the better. I found people I fit in with, and I hardly ever see the "favourite" kids from grade school. My teacher's were much nicer too. They had favourites but it was usually the shy kid that kept to themselves, a.k.a me. I got the choice of picking some classes that were better suited for me and my interests. Drew and I were right back to being two peas in a pod again. We would play video games together almost every night, well, whatever nights he wasn't with his new girlfriend Alexis. She was great too, she lived up the road and would come over often for dinner and to hang out. Dad worked a lot so I did all the housework and the cooking. Although I didn't mind, it got to be a little tiring sometimes. I felt like I had a sense of superiority over my school mates because I already behaved like an adult. I went to school all day then came home and maintained a house by myself and made beautiful dinners. Cooking is something I really enjoy doing and cleaning was just my way of showing off our house and how much I appreciated our normal life. I took pride in how our house looked, plus the two slobs I lived with always left a messy trail throughout the house wherever they walked, but poorly raised boys will be poorly raised boys. Grandma and Grandpa also lived a few doors down, our visits there turned into multiple days a week instead of just a weekend here and there. One of my favourite things about our home was that the entire backyard was the woods, except it was massive! Acres, and acres of woods to explore. This made me very happy because I felt completely at peace when I walked in the woods, and it reminded me of how I used to escape mom and dad's fighting by running off to the woods. Although the woods here felt different, they were amazing but I always felt like someone was watching me whenever I would go for walks in there. Although I'm certain it was impossible because I always hiked to the hardest parts of the woods and the parts that were the most dense. The woods always stood silent when I was there, I'd be able to hear someone coming from a small distance. Yet I always seemed to feel eyes on me.

We would go to moms once during the week for dinner. Usually on a Tuesday or Thursday. It almost always turned into a big fight because Liz or mom would say something passive aggressive about dad and it would tick me and Drew off and start a big fight, or Liz would sit there and talk about herself all the time and Drew and I would sit there in silence. We also hated mom's new boyfriend Ken, he wasn't bad when he was sober, but the minute he got a few drinks in him he turned into a jerk that picked fights with everyone. Seems everyone in that house just wanted to fight all the time, then cry wolf when a fight began. He also encouraged mom to drink all the time, I felt he brought her down a lot and used her demons to his advantage to guilt her into doing the things he wanted. The weekly dinners turned into every couple weeks, then once a month, then once every few months. Drew and I grew more and more distant toward mom because of how things were there. It was a lot better just staying away from all that drama and nonsense.

Our house was small and simple, but it was perfect. We all used the back door which was the entrance to a small mud-room. Then there was a big door that led into the small farmhouse kitchen. The kitchen had two doorways and one archway, one door led to creepy old narrow steps to the entire upstairs, and the other door led into the basement, the archway led into the big open dining room and living room. The upstairs was one giant room, it used to be an attic but dad converted it into one big room for Drew. He had a projector TV in there, a drum set and a guitar, so obviously he needed the bigger room. Dad's room was off to the left of the dining room, my room was off to the right of the dining room against the living room. The bathroom was in between dad's room and mine. The back of the living room had a front door that led to a screened front porch, it was nice to have brunch out there during the summer/fall months. There was a window going from my room to the front porch as well, which would have been convenient for sneaking out, although I never needed to because dad let me do whatever I wanted basically. The same way mom was with Liz, except I never partied or did anything like that, maybe that's why dad trusted me more. He understood Drew and I were not "partiers" or bad teens like Liz was, therefor we got more trust than she did. Through the basement door, was a creepy cement stairway to the basement. It was unfinished and all cement, it was damp down there because the sump pump would always drain later than needed, and water would sometimes fill the floor a couple inches. Sometimes we would have to hit it with a broom to get it to drain. The washer and dryer were stationed downstairs and we also had a big fruit cellar that we never used, it was extremely creepy in there so the door remained shut all the time usually. The ceiling was also not completed in the basement, you could see all the duct-work and where it broke off into vents throughout the house for the furnace.

Wires and pipes filled the ceiling beside the duct-work, and some rotten insulation. We didn't use the basement much due to it being so scary and basically a dungeon, dad used it to smoke his cigarettes during the colder fall nights and during the winter. It was a rough old farmhouse to say the least but it was absolutely perfect and charming in every way, it was finally a comfortable home where we could be somewhat of a normal family. It was only a rental, but it was ours.

Across the road is an old church that is usually filled up every Sunday morning from all the old town folks. This was a very small town, not known to most people at all except for the few people that lived here. It's name even sounded small, Woodfellow, it screams small secluded town. Beside our house was a little gas station/convenient store that all the neighbourhood kids went to for ice slurpies or five cent candies. Typical small town that is full of farmers and bored old ladies that gossip because they have nothing better to do. The teenagers around the neighbourhood usually would hang out at the grade school after hours or stand on all the play ground equipment and chat. There was a boy that came to the school yard often, his name was Jackson. He didn't talk much and he was very shy, but for some reason I got excited every time I saw him. He hung out with Drew a little as well, they would go dirt biking together sometimes and I always got the biggest butterflies when he would show up in all his dirt bike gear covered in mud. We were both too shy to talk to each other, but I think he liked me too, only judging by the way he would glance at me and seeing his eyes checking me out here and there. We didn't ever hang out alone because dad wouldn't allow that, he wasn't a fan of boys coming around. Usually if I had girls over, we would meet Jackson and his friends to all hangout together. Dad was okay with that because he knew we were staying out of trouble if others were around. My Grandma always had the impression that I was sleeping with all the boys in this town because we all always hung out. Meanwhile I was the biggest scared-y-cat ever when it came to anything like what she was thinking.

I still had my regular visits with Children's Aid twice a week at dad's house. It was getting to the point where we would run out of things to talk about because life was so normal. She eventually told me she didn't need to come for visits anymore and I could finally get on with my life without dealing with them. It took a great deal of weight off my shoulders to finally have Children's Aid off my back and I could finally move on with my life, after all, things were perfect at dads.

Dad often encouraged me to have my friends over on the weekends, he liked the life around the house. I had Tania over most of the time because me and her got along very well. Dad enjoyed having her around because she was very funny and had a good sense of humour and he could joke around with her without offending her. Tania would come over to my house before a house party or bonfire and we would get ready, dad would drive us and pick us up. She usually spent the night after so her parents wouldn't know we were at a party or drinking, even though this rarely happened. We didn't usually go out because I was a home body and preferred to stay home, plus I had the freedom to really do whatever I wanted because dad treated me like an adult. We would go for walks in the woods or around Woodfellow. She didn't think much of the woods because she was a little bit of a princess. She was over one night and we were finishing up supper, and she was helping me clean the dishes and put them away, and make sure the kitchen was neat and tidy.

"If you girls are planning on going in the hot tub tonight, let me know and I'll go pick you guys up some coolers or a mickey of vodka if you want." dad said.

Drew was gone that night to Alexis's house and I was excited for the girls night me and Tania had planned. We had a big spread of junk food and pop we were going to bring in the hot tub gazebo. It was a big closed gazebo dad made out of old wood scraps for the hot tub to be in, almost like a mini secluded party-room. Instead of walls he used old patio doors he found on the side of the road so all the walls were glass. There was a wood burning stove in it so it was like a tropical paradise in there. White Christmas lights hung from the ceiling to create a cool relaxing ambience. We had a TV and DVD player in there that we played CD's for music or a scary movie while we relaxed in the hot tub.

"Yeah dad we would love some coolers, some Vex or Smirnoff would be cool, thanks dad!" I replied.

"Yeah that's really nice Robert." Tania replied.

Dad brought his plate to the kitchen, grabbed his wallet and proceeded to the door.

"I'll be back girls, I'm going to run to the liquor store for you's." dad said.

"Okay thanks dad!" I replied.

It was so cool that dad let us drink at home and we were under age. His theory was that if we got all our "partying" done in high school, that we wouldn't want to do it in our college years and we would be able to focus on the schooling that actually mattered or if we were working then. We had some rules to follow though; we weren't allowed to leave the property if we had drank that night, we weren't allowed to tell anyone so dad doesn't get in trouble, and we couldn't act like idiots. Pretty simple rules to follow and we always did. I could always handle a few drinks, Tania on the other hand would be drunk after one drink, sometimes two max. It was a little embarrassing sometimes, but it was usually just us two so I didn't mind, unless we were at a party and I would have to babysit her while she was all drunk.

Later on, we were out in the gazebo sitting in the hot tub, we picked a scary movie to watch while we poured our coolers into tall glasses with ice. It was always a little creepy in the gazebo because it was at the back of the property, along the edge of the woods. The house was at a distance which made it a little more secluded. We filled our bowls with assortments of chips and candy we picked up and placed them on the ledge of the hot tub to be in reach. It was an exciting night, and I was excited to talk about all the high school gossip, and I was excited to talk about Jackson. I mentioned Jackson to Tania previously and she was always weirdly interested to know more about him, but she was like that with any boy. She had a thing with needing every guy on the planet to want her, and she was a very obvious flirt. Dad always thought it was because she didn't grow up with her biological dad, and her step dad wasn't the nicest to her. I agreed with dad, but I still liked to hang out with her because we always had fun, even when she was being a little stupid. We were sipping our cherry coolers while watching the movie, when Tania peeked up and said.

"Where can I go pee?" she asked.

"Well you can walk all the way to the house but it'll probably be really cold. I was just going to go pee outside near the bushes along the wood line." I replied.

"Oh my gosh, I'm not going to pee outside! What do I wipe with?" she replied laughing and a little embarrassed.

"Why not? It's black outside and nobody can see us. Nobody is going to be trucking around in the woods at this hour. And just shake a little before you pull your bathing suit up. It's no big deal, boys shake their dicks after peeing and that isn't gross?" I replied.

"I guess you're right, I've never done this before. Wish me luck!" she said while stepping out of the hot tub.

"Yeah sometimes I'm right!" I replied while laughing.

I paused the movie to wait for her. It was really quiet in there and I couldn't see exactly where she was because steam fogged up all the glass, It didn't help that it was light inside the gazebo and black outside. I heard the sliding door to the gazebo open, it was Tania coming back form her first outdoor pee.

“That was quick!” I said.

“It's so creepy out there! I hurried up and went really fast. I feel like I'm going to get poison ivy all over me!” she replied laughing.

“You'll be fine. However not sure how fine I'll be if we don't get some refills! The others have been in the fridge for a bit now and should be cold. We probably don't need the glasses anymore.” I replied.

I snuck out of the hot tub and opened the mini fridge to grab some more coolers. I placed the cap of the bottle along the edge of the wood stove. Tania looked at me with a very confused face.

“What the hell are you doing?” Tania asked.

“Chill out and trust in the ways of science!” I replied mocking a fake British accent.

I hit the top of the cap with my hand and the cap flew off the bottle. Tania looked at me with her jaw to the floor.

"That was sweet Charlie!" she said in shock. "Can you teach me how to do that?" she added.

I laughed and crawled back into the hot tub. It felt like burning hot water because my body was so cold from sitting outside the mini fridge. We pushed play on our movie and continued to watch. That's when my eye caught something outside. I turned my head to see, but because of the steam, I couldn't really see anything out there.

"Whats wrong" Tania said looking in the same direction I was.

"I don't know, I thought I saw a shadow or something, but it's probably just me feeling creepy because of this scary movie and the booze." I replied.

We thought nothing of it and continued to watch the movie and have our drinks. I reached over to the table beside us and grabbed a handful of chips. In that moment I saw this shadow figure again, it ducked down behind a large bush as I turned to grab the chips.

"Okay what the fuck was that? I swear I'm seeing something out there!" I said aggresively.

The expression on my face got serious, I put my bottle down and paused the movie, still staring outside in the same spot. Tania was beginning to realize I wasn't joking or messing around, I was dead serious. She got really quiet and we both continued to stare at the last place we saw this shadow figure. It was the edge along the woods where we saw it, almost the same spot Tania went to the bathroom at. There aren't any houses for miles back there. What the hell was someone doing on our property at this time of night? How the hell would they even know we were in here? I got the courage to climb out of the hot tub and creep to the sliding door of the gazebo. I slowly slid it open, still staring at the bush. As the door opened, steam poured out the door and made it close to impossible to see anything.

"Is someone out there?" I called out.

Nobody replied.

I listened quietly if I could hear any feet moving in the grass, or if I could hear any rustling in the leaves. I had a good ear for uncommon noises in the woods because I spent so much time in the woods hunting or fishing in the creek. Your ear tends to tune to things moving around in the trees or on the ground.

"Hello?" I called out again.

Still no response.

I slid the door shut and locked it behind me, making my way back into the hot tub. Tania looked at me terrified and blank.

"Well what the fuck?" She asked.

"It was probably a deer or a raccoon or something. Nobody would be out there right now." I reassured her.

"Should we call someone?" Tania asked.

"Naw...... We're good." I replied.

I hit play on the movie and Tania calmed down a little bit. I reached over and picked my drink up and took a big swig. I picked my phone up and texted Jackson.

"Are you creeping on me and Tania right now?" I texted.

I waited for his reply while we watched the movie and continued to stuff our faces with chips and Sour Patch Kids. A few minutes later, my phone buzzed.

"No? I'm at Carson's house right now playing video games." he texted back.

I knew he wasn't lying, and I knew he wasn't the type to be a creep and spy on girls hanging out in a hot tub. I thought to myself, for sure that was an animal of some sort. For the rest of the night we didn't see anything else. We finished up our movies, chips, drinks and gossip and started packing up the rest. We closed the hot tub and shut everything down.

"You ready for the coldest run ever?" I said giggling while I slowly slid the door open.

"Holy shit you weren't kidding!" Tania said.

We both ran back to the house. We walked in the back door in our bathing suits wrapped in towels. We patted ourselves dry and started making our way to my room. Tania had a good buzz on at this point, but it was nothing out of the ordinary because she was always like that after one or two drinks. Sometimes it felt like she faked drunk so she could get attention, not sure why she felt she always needed attention. We walked past dad's room and he was sitting on his computer, I assumed playing an old Sci-Fy war game he liked.

"Hi girls, did you close the lid to the hot tub?" dad asked.

"Yeppers it's all shut down." I replied.

He didn't get up off his computer, which wasn't out of the ordinary. Every night he was always glued to his computer working on something or playing that game. He kept the door mostly shut and you could only see the bright light of the computer reflecting off his bedroom walls. Tania and me got into my room and shut the door.

"It's fucking cold out there!" Tania said shivering.

We got changed into our pjs and called it a night. Whenever I had friends over we always slept on the two couches in the living room because I got grossed out if anyone slept in my bed. Dad was still awake in his room but the light from his computer didn't bother us. Tania was tossing and turning on the couch, I assume because of the cooler she drank maybe she was dizzy a little, however I quickly passed out.

I woke up really late at night, half asleep I turned over to see if Tania was sleeping and if she was okay. She wasn't on the couch. Confused and slightly annoyed, I got up and walked to the bathroom to see if she was puking or something, but she wasn't there either. I turned to my room and pushed the door all the way open, it slowly squeaked open to reveal Tania wasn't there either. Dad's computer light was on in his room, weird, why was he still up? I pushed his door open to find nobody there and his computer left on. I walked over to shut the screen off as it was blinding. The screen savour disturbed me a little, it was a naked photo of some girl that looked like he got it off the internet.

"Fucking gross." I thought to myself as I looked on the bottom corner to see the time.

3:05 AM. Still no sign of Tania or my dad. I shut his computer monitor off. Dad's desk was always a spot I hated touching because it was always full of different porn CD's left all over his desk, I assumed that's why he was always glued to his computer every night, other than the war game. He didn't try to hide them, but it was his room and I rarely went in it. I usually only went to his desk if I was finished folding his laundry and I would put the pile of clean clothes on his desk for him to put away later.

I cringed at the pile of porn there, it was very dark but I could still see what was on the cover of the disks. The CD on the top of the pile had a picture of two girls on it, one naked bending over while the other held a purple plastic dildo up to her vagina.

Why the fuck does he leave this shit out, I thought to myself while pushing the disk off the corner of the desk. It fell behind the desk against the wall and I thought, good riddance. I turned to continue my search for Tania and Dad. As I left dad's room I could hear very faint talking coming from the front porch. I walked over through the living room and swung the door open to the front porch. Sure enough Tania was sitting on a chair out there and my dad in the other chair having a smoke.

"What the hell are you two doing? It's fucking late!" I said grunting.

"We are just talking, Tania had some things about her family life that she needed my advice on." dad replied.

"We are almost done talking, go back to bed and I'll be in soon." Tania added.

I scuffed and shut the door slamming it. I grabbed my blanket and pillow and began walking to my room. If she's going to stay up talking with my dad then I'm going to sleep in my damn bed. She can sleep on the couch alone, I thought to myself.

I crawled into my bed and quickly passed out. The night quickly went by and before I knew it, morning was here. I walked out of my room to find Tania awake on the couch, which was pretty weird because usually I was awake before her, she enjoyed to sleep in really late and wasn't much of a morning person.

"Morning, where's my dad?" I asked in a bitchy tone.

Tania had a worried look on her face and she sat up to face me. She already had all her bags packed ready to leave to go back home, which also was odd because she typically stayed the entire next day after a sleep over.

"Your dad went to work early this morning..." Tania replied.

Weird I thought, it's Sunday. He doesn't work on Sunday's, she probably misheard him and he went somewhere else. I had no reply for her as I was kind of mad still about last night.

"Charlie can I tell you something?" Tania said anxiously to me.

"What's wrong with you...?" I asked.

"You need to tell your dad to lay off of me a bit man..." she replied.

I will admit, I immediately got defensive as Tania pulled crap like this all the time. She always had it in her mind that every guy on this planet wanted her.

“What do you mean?” I asked.

“I sort of feel like your dad was coming on to me last night but I’m unsure really.. It felt like he was undressing me with his eyes... It was really weird and I’ve always thought of your dad as a close friend.” she said.

“He was probably just drunk and trying to help you with your personal shit at home.” I replied.

Tania always pulled stuff like this, I felt a little angry at her at the time. She craved male attention, she had a history of coming onto men much older than her, I chalked it up to that typical stereotype of “daddy issues” that my dad mentioned about her. I assumed my dad was just having an intimate conversation with her about her family and she took it the wrong way as my dad would never do anything gross like that. He often had conversations like that with me. He spoke about the world how it was and he never sugar coated it. I assumed dad was telling Tania how to handle her step dad and Tania probably felt weird about it because she never had an adult speak to her like a friend and not a parent figure. She probably felt intimidated.

"I'll talk to him about it for you.' I added.

"My mom is on her way to pick me up this morning, we have a family breakfast." she said.

This was all very weird, Tania never did anything with her family, she hated them. Now she's randomly having a breakfast with them? Her mom also never picked her up. It was always my dad driving her back and forth or I would bike to her house and she would bike back to mine with me.

"Okay enjoy your breakfast" I said sarcastically.

We were a little short with each other for the short time before her mom got there. She pulled into the driveway to pick her up, she hugged me and left like nothing was wrong. I picked up my phone to call dad as I was feeling really angry. As I picked up the phone, dad pulled into the driveway right after Tania's mom and her left. He came inside and looked stressed and anxious.

"What happened last night?" I asked angrily.

"Charlie the weirdest thing happened to me last night. I'm not sure you should have that girl over anymore. She's got some issues." He replied.

"What do you mean?" I asked.

"I was in my room on my computer, I thought you guys were asleep when I heard a small knock on my door. I opened the door and it was Tania, she was crying and said she wanted to talk. I shut my computer off and grabbed my cigarettes and we both went in the front room to talk. She said her step dad is an ass hole to her." he replied.

I thought to myself, I shut his computer off… But whatever, small detail who cares, maybe I was dreaming for that portion as I seem to have had some vivid dreams in the past. I cut him off mid sentence..

"I know her step dad is an ass hole, I hear the way he talks to her when I'm there. He hates Tania and makes it very obvious that he does. Sort of the same thing as mom and me." I explained.

"Yeah she mentioned that about him and she was having some problems with her boyfriend too." he added.

"Yeah she always has boy problems. She dates a guy and cheats on him with the next, then cheats on that guy with the next and the next and the next. Shes always been like that. I don't take the time to get to know her boyfriends because I know they won't be around for very long." I added.

"Well last night when she was talking to me she randomly got up and sat on my lap while I was smoking. I was just wearing my robe and it was extremely awkward and uncomfortable for me. I didn't know what else to do so I told her to go back to bed and I put my cigarette out and walked to my room. I got to my room and to my surprise she was standing in the doorway staring at me. I asked her to go to bed but she asked if we could talk more. I told her we could only for a little. I sat in my office chair while she sat on my bed. She was being very flirtatious and asking me what I wanted to talk about next. I told her to go to bed as it was really late and I was tired and the situation was all quite weird. She got up impatient and walked out, I can't help but feel she wanted to sleep with me." he explained.

"What the fuck!" I said in anger. "That is so fucked dad. But honestly that doesn't surprise me, Tania is completely messed up sometimes in regards to men." I explained.

I didn't want Tania to come over after that, she was so mentally unstable I didn't want her around. The weird thing was, she never asked to come over ever again. I didn't hear from her, she didn't say hi at school, nothing. She just dropped me.

Life went on after that. I had other friends I could hang out with. My cousin Sara started to come over more often, she wasn't too big on drinking or anything of that sort. Whenever she came over we would do our own remakes of funny or scary movies we liked. Or we would go watch the baseball games up the road. My friends Jessica and Bianca came over once in a while too. Jessica actually came on a family vacation with us as well, dad always kept trying to pick her up while at the beach and throw her in the water because she was from the city and maybe dad thought it was funny for a city girl to go in the lake. Most of my friends felt really comfortable at my house because my dad didn't have very many rules, he didn't need rules either because Drew and I were good teenagers. Dad would often buy me and my girlfriends coolers or alcoholic mixed drinks that we would drink on the weekends. He always encouraged me to have Bianca and Jessica over the most. Bianca was a foreign girl with tan skin and long dark brown hair, she was very pretty. She was also extremely funny. Jessica was a more shy girl, she was also stunning but was way too modest and shy to ever see herself as anything beautiful. Dad seemed to like them the best because he said they were good girls, good influences, and not party girls like Tania was. I began to see a swift in dad about how he spoke about my friends, it was very slow but it was apparent.

Drew spent almost every night at Alexis's house at this point. They were practically married and always together. Dad and I got really close, you could say we had a very good relationship because it was always just me and him all week. I wasn't allowed to have friends over during the week, and Drew was always gone during the week. I would often sit with dad in the front room while he had his smokes. The weather was beginning to get a little colder and dad began smoking in the basement to escape the cold weather. We often talked about the world and society and how much it has changed from back in the day. My dad truly believed society was much better when women weren't allowed to work and their duties included cooking, cleaning and tending to their husbands needs. He always spoke about women as if they were objects, but he was very slow with how much he tried to convince me of this everyday. He would explain that after women have kids they are pretty much useless to their husbands. And when I would disagree he would reassure me that every man thought this way and I should just accept it now so I don't end up disappointed as an adult when my husband will not want me anymore after I have a kid with him. He was halfway right, a lot of men see women as objects and gross after having a baby, but I always knew it wasn't all men that thought that way. I knew in the back of my mind he wasn't completely right because I knew lots of happy healthy couples. He would explain that if you lined up fifteen naked women in a line and opened there legs, you could tell right away all the women that had babies and how gross their vaginas were and how it was unfair to men that they had to have sex with that after. Him saying these things made me feel a little hopeless for my future with men, it scared me away from Jackson a little as well. Part of me felt as if I was just an object and it's okay to be an object to men because like he said, all men thought like him deep down. He explained that the men that acted happy with their wives were secretly faking it and were unhappy and too cowardly to admit it. He often talked about how all men wanted a younger woman's body because they weren't covered in stretch marks, cellulite or saggy skin. I often looked at my body in the mirror in disgust thinking, no man will ever want me because I have cellulite, being self conscious devoured me slowly everyday the more dad opened my eyes up to how the world was. He spoke about how if teenage girls, virgins specifically, would have sex with him, that they would never want to sleep with inexperienced younger boys because older men know how to do it correctly. He would often use specific friends of mine as examples in his ramblings. He though Sara wouldn't ever find anyone to love her because she was ugly, and how shes going to need to learn how to please a man really good in order for him to ignore her ugly face. He spoke very highly of Bianca and how she's the perfect example of what older men want in a girl, big butt and not an ounce of cellulite, saggy skin or stretch marks.

He would prove his theory by giving specific examples about his sisters, how all the guys in high school wanted to hang around them all the time until they got fat, then they all disappeared. He would use examples like this to show me how right he was about it being all men and not just him. He was the only one with big enough guts to say this stuff out loud, he claimed.

And then he brought up Tania. A name that became foreign to me as our friendship ended months before. My mind immediately went to the last night she ever slept over. He said things about her face and how perfect it was because it looked like a 25 year old's face on a 15 year old's body. He would add that it's too bad her mental health is so screwed up because she's the perfect image of what men want. I knew these conversations weren't typically ones a dad had with his daughter, but he was my dad. I knew he was just trying to open my eyes up to how the world was. I felt like I had this knowledge about society that no other kids in school had. I felt superior to everyone else at school.

We were sitting at the dinner table that night having some spaghetti I made. Drew was gone to Alexis's house as always.

"The pasta noodles are a little over cooked, they are falling apart." he said with a smirk on his face as he twisted his fork around the noodles.

"I'm sorry, next time you can make it yourself then." I said jokingly and laughing.

"Just trying to help you so you can make better food, nobody your age cooks as good as you so you should be proud of that at least." he replied.

"Alrighty! I'm going to clean up and take a shower, unless you have to use the bathroom?" I asked.

“Nope! It’s all yours. While you shower I’m going to go have a smoke downstairs.” he replied.

“Okie dokie!” I said as I began to clean up the dishes and put away all the left overs while dad went into his room to get out of his work clothes.

“Are you going to shower yet?” Dad asked while peeking his head into the kitchen.

“Nope still have more dishes left, why?” I replied while looking at him confused.

He nodded his head and went back into his room. I finished up doing the dishes and made my way to the bathroom. I turned the shower on to warm up while I went to my room and grabbed my pjs and returned to the bathroom.

“You going to shower now?” dad asked while walking out of his room.

“Yeah I was just letting the water warm up. Why?” I asked.

“Oh nothing, I just didn’t know what you were doing with the shower on and the door open. I’m going to go for a smoke.” he said.

He walked into the basement and I went into the bathroom. The bathroom was always very steamy before I even got into the shower, I liked the water boiling hot. My showers were always pretty long as well, I often just sat in the shower with the water beating on me for a few minutes when I was done shaving and washing my hair. I usually shaved everything and washed my hair every single night because I liked the clean-feeling. I enjoyed my showers and really looked forward to them as they always seemed to relax me. They were my relaxing time, my own time. I wasn't at school, I wasn't cooking or cleaning. I got to relax for 15 minutes in the hot water. After my long shower, I got out and wrapped the towel around my soaking wet hair and put my pjs on to get ready for a movie and bed. I got out of the bathroom and dad was still downstairs. I walked down the creepy cement stairs to go see him downstairs, he had an old wooden rocking chair down there that he would sit in to smoke his cigarettes.

"Hey dad, that's one long ass cigarette." I said jokingly.

"Well I smoked a couple and I'm just playing on my new Blackberry my work got for me. The buttons are way too small for my fingers so it's hard for me to figure it out. I'm done this second smoke so I'll probably come up now. What are you doing the rest of the night?" Dad said.

"I'm going to either watch a movie in my room or play some video games, I'm not sure. It would be nice if Drew ever came home and we could play video games together, but whatever I'll just play a single player game." I replied.

“Yeah he’s always at Alexis’s now. Is it just me or does she have weird boobs?” he asked.

“I’m not sure I don’t even look at her boobs dad, I’m not a lesbian.” I replied feeling slightly weird.

“Haha I know but I’m just saying.” he replied laughing.

I went back upstairs and got myself a glass of water to bring to my room. Dad followed behind me.

“Goodnight Char.” dad said.

‘Night Dad.” I replied.

He went in his room and closed the door. There was a gap between his door and the floor of maybe two inches because the floor had sank over time. I knew he was on his computer because I could see the bright computer screen light under the crack of his door. I didn’t like shutting my door because the air didn’t circulate properly because it was an old house and my room would either get blasting hot or ice cold depending on the weather outside. I had a weird feeling in my gut that night, I couldn’t explain it. Like a faint twist or knot in my stomach, but not noticeable enough for me to really care.

Life was still very simple and routine, which was something I really liked because it made me feel normal. I went to school during the week, dad worked and the weekends were for fun. I would have my friends over, dad would sometimes have his friends over, which were few as he didn't seem to get along with people for a long time. The one who stuck around the most was Kevin and his wife Christy, Kev seemed to think my dads sick humour was funny. They often came over on the weekends and we would sometimes go hunting together, or he would help my dad out with something outside. Christy eventually stopped coming over so much, but Kev was over almost every week. For months dad would go for his smokes after I was done cleaning and in the shower. He would always sit on his computer working on stuff while I went to bed. It was all very routine. I didn't mind dad smoking in the basement because the smell always stuck down there instead of coming upstairs. Whenever he smoked in the front room it would always smell up the entire house when he opened the door to come in, and it made me feel like the house wasn't sanitary or it was dirty. Dad often asked me about Liz and how she was doing. Sometimes he would ask for my password to my social media accounts so he could log in and see pictures of her. I felt bad for him, that was his daughter and he missed her. Even though she wasn't blood related to him, he still raised her from a toddler and now she was too spoiled to even care he was there for her when her dad wasn't. Kevin seemed to have a weird hate for Liz as well, although he never met her. He usually just generated an opinion on whatever he heard from my dad, almost like my dad's little puppet. Kev must of been bullied in school, because he tried hard to fit in with my dad.

One night I was laying in bed trying to sleep, and dad was in his room working on his computer with the door shut. It was just like any other night, except the weather was aggressive that night. It was storming, and the wind was blowing the trees so hard you could hear branches randomly falling around the house. The thunder rumbled the earth, and the lightning lit up the entire inside of the house with every flash. I was trying to ignore it so I could fall asleep, but it seemed nothing was working. I took my phone out and put on some white noise to try to drown out some of the loud storm and maybe get some sleep. It was really late and I had to get up early for school tomorrow. Eventually I fell asleep. I woke up to the sound of a door opening. I lifted my head to peek around my room to see what door opened. Nobody was there and the house was dark but I could see dads door open to his room, but his room was completely black and I assumed he went to bed.

As I laid my head back down to sleep and close my eyes, I began to hear footsteps in the house. I lifted my head once again to look towards my dad's room from my bed. I couldn't see what was making the footsteps sound. The thunder and lightning are still coming at full force. I'm beginning to get creeped out with what I'm hearing, dad was asleep and Drew was gone so who could be walking around right now this late at night in the house. We always left our doors unlocked, maybe it was a burglar or an intruder. I stayed frozen in my bed peeking into the dining room from my bed waiting for something to happen. It was quiet, not a sound anymore. I laid my head back down assuming it was maybe a branch that fell on the roof. I turned the other way facing the opposite direction of my door, I peeked at my phone to check the time.

1:45 AM.

My heart rate was starting to relax a bit back to normal. I clicked the white noise up a little louder and laid my head back down on the pillow to try to go back to sleep. I heard it again, footsteps in the house. What the hell, I thought to myself. I rolled back over toward my bedroom door to see if I could see anything. When I realized what I was looking at, my heart froze. I could not believe my eyes at what horror I was seeing.

# Chapter 5

I turned my head away in disgust, clenching my eyes shut I laid my head back in bed. My stomach twisted in a knot and my heart stopped in shock, I saw dad walking around the dinning room and around the house completely naked. I had never seen a full naked man before, it was traumatizing that my own father was walking around the house naked during the night. What was he doing? Why did he feel it was okay to be naked in front of his teenage daughter? Maybe it was because he figured I was sleeping? My eyes still clenched shut, I heard his foot steps approaching the doorway of my room, then they stopped. I heard him breathing and I knew he was just standing there, naked watching me sleep. I rationalized in my head what he possibly could be doing. I tried so hard in my head to rationalize how this could possibly be okay. I thought, he's my dad, he's supposed to love me, he would never hurt me. Maybe he heard a sound outside and it was coming from near my room, or my windows? Maybe he was sleeping naked and simply forgot to put a robe on before leaving his room. Maybe he's drunk. Then a small thought popped into my head, and for a moment the thought wouldn't leave, and bounced from one side of my skull to the other.... M*aybe Liz wasn't lying?*

Dad drank often, not enough that I would call him an alcoholic though. If he was drunk was that a good enough excuse to traumatize your daughter like this? He stood there for maybe one minute looking at me, but it felt like an eternity of hours. I kept my eyes sealed shut, pretending to be asleep. I didn't know why, but I knew I was afraid. I knew that maybe if he knew I was awake he would do something worse or maybe there is an explanation to this and if I jumped to conclusions it would just make everything awkward? It's hard to express what I'm feeling in this moment, I feel my love for my father as his daughter, but I also feel maybe he did things like this to Liz. Maybe she got sick of it and that's why she said something about him. I heard his footsteps retreat back toward his room, I glanced up in fright to see he had gone back to his room. I laid awake for the rest of the night, scared maybe he would come back and watch me again. But he didn't, he remained within the walls of his room. I wish I could say this was the end, but unfortunately from what I was coming to learn, this was only the beginning.

During the day you could say dad might of been normal. He often joked and made silly comments, that was the dad I loved and the dad I had been used to since I moved in here. The longer I lived there, the more he slowly would progress worse. I kept making excuses for him, he's my dad. He would walk around some nights naked, wandering through the house after I went to bed. Drew was lucky, he had Alexis's house he could hide in. I felt I didn't have any options, I felt moms house was all drama, and Liz would get treated like royalty again and here I had to deal with a demon that took over my father every night. I thought, maybe if he got a girlfriend or if I got him counselling it would stop? Before he would walk around naked he would lock himself in his room on his computer. I always thought maybe he was playing his war game or doing something for work, eventually I came to learn what he was doing on that computer late at night. There was a reason his desk was filled with porn CDs. Instead of shutting his door like any normal prudent person would, he slowly began leaving his door open slightly. Over time he would open it a little more, then after months, his door would be wide open. I would lay in bed hearing faint moaning of the porn he watched on his computer. I could hear a slippery pounding sound while he watched his screen. Even if I shut my door, you could still hear it. Every pound he made would run awful chills up my spine. He would keep a big bottle of lotion beside his computer on his desk as well. Every night I would hear him masturbating at his computer, I knew when he would be done as he would moan and then all the pounding sounds would stop instantly. This went on for months, he would get louder and louder every night. Almost like he was getting more and more comfortable doing this stuff in front of me as time slowly went on, almost like he was trying to get me accustomed to this... I've come to learn this is called *grooming*... It's were you slowly condition someone's mind to abuse, then eventually they have no concept of their own boundaries and they don't even know how they got to where they are.

One day I got the courage to speak to Drew about it, he didn't seem shocked. Nor was he bothered or disgusted with dad's behaviour, he remained aloof and numb.  Almost like he was living in a cave and

Alexis was his escape. He made me feel like it was normal that single dad's do that. I felt stupid, I felt like a cry baby or a spoiled brat

"I know dad leaves his porn everywhere, I watch porn too. It's just the way it is. I don't have to watch it that often though because I have Alexis. Dad doesn't have anybody, so cut him some slack." Drew said.

"But I can hear him. It keeps me up at night! It's nasty!" I expressed.

"Tell him to shut the fuck up then, not sure what you want me to do, it's better than moms house." Drew snapped.

I felt our relationship dwindling away the moment I tried to express anything negative about dad. Drew excused his behaviour like it was normal and for a moment I knew how Tania felt and how Liz felt when I did what Drew is doing, excusing dads behaviour.

The following night I mentally prepared myself to tell dad to be quiet when he masturbates. Before getting into the shower I would look at myself in the mirror and give myself the "I'm a strong woman" speech while I practised what I was going to say. I could smell dads smoke from the basement he was smoking in, it was coming through the vent from the basement into the bathroom. I figured once I turned the shower on and cracked a window, the steam would wash out the smoke smell. I undressed and got in the shower, I was feeling uneasy that night and decided not to shave anything. I had some clear stubble going on everywhere but I didn't mind, I'd just do it tomorrow night instead. After getting out of the shower I sat in the steamy bathroom, naked brushing my teeth still trying to mentally prepare to say something. I cleaned the steam off the bathroom mirrors and stared at my body in shame. I had so many flaws that dad spoke about on other women, maybe Jackson will think I'm gross as well? Just as I thought about him, I heard my phone vibrate. It was a text from Jackson. I sat on the toilet lid still naked from my shower, sitting in the steam and opened the text.

"Hey pretty lady!" a text from Jackson.

"I was just thinking about you..." I replied in an attempt to be flirty.

"Oh yeah? What were you thinking about?" He replied.

"Well I was in the shower.. Naked… Thinking maybe……… We could play video games together." I said jokingly.

"Wow you had me going there for a minute LOL!" Jackson replied.

"Maybe we could hang out this weekend since tomorrow is Friday?" I asked.

"Absolutely, meet me at the old elementary school for 8 PM?" he replied.

"Perfect!" I answered.

I sat smiling on the toilet before I came back to reality of what I had to face tonight, I put my pjs on and brushed my hair and got out of the bathroom. To my surprise dad was already upstairs from his smoke. As I walked out of the bathroom you could tell I had been blushing from Jackson's messages.

"What are you so smiley about?" Dad asked jokingly.

"Nothing just going to meet up with Jackson tomorrow, I think I really like him." I replied.

"Well be careful, you're burning the envelope from both ends so make sure he knows what a great girl you are." dad replied.

"Thanks dad." I said.

The compliment from him was nice, maybe he wouldn't do anything tonight? Maybe tonight would be a normal night, like it used to be. Maybe he was just going through a rough phase. I felt the optimism rush through me.

"You know when I was a kid and I was going to be meeting a girl, I would sit in front of the mirror and give myself pep talks." dad added.

"That's so weird because I do that too!" I laughed.

"Yeah I also used to sit on the toilet while I was talking on the phone with that girl too." he added.

I sat there, perplexed on how specific he was, I didn't understand why he was saying these very specific things to me. I had just done the same things in the shower I just took. How odd that he did that exact same stuff too and mentioned it right after I just did it...

"I also always asked girls I was hanging out with to be freshly shaved, no guy likes any hair on a girls body." he added again.

I froze, it's like he knew everything I did in that shower. And why was he so eager to tell me this stuff? I couldn't say anything back to him, I was in clear shock. I walked past him into my room and shut the door. Maybe everyone did that stuff in the bathroom and it was just a coincidence? I always tried to create rational thoughts in my head to explain what was happening. There's no way he could see me anyways, right? And why would he even want to see me, his daughter, in the shower?

I went to bed that night confused. So many thoughts were running through my head. I felt maybe there was no way to help dad, maybe he was doing this to Liz. I wonder if mom would support me if I told her, the way she supported Liz. Maybe every single dad was like this and I was just being a cry baby. My friend's dad's didn't act this way, Jackson's dad didn't act this way. I thought about how my life would be if I just moved back to moms, would she even want me there? The level on confusion going on inside my head was crazy, because dad seemed pretty normal during the day and every thing was routine and great, and then once it started to get dark, his hidden agenda took over.

All these thoughts filled my head from ear to ear. That's when I realized it was quiet in the house. Maybe he wasn't masturbating tonight and I could open my door to get the warm air in here. I slowly crept out of bed and opened my door a crack. Immediately I could feel the warm air kissing my face as it blasted into my room, even if the door was only open a crack. Dad's light was off, I couldn't see any computer lights either. Maybe he went in the gazebo to watch his porn tonight, I thought, thank goodness!

I swung the rest of the door open and climbed back into bed. I felt so relaxed and cozy in my bed, it was so nice to get a break from hearing that crap tonight and it was nice I got some warm air in my room. As I was calmly starting to drift off to sleep, I began to hear the pounding. He's inside the house? I could hear his faint moans while he continued to pound himself. The sound gave me repeated kicks to my gut. It sounded like two wet or moist pieces of flesh rubbing together. I laid in my bed sick to my stomach. I crept my head up towards dad's room, but the lights were out and nobody was there. Where was he masturbating?

I got up out of bed to shut my door, once I was at the doorway I could see the TV on in the living room from my door. He had porn playing in our family living room. He was on the couch masturbating, which was against the same wall my bed was on. I cringed and shut the door slamming it so he knew how disgusted I was. I don't think he cared, I think he wanted me to hear him. I felt like he wanted me to see him doing this, almost like he was trying to make this behaviour normal to me. I could hear his faint moans and the sounds from the women on the TV. I laid in bed putting the pillow over my head so I didn't have to hear him. I reached beside my bed and grabbed my phone. The light burned my eyes as I clicked the screen on. I opened a text to mom and began to type. Somehow, I couldn't hit send. No matter what I typed to her to save me, I would delete it all. She didn't care about me before, only Liz and herself. Why would she care now. If anything she will use this scenario as a way of saying "I told you so" and shame me more. That word, shame. I never understood the true feeling of the word until this point in my life. I was filled with shame. I wanted to protect my dad, but I wanted him to stop doing this to me. I didn't know how to make it stop without him going to jail or him getting into trouble. I felt he needed a counsellor or rehab or something. I thought, maybe he's going through a phase? Maybe he will stop once he gets bored of it and we can all be a happy family again like when I first moved here. Yeah, maybe I need to just deal with it till his phase is over, then we will be normal again. He seemed to act worse when he was drinking, but it was hard to tell because he drank every night.

I woke the next day trying to ignore and forget what happened. I tried to fill my head with excitement about seeing Jackson tonight, although it was hard to get that awful pounding sound out of my head. The school day flew by with him on my mind, every time I caught myself thinking about what dad was doing, I would force myself to think about the fun I was going to have with Jackson. I thought about his long flippy brown hair kissing his shoulders. His perfect green eyes with an orange circle in the middle. He always wore a beach bead necklace around his neck, even though he wasn't much of a "surfer-dude". He was an everything type of guy. He drove dirt bikes with Drew, he rode BMX bikes all over town. He always knew how to fix anything with a motor. And that look he gave me was my favourite above all. It was warm, familiar, comfortable and I felt like I've known him my entire life. He was always on my mind, well, whenever I wasn't cringing in disgust about what dad was doing. As soon as I got off the bus I flew into my room. Dad wasn't home yet but I wanted to make sure I looked perfect for Jackson, as I struggled with my confidence from the things dad would say about women. When I was straightening my hair I heard Drew come down his creaky stairs from his room.

"Charlie? Are you home already?" he called out.

"Yeah there was no kids on the bus today so it was a short trip." I replied getting out of my chair to meet him in the dining room.

Alexis was walking down the stairs right behind him. Both of their faces were red and sweaty. Alexis's hair was a mess and she forgot to put her bra back on. I knew they had been fooling around upstairs. It seemed that was the only time Drew came here, was when nobody else was so him and Alexis could play house till we got home. Then they usually immediately packed up and went to her house, her parents didn't care much about what they did so it was more desirable to go there. Part of me felt Drew always wanted to be there so he could escape my dad, I feel like he knew what dad was doing and he tried to stay away. He knew dad was a "horn-dog", his words. I think he may of felt a little embarrassed but also he loved dad and didn't want to see him hurt. The few girls that Drew brought over wouldn't ever come back much after they met dad. I later found out why. I knew Alexis was safe from my dad because he always made comments about how her body was gross and Drew probably only likes her because she puts out. I knew that wasn't true, Drew was crazy about Alexis.

"We are going to have dinner here tonight, then head off to Alexis's house. What are you doing tonight?" he asked.

"Making dinner for everyone I guess, then going to see Jackson at the school." I replied.

"You two dating or what?" Drew joked.

"I don't know what you want to call it." I replied grinning.

"Charlie's got a boyfriend! Charlie's got a boyfriend!" Alexis's joked.

"Shut up!" I said laughing. "What do you two want for dinner? Spaghetti good?" I asked.

"Whatever is good. Can you make that same sauce you made last time? It was really good that time!" Drew replied.

"Okay sure!" I answered.

I went back into my room to finish my hair and makeup. I put on the nicest pair of low rise jeans I had. They were dark and made me look flawless. I put on a tight T-shirt with a V-neck because it took away the attention from my wide shoulders. I gave one last look at myself in the mirror. After feeling satisfied by the way I looked, I left my room to start dinner. I took the ground beef from my uncles farm out of the fridge. We didn't usually buy meat, we either got it from family that had cows or dad would stock the freezer with meat that he hunted. The stuff from the store tasted so fake we all didn't like it. Spaghetti was my favourite thing to cook, it was easy, cheap, it wasn't time consuming, and everyone couldn't get enough of it. Alexis and Drew were sitting on the couch watching TV when I saw dad pull in the driveway.

"Is that dad? He's home from work early today, no?" Drew questioned.

"Yep he is." I replied sarcastically.

I was beginning to dread dad's company, even when he wasn't drinking. Even when he was being funny and not being "weird". Having him in the same room as me was beginning to make me cringe from being so uncomfortable. The only time I wasn't repulsed by him was when he had friends over, or we had other family members over, because I had something better to focus on. Kevin would usually stop in here and there, dad seemed to act normal with him around, which was a good reminder of the better side of my dad. Dad came in the back door and dumped his half eaten lunch in the sink.

"Hey Char, how was your day? What are you all dolled up for?" Asked dad.

"It was good, and I'm meeting Jackson at the school later on to hang out." I replied.

"Well don't be out too late, especially with a boy. Grandma has been saying stuff about you to the rest of the family because you are always hanging out with that boy all over town." Dad said.

"I really don't give a shit. Grandma can think what she wants about me because no matter what I do, there is no changing her mind. Little does she know her favourite grand children have slept with half of Woodfellow and she doesn't say one bad thing about them because they encourage her shitty behaviour and favouritism." I snapped.

"I know.... I know... I know how it is and I know how Grandma is. I'm just letting you know she is passing judgment like she always is. Just be discreet around town with that boy." dad replied chuffling his keys from his pocket onto the counter.

"Hey Drew and hi Alexis." dad said walking to his room to get out of his work clothes.

"Hi Robert!" Alexis called out.

"Howdy..." Drew replied back to dad.

Drew seemed uninterested. He seemed shut down., and not here mentally. Maybe because he suppressed guilt for knowing something was wrong with dad but didn't have any courage to be a man about it. Him shutting down made me resent him. He was dismissing me, ignoring what is happening to me. Leaving me alone every night with dad, almost like he was helping dad do what he does. It filled my heart with resentment and anger.

Once dinner was ready we all sat down together for the meal. For a minute it all felt normal, like it used to. We were laughing and joking around. Things were pleasant, dad wasn't being a creep. This only reassured my feelings that dad was only going through a phase, and he would eventually stop. See how normal he can be? I seemed to have forgotten everything for a brief moment, realizing maybe I was being ridiculous and things were normal and maybe I was just being sensitive or over emotional.

I picked up everyone's plates after we finished and brought them to the kitchen. Drew and Alexis quickly said their goodbyes and left for the night. Dad helped clean the rest of the table off and brought things to the kitchen for me to wash.

"Make sure you dry my lunch dishes completely off because they smelled a little bad when a little water was sitting in them all night." dad instructed.

"Yep." I replied.

Where did that comment come from? Why did I need to make the meal and clean up from it? And why did he have the nerve to tell me to do his dishes better, why doesn't he do them himself because he's the parent? I was beginning to hate parts of him, but at the same time I loved some parts of him. I loved his good side, not his bad side. But what I was quickly learning was maybe there isn't a good side? Maybe he puts on a show for everyone so they think he's Mr Amazing. He sure does paint a pretty good picture of himself. I felt like only me, Liz, mom and now Tania all knew this dark side of him, the manipulative side, the grooming side, the vile side. I felt like he was trying to make me into the wife he never had. The one that cooked every meal and kept the house spotless, and not bitch or complain, all while he took all the credit.

"What's wrong with you?" Dad asked.

"I haven't slept in weeks dad." I snapped.

"Why haven't you slept Charlie?" dad asked stupidly.

I felt my entire body become stiff. My heart was pounding at a million miles per hour and never winning the race. I could feel my breath getting lighter till the point I was holding it. My hands still plunged in the sink washing dishes, I frozen for a moment.

"You are loud at night that I can't sleep." I replied blowing all my air out. I felt the weight come off my shoulders.

"Loud doing what?" he replied with a small smirk on his face.

He was standing at the edge of the counter near the doorway into the dining room. Not moving a muscle, waiting patiently for my answer. He wanted me to say it, he knew exactly what he was doing every night but he wanted to see if I had the guts to say it out loud.

"You jacking off! It's disgusting and I want you to stop!" I yelled.

"Oh well I'm sorry, didn't know you could hear." he replied, still with the stupid grin on his face.

Bullshit. I thought to myself. You know I can hear you. You purposely do it loudly so I can hear. Then when I was too scared and embarrassed to call you out, you started doing it in the living room. I thought to myself. So many arguments ran through my head, but none could come out of my mouth. I shouldn't even have to ask this of my dad. He should be adult enough to know that stuff is so inappropriate. He didn't care.

Things were immediately awkward. He was silent and embarrassed, I was embarrassed and annoyed. I kept facing the sink while I washed the dishes. I heard his foot steps retreat to his room. I finished up the dishes and went to my room to grab my things. I sent Jackson a quick text to let him know I was on my way. I grabbed my bag, and sweatshirt and headed for the door.

"Bye dad, I'm leaving." I called out.

"Bye Charlie, BEHAVE!" dad instructed.

I scuffed and walked out the door. The hypocrisy coming from him was unreal. I grabbed my peddle bike and began biking to the school. It was chilly out tonight but I didn't mind. I liked the small bike ride alone, gave me time to think. Pulling up to the school I could see Jackson's bike was already there leaning against the fence. The bottom of my stomach quivering in excitement as I turned the corner and saw him throwing a basket ball into the net by the school wall. He smiled and put his hand out as an invitation to come play ball. I smiled and learned my bike against his and walked up to him. We never said a lot of words to each other, but we didn't need words. We were both a little shy with each other and nervous. We always had fun playing around the school when we were with friends, so this should be no different. We climbed on the roof to lay down beside each other and watch the stars. This moment was perfect and I wished I didn't have to go home tonight. I hung out with a lot of people from Woodfellow, but not like this. Jackson sat up and put his hand on the side of my face, he sat there for a moment looking at me with the softest look in his eyes.

"What?" I giggled and blushed.

He leaned in and kissed me. It was the first time I had ever kissed Jackson and it felt like nothing I had ever experienced before. His lips were soft and hugged mine like two puzzle pieces coming together. I could feel the imaginary sparks flying all around us, the butterflies in my stomach were flying around like a bunch of psychos. For a moment I forgot about my fucked up life, all the bad just went away. Jackson slowly pulled his lips away from mine and began staring at me again with a huge smile on his face.

"I have my Aunt's wedding tomorrow night. I know it's last minute but I really want you to come with me as my girlfriend." Jackson said.

"Girlfriend?" I replied smiling.

"Yes my girlfriend." He said leaning back in for another kiss.

"I would love to go with you as your girlfriend Jackson." I replied, then embracing his lips against mine once more.

We watched the stars for another hour and I knew I had to be home soon or dad would come hunting for me around town. Jackson climbed off the roof first and helped me down. We rode our bikes beside each other all the way back to my house. He was in front and kept turning to look at me with a smile on his face. Once we approached the door, he kissed me one more time. I held onto him in a deep hug, I think he could tell I didn't want to let go of it.

"I'll see you tomorrow, I can pick you up around 5 since we aren't going to the ceremony and only going to the reception." Jackson said.

"Okay I'm really looking forward to it. I'll see you tomorrow." I replied with a big grin on my face.

Jackson got on his bike and peddled off into the darkness towards his house. I pulled my phone out and texted mom to ask if she could do my makeup and hair tomorrow for the wedding. It was late and she probably wouldn't get back to me right away tonight. I could see my dad waiting for me on the couch in his dreadful robe. I placed my hand on the door knob, it felt cold. Maybe it was the temperature, or maybe it was because dad was in this house sucking the warmth from it. I swallowed my breath and twisted it open.

"Hey dad." I said.

"Well its about time you got home, I was about to come find you." Dad joked.

I laughed nervously at his joke, closing the door behind me. The only thing on my mind was how much I hoped he was wearing clothes under that robe. And thank goodness he wasn't masturbating in the living room to porn, what if Jackson saw?

"I'm going to a wedding tomorrow with Jackson, is that okay?" I asked.

"Well yeah that's okay… That boy sure is taking a liking to you eh." dad remarked.

"Yeah he's a good guy.. Do you think maybe I could ask mom to come do my hair and makeup? I don't have money to pay someone to do it and I know you don't either. I also haven't seen mom in quite some time. If you aren't comfortable with that then it's okay I can do my own hair and makeup." I asked nervously.

"Well sure! If she's okay with that!" Dad said.

He seemed weirdly happy about my idea. I thought to myself, maybe he missed mom. Or maybe he just wanted to shove it in her face our fake amazing life we had here. Dad seemed to have inherited a lot of qualities from Grandma, the narcissism, maintaining a good reputation despite how much of a shitty human being you are deep down. They both painted a perfect picture of themselves to everyone, but only very few knew the truth about them. And if that person was to ever reveal the sick and demented truth about them, they would be ridiculed and somehow, they would make themselves the victims, gas lighting and crying wolf were regular characteristic traits of them. The longer I was around dad the more I saw his narcissistic personality coming out, it scared me. But when you are this young you don't often recognize these things easily, especially when this is your parent, someone who is supposed to love you and take care of you. But in this exact moment, I still had no knowledge of the horrors that were headed my way.

"I'm going to hop in the shower, then find something to wear for the wedding tomorrow. If I don't see you before you go to bed, goodnight then." I said.

"I'm going to head downstairs for a smoke, then probably go to bed. Goodnight Charlie." dad replied.

I felt a huge feeling rush over me, almost like a light bulb lighting up inside my head. I knew deep down something was very wrong, or something very bad was about to happen. I didn't know why my gut was doing what it was doing, but my gut was very uneasy all of a sudden. I went into my room to get my pjs and towel, I waited till I heard the basement door shut behind him and I knew he was downstairs.

Why does he keep going downstairs every time I take a shower? How does he seem to know exactly what I'm doing in there all the time? I'm going to wait in here till he comes back upstairs, then I'll take a shower? I thought to myself. Seemed like a good plan to try to figure out if maybe I was just overthinking or if something was indeed wrong. No matter how much my brain made excuses, my gut kept twisting in a knot to try to warn me. I sat in my room, quietly waiting for dad to come back upstairs. After about 20 minutes, I heard the footsteps coming upstairs. I immediately pretended to be doing something in my room. My door was open a crack and dad walked up and slowly pushed it open.

"Aren't you going to shower?" Dad asked.

"Yep I am just grabbing my stuff. You going to bed now that you're done your smoke?" I questioned.

"Yeah I'm pretty tired. Goodnight." dad said as he walked into his room.

How did he know I didn't shower when he was down there for 20 minutes which is how long my usual showers are? Why does he care so much when I shower? All these thoughts were running through my head as I walked into the bathroom. Something is indeed wrong. I shut the door behind me and the bathroom ceiling fan off so I could listen. I stood leaning against the bathroom door quietly listening to hear if he would leave his room. Not one sound came from outside the bathroom door.

I'm crazy, no way he would be that messed up, I'm just anxious and overthinking. I thought to myself, shaking my head feeling like an idiot. I clicked the bathroom fan back on and turned the shower water on. That's when I heard it, the faint footsteps coming from dads room going towards the kitchen. When I heard them disappear, I snuck out of the bathroom to pretend to get something from my room. With the water still running and the bathroom fan on it was the perfect cover for me to figure out what the hell he was doing downstairs while I showered. I tip-toed towards his room, his door was wide open and I could see nobody was in it. I crept around the doorway of the kitchen and saw the basement door was wide open, he was back downstairs. I snuck down the creepy old steps going into the basement, it was extremely hard to not make a sound because the boards on the stairs were so old and the wood was extremely rotten. I turned the corner halfway down the stairs and could see the entire open basement. There he was, standing under where the bathroom is directly above his head. He was looking at the ceiling above him which would be where the bathroom is. My gut sank, but I felt a small amount of courage run through me.

“What are you doing?” I called out.

Dad’s face immediately turned to look at me in surprise and his face went as white as a ghost, completely blank. He looked like a deer in headlights. He stuttered while trying to answer me, he was doing his robe back up as he turned away from the ceiling.

“I-I-I was-looking at the duct work and-and seeing what I have to re-replace.” he stuttered.

He looked so guilty, but guilty of what I wondered. I knew he was lying to me, did he think I was stupid? My mind knew he was lying to me, almost like I had another person inside of me that was telling me he was lying. He followed me upstairs and went in his room and shut the door behind him. I turned the fan off in the bathroom so I could hear if he was going to leave his room again. I checked all the walls of the bathroom for a camera, or a hole. I couldn’t see anything and it looked like a completely normal bathroom. I struggled to take my clothes off and take a shower, something didn’t feel right about this. I decided to skip my shower tonight.

Maybe he was looking at the duct work? Maybe I’m just overthinking all this. I thought to myself. What the hell was he looking at down there? I thought over and over again. I stayed up that night, very late. I’m going to wait till I know he’s sleeping and go downstairs and see what he was looking at, then maybe I’ll have some answers as to what he is all about and if Liz was indeed lying. This is fucking crazy I thought, why should I even have to do this stuff? I put on some video games to make the time pass by quickly into the night. I knew I couldn't get tired from the stimulation of the video games and shooting, this was something I could use to preoccupy my mind while I waited to make sure he was passed out.

11 PM

12 AM

1 AM

2 AM

I knew he'd be asleep by now. I crept out of my room. The house was dark and silent. I snuck to dads door of his room and listened to see if I could hear him awake. Not a sound came from his room and I knew he was indeed asleep and I was safe to go downstairs to see what he was looking at.

Now to get the courage to go in that terrifying basement alone, in the dark at 2 AM. I thought. The house was completely black and silent. For some reason I didn't feel alone, I felt someone else there watching me but I didn't know what it was about.

I tip-toed to the basement and opened the door to the creepy old wooden steps that I hated so much. Not one sound came from down there but instead a rush of leeriness pushed itself up the stairs to my feet that waited to take the first step down. I walked down to the bottom of the steps as slowly as I could to not make a sound and risk waking dad, there were no lights down here but I brought my cellphone to use as a flashlight. I turned the light on and began to look at the ceiling where the bathroom was. I was on edge, like dad was going to know I was onto him or something was going to come out from the fruit cellar and kill me. I felt eyes on me even though I was alone, or at least I thought I was alone. The ceiling was full of cob webs and dust, wires and exposed duct tunnels filled the ceiling as I squinted to try to figure out exactly what was what. Copper pipes and other metal pipes, it's crazy that we have all this inside a house. Because our house was so old, the vents were much bigger than a traditional house nowadays, maybe a foot and a half wide each side. About double the size of a more modern home. This means the duct tunnels were much bigger wherever a vent was located, having to compensate for the large vent size. Something caught my eye on the edge of the duct work where the vent opening was going into the bathroom. I turned over to get a better look at the duct work. There it was, a hole the size of my head. You could see the entire bathroom through the vent, the shower, the toilet, the sink, everything. I gasped. He's been watching me shower all this time. That's how he knew about what I was doing in there, and when I wasn't in the shower. From that moment onward so much made sense to me. *Liz wasn't lying.*

*My dad is a creep.* Those words echoed inside my head, making me numb every time the echo went off again. I walked back upstairs feeling double my body weight. I plunged into bed, laying there in shock. How can a father look at his own daughter in the shower and be sexually attracted to her? Suddenly I wasn't afraid anymore of a ghost in the basement or the awful man in black that haunted me in my dreams, because I knew the real monster was asleep in his bedroom directly across from me.

# Chapter 6

I woke up that morning feeling hopeless about my situation. I didn't want to leave my room. I felt so violated and exposed. It was almost as if I was naked all the time even though I wasn't. My body was full of shame for hating my dad at the same time as loving him. It was the most confusing, mentally draining battle inside my head that seemed to never go away. I also know now my dad is sexually attracted to his own daughters, his own blood. Yes I say daughters, because now I know he must have done something to Liz. What did he do to her? I wondered. I heard my phone buzzing and rolled over to grab it on the night stand beside my bed. Two texts and one missed call.

"Hey Charlie, I'm super excited for tonight! Can't wait to see you all dressed up!" a text from Jackson.

"Hi baby cakes. What time did you need me to come over to do your hair and makeup?" a text from mom.

I also had a missed call from her. I must have slept in a little longer than usual, probably because I didn't get any sleep last night. How was I going to pretend in front of dad that I don't know what he was doing? How was I going to walk around and without these events filling my mind?

'Hey mom come around 3 please, looking forward to seeing you." I replied back.

I could hear dad walking around the house and knew he was awake. My room felt like the safest place for me now, I didn't want to leave till I had a solution for the showers. I pondered ideas back and forth in my head, how can I stop him from seeing me? Then maybe if he can't see me he will lose interest and be normal again? Maybe I can put my pjs or dirty clothes over the vent before getting into the shower. That means he won't be able to watch me, he won't know that I know, and things will go back to normal. I walked out of my room and dad was making a big breakfast, Drew and Alexis were here sitting at the table waiting to be fed like a bunch of vulchers.

"Good morning sleeping beauty! You okay? You never sleep in..." Dad joked.

"Morning, yeah I'm fine." I replied.

It was almost impossible for me to not sound so monotone. I felt like I wasn't even myself, my spirit had left and I was on autopilot. Just a walking ghost, not even in my own body, constantly calculating what dad was doing.

“Hey dude!” Alexis shouted.

“Morning guys!” I replied rubbing my eyes.

“You look tired man, not good to have bags under your eyes for a wedding.” Alexis added.

“I’ll be fine. I didn’t sleep well.” I said.

Dad came in with bacon, eggs and toast. For him to cook anything was rare. I could feel myself judging his breakfast making skills. The memory of mom’s breakfast for dinner so long ago was so demeaned by him, meanwhile her “breakfast” looked much better prepared than dad’s. I wondered why he felt he could judge mom’s cooking then, when his looked like this.

“Dig in guys!” Dad said.

“Mom will be here for 3 to do my hair and shit.” I muttered.

“I’ll probably be gone then, I don’t want to be here when she’s here.” Drew said.

The rest of breakfast was a quiet one for me, I didn't say much. Although it was hard to get a word in regardless because Alexis never stopped talking to even take a breath. Drew and Alexis hung around all day before mom got there. You could tell they really had no interest in being here, almost like they were just hanging around here so we couldn't complain that they were never here. Drew, me and Alexis played video games most of the day and they left to go back to Alexis's house right before mom pulled in, they planned it for sure. Mom saw me in the window and she smiled as she put her car in park and got out, but she looked a little uncomfortable being here, I could tell watching her from the window as she got out of her car and walked up the rest of the driveway. Did she want to be here for me or did she want to be here just to get a glimpse of dad's house and what our set up was. I didn't know the answer to that, as much as dad likes to play "show off" mom was equally as nosy.  I was just relieved I didn't have to be alone with dad, it was a great way to keep my mind preoccupied. She approached the door and I was waiting right there to meet her.

"Hi mom!" I said with a smile.

"Hi baby! Your dad's house is cute! I like the gardens." she said.

Dad walked out from his bedroom, wearing actual clothes and not just a robe. It felt like I hadn't seen him in real clothes in so long because he was always in that god awful robe. That was the only time he wore clothes, when someone was here or he had to be good in front of company. He did wear the robe a few times in front of Kevin when he would show up unannounced. But for the most part, he had an image to maintain, so the robe was only when it was just me and him.

"Hello Christine, thanks for coming to do this for Charlie." dad said.

"Hi Robert. And yeah I wasn't doing anything anyways. You have a nice house." mom replied.

"Thank you, would you like a tour before you girls do your thing?" Dad asked.

"No dad, the house is tiny she can see the entire thing just by walking to my room." I snapped.

"Okay I'll leave you girls to it! Christine would you like a drink? Water, pop, a glass of home made red wine perhaps?" dad asked.

"Yeah I wouldn't mind a glass of wine. You say it's home made?" Mom replied with an impressed look on her face.

"Yes I made a batch of wine. It has a hickory-type taste. I keep the bottles in my room for special occasions." he replied.

Dad walked into his room to get the glass of wine. I lead mom to my room and began showing her all the makeup and hair things I had. It wasn't much but it was all I had, dad thought makeup and stuff was a waste of money. As mom checked out everything that was in front of her, I pulled the dress out of my closet that I was planning to wear that night. It was one I borrowed from Liz a while back. It was long at the back and short at the front. The dress fit tight to my body at the top and had a deep v-neck. It was a lighter burgundy colour and accentuated my body beautifully, it was similar to a tango dress. I was really excited for Jackson to see me in it. Even with all the bad going on in my life, I seemed to have tonight to look forward to. The anticipation of tonight made the bad things sit in the darkness for a while, waiting to pounce again, but for now at least it was in the darkness.

"Here you go Christine." dad said while handing her the small glass of wine.

"Thank you Robert" she replied politely.

Dad sort of lingered there for a moment, his eyes were deep looking at mom. He seems to have the same look on his face when he's hunting a deer in season. He was so focused on her he didn't even notice me staring at him, wondering what the hell he was looking at her for. Nothing can explain his eyes though, they were dark and focused, like a predator looking at its prey waiting for the best moment to sink its teeth in. I continued to watch him, mom was completely oblivious to what was happening in this moment, but I was just as focused as dad was. I gazed at him while he just stared at her with his awkward body in the doorway.. Then once he saw mom begin to sip the wine he slowly walked away and left us alone, I felt an unusual feeling of comfort with mom right now, which I never really experienced often with her. We both sat on the floor while she loosely curled my long hair, this always took forever because my hair is insanely thick and as long as my waist. But sitting with her and chit-chatting was sort of nice, it was calming that me and her were actually having a moment together. Is this how Liz felt getting all this attention from her? It was almost like I was finally a priority to her, at least it felt like that in this moment. I was looking at the different makeup I had, to see which eye shadow I wanted and what matched my dress the best, I wasn't too good at makeup and matching things, that was more Liz's type of thing.

"I can see why you like it here Charlie, the house is really cute and you have a nice room." mom exclaimed.

"Yeah it's nice." I said in a narrow voice.

We kept up the small talk till she was done my hair, which felt like hours. I turned and faced her to give her the makeup I chose. Her eyes looked glazed, and her cheeks were turning slightly red. The bags were beginning to form under her eyes and she was starting to blink slowly.

"Mom are you buzzed from that wine?" I asked unimpressed.

"A little yeah, I can't believe it either. I normally drink 2-3 big glasses before I feel anything. I haven't even drank half of this small one and I feel like I got hit by a horse! I'll be okay though, I'm not going to finish it." mom explained as she moved the glass from the floor to my desk beside her.

She's right though, it was weird that she was feeling buzzed, she drinks wine all the time, why was this one so different for her. She barely drank any of it and it was a very small glass to begin with. She finished up my makeup and I turned to look at myself in the mirror. Even though I probably looked so beautiful, I couldn't help but pick out every one of my flaws. The comments dad would say about other girls would repeat in my head and I always felt less than beautiful, like I was never good enough.

"You look so pretty it's crazy baby girl!" mom said.

"Yeah thanks mom" I said in a narrow tone.

"You okay hunny?" mom asked.

"Yeah I'm good, just nervous." I replied trying to end the conversation.

"Jackson is one lucky guy!" mom said with a proud look on her face. "You look like Liz a little bit now." she added.

My heart skipped a beat, is that why dad does what he does to me? Is it because I look like Liz sometimes and maybe he's obsessed with her. She was right, I said to myself as I stood there staring at myself in the mirror. I normally didn't do much to my hair or wear this much makeup, but she was correct, all I could see was Liz looking back at me in that mirror. Mom got up stiffly from the floor and turned to help me get up. I stood up and walked to my bed to pick the dress back up and take it off the hanger. I moved into my closet and shut the door behind me to change.

"Why do you change in the closet?" mom asked confused.

"Its just something I do." I replied hoping she would leave it at that.

It worked, she sat on my bed silently while I wiggled into my dress. The closet felt like a private place for some reason, when I changed in my room I always felt eyes on me, but my closet felt safe. Once I was finished, I stepped out of the closet with my dress on and my heels in my hand.

"Wow Charlie, you look great!" mom said.

"Thanks mom." I replied.

In that moment, I knew mom was proud of me. I rarely had moments like this with my mom. I felt accepted, which was something completely new to me. But I also knew she may have only felt this way because I was basically a mini Liz tonight, all girly and all. Then for a brief moment, a thought ran through my head, *should I tell her?* Probably telling her here isn't the best idea, it's dads house and it could get ugly, especially since mom had alcohol in her system. I better not tell her here, maybe I better not tell her at all. Mom was already struggling to cope with Liz, I knew she blamed herself for a lot of things when it came to whatever happened with Liz. I didn't want to add to that, I didn't want to be a reason to cause people stress. I was at a place in my life where I'd rather adjust to people crossing my boundaries, than to risk causing drama or having someone upset with me. In these types of situations, you also always have it in your mind that *this would never happen to me so there must be a logical explanation to what is going on*. That mentality is what caused me to doubt myself or to not want to rock the boat.

We both stepped out of my room and mom walked into the doorway of my door as we were walking out. She looked drunk almost, or buzzing really hard. It was very odd for her.

"Mom are you okay?" I asked concerned.

"I cannot believe what that half glass of wine is doing to me! I probably shouldn't drive home, I better call Ken to pick me up. Robert is it okay if I leave my car here tonight and come get it in the morning. I think maybe I'm having a reaction to your wine or something because I'm feeling like I had 8 glasses instead of the half glass I had. I've only had a few sips and I feel like I've drank an entire bottle!" mom said.

"Sure. You can always sleep in my bed and I'll crash on the couch." dad replied with the same predator look on his face.

I knew it made mom uncomfortable, I could tell by her face after he said what he said. I've seen that face before, years ago when they were still married. It was very familiar to me but I always just assumed it was moms resting face, when in reality it was dad making her uncomfortable all along all those years ago. I couldn't help but ponder what he may have done to her during their marriage.

"No I'll call Ken to get me it's fine." she repeated.

Dad stood silently as mom walked into the kitchen to call him. Dad stood in the dining room turning his attention from mom to me instead. He stared, the same awful look he previously gave. Not in the normal way a father would look at his daughter, this was different. I could feel his eyes overlooking every inch of my body, it made me feel disgusting and dirty. I stood there awkwardly straight trying to hide any of my curves or to make myself look as unappealing as possible and maybe he would stop.

*He didn't.*

"You look absolutely amazing Charlie. Jackson better mind his hands." dad said breaking the silence and awkward staring.

"I know dad, Jackson isn't like that." I replied.

"Just making sure he's being appropriate to you." he replied.

It took every bit or my entire power as a human being to hide my facial expression. Was he joking? Appropriate? Did he know the definition of that word? Dad didn't seem to care when he was being sick as hell to me but he cared if another man even laid a finger on me? The hypocrisy was baffling to me. I couldn't help it anymore, my facial expression was beginning to poke out, it became sarcastic and dull. A knock on the front door broke the silence in the room,  and I peeked over my shoulder towards the window. It was Jackson in his tux waiting for me. I ran over to the door to greet him with high excitement.

“Hi Jackson! You look so good!” I yelled as I flew into his arms for a hug.

He turned his head mid hug to whisper in my ear. “You look beautiful Charlie.”.

I felt the goosebumps on the back of my neck slowly moving down my body. His cologne was a deep dominant smell that rubbed onto my dress after the hug, but I didn’t mind. It made me feel protected, it made me feel valued.  Jackson seemed to want me, regardless of how damaged I was, even though he had no clue how damaged I was. He had no clue what was happening behind the walls of my house, and I planned to keep it that way. Maybe he wouldn’t want me anymore after he found out what dad was doing to me at night.

“Hello Mr. Knight.” Jackson nervously said to dad.

“Hi Jackson, make sure she’s home at a reasonable hour tonight. 12 AM perhaps since it’s a wedding reception after all.” Dad instructed.

“Yes sir, it’ll be my mom dropping her off.” Jackson replied.

“Alright, that’s fine. I known your mom very well.” dad said.

Mom walked back into the dining room. Still with glazed eyes on her face, she was even more groggy than before. It was slightly embarrassing for this to be her first time meeting Jackson and she was like this, although I knew it wasn’t her fault. Something was for sure wrong with that wine dad gave her, maybe it was spoiled or rotten.

“Mom this is Jackson. Jackson this is my mom.” I introduced.

“Hi honey aren’t you just so handsome!” Mom said. “Stand together so I can get a picture!” she added.

Jackson put his arm around my waist and we stood next to each other for a picture. I could see dad peek at his hand around me, he seemed unimpressed by it but I really didn’t care what he thought. Jackson was so much taller than me but my heels made up for the huge difference in height. We all walked out the front door into the front yard. Jackson’s mom was waiting in the car to drive us. Mom was standing on the pathway in front of the old wooden stairs to go inside while dad stood in the doorway of the front door.

“Okay we have to go now.” I said.

“Okay guys make sure you have lots of fun! Charlie you look amazing. Jackson I will make a plan to have you guys over for supper, I’m sure Ken would be thrilled to meet you! Ken is on his way right now to pick me up but he's still probably 20 minutes away, too long for you guys to wait eh?" Mom said.

"Dinner sounds good, we don't have the time to wait right now because we don't want to be late for the reception." I replied.

Dad said nothing and watched us get into Jackson's mom's car. He did a brief wave at Jackson's mom as we began to back out. Dad turned to mom and said something to her but I couldn't make out what he was saying, the windows were all shut in the car. Mom did not react to dad talking at all, she looked utterly uncomfortable and did not turn around to face him. I stared again, forgetting I'm with Jackson. What did he say to her? The thoughts wandered in my head as to if she was going to be okay while I'm gone, even though Ken was on his way to get her.

"Hope shes going to be okay." I said to Jackson.

"Why wouldn't she be okay?" Jackson asked confused.

For a moment I forgot that nobody knew about what was happening to me. Nobody knew the sick things dad had been up to in our house every night. It almost slipped out just then. Shame filled my body and began to weigh down on me. I felt like an idiot for not using my brain, I almost just spilled what was going on to people I barely knew. I tried to think of ways or words I could say to dig myself out of this small hole I dug for myself.

“Oh nothing. The wine my dad gave her was a little strong, but Ken is on his way to get her so she should be good.” I replied.

Jackson’s mom cranked the music and the ride to the wedding turned into a mini party. After some driving we arrived at the reception. It was nice to get away from home and enjoy myself a little. The food was never ending, course after course we stuffed our faces. Smooth Jazz playing in the background by the live band. Tall candles placed in the centre of the table and the lights were turned dim to create an amazing romantic atmosphere. This place was beautiful. After we finished eating, Jackson and I went and danced to a couple slower songs, he was too shy to dance to any fast songs, but I didn’t mind. To be here, away from my life for a moment was enough for me. I was thankful to be out of dads for a night and forget about everything that was happening there. The horrible secret I found out the night before was being suppressed deep down so I couldn’t feel it anymore, I needed it to be suppressed, then it was easier for my brain to process things. It was easier to ignore, than to face the trauma... *so I thought....*

“Well babe we should probably get going, your dad wanted you home for 12 AM latest and we are cutting it tight.” Jackson said.

I smirked at him after he called me babe. It was something I had never been called before by anyone. I agreed that we should probably head back home and we began to gather our things and leave the wedding. Jackson’s mom unlocked the car and we loaded all our stuff in to go, she looked a little exhausted and worn out from all the dancing.

"Did you guys have fun? Boujee-ass wedding eh? I took my heels off right after dinner." Jackson's mom said.

"Yeah it sure was fancy. But I had a great time." I replied.

"The food was the best part!" Jackson joked.

"I've never been to a wedding that nice before. They did a really good job, and yes Jackson the food was amazing. Why am I not surprised that was your favourite part?" I added.

Everyone in the car chuckled and we continued the small talk as we drove home. The ride felt short, even though it wasn't. I was dreading going home, I was wanting the drive to last as long as it could but I knew dad would be really mad if I was home after the curfew he set. We pulled into the driveway and the house looked dark, no lights were on and the back door was locked. That's odd I thought, we never lock the door. I fiddled in my purse to find my keys, Jackson was holding his phone light over me so I could see what I was grabbing in my purse.

"There they are." I said.

Jackson leaned in for a kiss, his lips always felt so good against mine. I cut the kiss short because his mom was sitting in the car parked in the driveways and I knew dad may have still been awake waiting for me to get home.

“Sorry I feel awkward kissing you when your mom is waiting in the car right there and can probably see us.”I explained.

“You are probably right. Thanks for tonight. I’ll talk to you tomorrow.” Jackson said.

We gave each other one last small kiss and then he made his way back into the car. His mom waited until I had the door opened and walked inside before she began to pull out of the driveway. The house was silent and eerie. My heels echoed through the house and I decided to take them off in the kitchen before I walked through the house. If dad was asleep, I didn’t want to risk waking him up. Drew’s car was gone, I assumed he was at Alexis’s house once again. I walked into the dining room and saw dads door half open and the lights off in his room. I leaned more into his room and I could hear his deep snores. He must be passed out, I thought. I turned around quietly and walked into my room closing the door behind me before turning my light on. This was a great way to end a great night, dad is asleep and I don’t have to deal with his crap tonight. I took my dress off and put my pjs on, I was feeling too lazy to wash my makeup off tonight. I also didn’t want to risk going into the bathroom and possibly waking dad up. I clicked the TV on as I relaxed in bed and my eyes were already trying to close, I was utterly exhausted from all the dancing and loud music. I turned the TV off within 10 minutes and drifted off to sleep.

# Chapter 7

I awoke to a loud thumping noise. I jolted my body up in my bed to see what was going on. My room was dark but it looked quite different than how it usually looked. The windows were all boarded up and the curtains were filled with dust and hung half ripped off the window ledge. My bed sheets were torn and old, my closet door hung halfway off the hinges and the air smelled of old musk and mould. My heart was pounding and my body was stiff like an arrow as I scanned the entire room from side to side. My bed was damp from all the sweat dripping off my body as I looked around nervously. I stood up out of bed and ran out of my room into the dining room trying to catch my breath. I didn't know what was going on and why the house appeared so different, almost like I was in a different realm but in the same house.

"Dad?" I called out.

Nobody replied.

I slowly walked towards dads room and pushed his door open. It was dark and his windows were also boarded up, it appeared all the windows in the house were boarded up for some reason. Like the house was abandoned. Dads bed was missing the mattress and it was just an old metal bed frame. His room was so quiet, almost like the room was sound proof, and the air was stagnant and rotten.

"Hello there." A creepy low toned voice said.

I turned to look around the room to see who was in there with me, nobody was in sight but I could feel someone there.

"Who's there?" I cried out.

No reply.

I crept slowly more into dads room to get a better look around. His closet door slowly began creeping open behind me. My body froze while hearing the slow creaking behind my back. Every muscle in my body was tense as I tried to figure out what I should do. I got a brief moment of courage and turned around to face directly into dads closet. It was completely black and I couldn't see anything in there at all. The heavy presence and weight from the closet vibrated all around me, I knew someone, or something was in there staring back at me.

"Hello there." The terrifying voice said again.

This time it was clear the voice was coming from the closet. I focused all my attention and energy at the inside of the closet to try to make out any shapes or anything moving, but I couldn't see a thing. The closet looked like a dark awful black hole that never ended and swallowed whatever happiness that happened to walk by. I slowly stepped forward toward the open closet.

"Dad?" I asked again.

No reply.

I could hear faint deep breathing from someone in the closet. As I got closer I could see faint glowing eyes staring back at me. They were dull and evil, they were so malevolent you could feel it in your bones while staring at them. It was the man in black again, I knew right away when I began to make out some facial features. A large comical smile began to form on his face as he stood in the closet looking at me. My body froze as I stood in terror gazing back at him. For a moment I felt almost paralyzed by him, unable to move or breathe. Once his smile reached close to each ear he slowly tilted his head, his eyes fixated on me and not blinking. He paused once his head was tilted sideways, we stared at each other waiting for a move. I let out a gasp and began to sprint into the dinning room and to the other side of the table. I could hear his deep breathing behind me chasing me. He was giggling and fiddling his fingers in front of him while he chased me around the table, almost like he was getting pleasure out of terrorizing me. I was running around the entire house trying to find an exit that wasn't boarded up. I turned to peek over my shoulder and immediately stopped running in my tracks. He was gone. The laughing man in black had vanished.

I could still hear him giggling but it sounded like it was coming from all around me. I turned and ran into the kitchen to go out the back door. The fridge door hung loosely and rotten food covered all the shelves in the fridge. Broken jars of preserves laid on the kitchen counters full of maggots and flies feasting on the remaining rotting fruit jams. I tried to free the door by pulling on the knob aggressively but it wouldn't budge. I turned around to look back at the entrance to the kitchen. The giggling had ceased and the house stood dark and silent once again. I wasn't going to stand around wasting time in case he came back, I turned back to the face the door again and tried to free it. The minute I turned to face the door I could hear someone walking towards me from the living room. Twisting my body around to see if it was him, once I turned the footsteps stopped. Nobody was there. I turned once again to try to free the door and heard the foot steps coming to me again but faster this time. I spun around to accept whatever fate was coming my way. Nobody was there. Screw this, I thought. I swung the basement door open and fled down the stairs. The basement was an even worse dungeon than how it normally looked and damper than before. I saw dad's wooden rocking chair sitting beneath the ceiling where the bathroom is. I took dad's big trench coat off the hanger and sat on the chair and covered myself with the trench coat hoping nobody would find me. Heavy angry foot steps came slowly down the stairs. Thudding on the old wood causing it to crack with every step forward. I quivered under dad's coat, hoping the man in black would get bored and leave once he realized I wasn't right at his disposal. I held my hand over my mouth to conceal any sounds or faint whimpering I was making. My eyes were glued shut. The steps reached the bottom of the stairs and paused. My body was so tense from feeling so much fear, I managed to force my eyes open a crack but I couldn't see anything from the trench coat being so thick and wrapped all around me. I waited, I couldn't hear any sounds at all. It felt like forever that I was hiding under this coat, a lost eternity of living in fear trying to hide. Maybe he left, I thought to myself. I slowly wiggled the coat to peek at the edge of the stairs, nobody was there. I quietly moved the coat around to expose the rest of the basement. Once I moved it a crack to the other side of me, there he was, the man in black. He was standing facing the corner of the back of the basement. He stood rigidly with his head tucked into the corner not moving a muscle, but his stance was so strong, almost like his feet emerged from the earth itself. I sat there with my eyes fixated on him, waiting for him to make a move, or waiting to see why he was standing in the corner facing the wall. His body slowly began to rotate to face me, almost like it was levitating at this point, but his head was still facing the corner. I watched in fear as his body slowly rotated, like seeing a demonic dis-morphed ghost. He paused once his body was entirely facing my way. It's anatomically impossible for someone to turn their body all the way around with their head still facing the other way, but this man did it, that's how I knew he wasn't human. His head began to slowly turn my way, a straight emotionless expression filled his face and he turned to look directly at me. He knows I'm here, I thought, it's over for me. Once he was facing his entire body and head in my direction, his cheeks began to stretch big and wide. That awful comical smile was returning to his face. I clenched my eyes in fear for what was coming next. I peeked them back open and the man was walking towards me with great speed, almost power-walking to me.

“This is my coat!” he yelled in his demonic voice while ripping the coat off me.

My body jumped up and my eyes flew open. I was in my bed covered in sweat. Fuck, I was dreaming again, I thought. I rubbed my face and glanced around my room. It was dark but you could still make out the composition of my room. I turned the other way to see my door, dad was standing there. He was in his robe and it was completely undone. He was naked underneath and his face was expressionless.

“Dad what the hell are you doing?” I yelled at him while trying to gather my thoughts.

“Oh sorry I heard you having a nightmare and came in here to make sure you were okay.” he replied.

He closed his robe and tied the string shut. He didn’t look concerned for me, he almost looked like he was happy I was having a nightmare, or he was using it as an excuse to come near my door. He had a sick twisted smirk on his face while I sat in my bed looking at him. That’s when I noticed the bulge of his robe between his legs. He had been watching me having a nightmare and getting himself aroused beside me.

“I’m fine can you leave please! Your freaken penis is sticking out and it’s fucking gross! Please fucking leave!” I yelled.

“Okay sorry.” He said with that same smirk on his face as he turned and headed back to his room.

No apology or anything of that sort came from his mouth. Something was very wrong with him, my gut was quenched and tied in knots. He slowly walked back to his room and shut the door behind him. I got up and closed my door and turned the light on. I sat on the edge of my bed rubbing my face and drying off all the sweat from my body. What the hell am I going to do, I thought to myself. Should I tell Grandma? No, she would just blame me. What about mom? Maybe. But then I will be forced to live with her, maybe that isn’t so bad, maybe that would be better than this. I stood up and creaked my door open to make sure dad was still in his room. Once I was able to confirm dad was in his room, I tip-toed into the dining room and picked up one of the dining chairs and brought it back to my room. Once the door was closed behind me, I propped the dining chair against the door knob so nobody could get in my room. At least I can sleep in peace now for the rest of tonight and I know for sure nobody can watch me sleep. Tomorrow I will figure out what I’m going to do about this.

As I took my time trying to configure all the options on how to proceed with the situation with dad, the days all blended together. Time went on but it felt like it was standing still in my mind during this situation. The days came just like many before it and what will be many after. Dad didn’t come into my room every night, maybe two times a week. Sometimes it was four times in a week, it fluctuated depending on what kind of mood he was in. He wouldn’t do anything, he would just stand there watching me. Sometimes I would wake up and turn over and he would be standing there, he would play dumb and say I was having a nightmare so he came in, seemed to always be the same excuse. He was always in his robe and it was usually undone. Eventually over time this became normal, he did it to Liz now he's doing it to me, this is normal and expected behaviour from a father, I thought. Things like this begin very slowly, they begin with a comment, or a small gesture. It's so small you may not even notice it, but they do it small on purpose. Slowly making it bigger and bigger over time, desensitizing you to the abuse almost, that way you are more likely to put up with it because you've been slowly accustomed or conditioned to it over years. One day you will look back and wonder where it all began and how you even got here, it's crazy how much grooming is hard to recognize from a young person, and even grown adults around you can't seem to spot it easily. It's also crazy how much work and effort is put into grooming someone.

I started putting the dining room chair in front of the door almost every night once I noticed he was regularly watching me. It was getting to be exhausting because I would sit in bed and wait for dad to go to bed so I could sneak out and grab the chair without him noticing. I also would have to get up before he did for work at 5 AM and put it back. Something about him finding out I knew what he was doing made it all seem real, I don't think my mind was ready for that acceptance yet. Looking back, I'm sure he knew I was putting the chair there when he no longer could open my door anymore during the night, but my fragile brain felt better with the mindset that he didn't know the chair was there. My school teachers were beginning to notice something was off with me. I became very irritable and miserable, I separated myself from my friends and became quite a loner around school. Normally I was more talkative and participated often in classroom discussions, those days slowly faded away. Almost like I wasn't even in my body anymore, I was just on autopilot in order to survive emotionally.

One day, I was sitting in class quietly writing a quiz when I heard a knock at the class room door. All the students picked up there heads from their desks to look towards the door out of curiosity. Our teacher Mr. Gibbs walked to the door and opened it a crack. The student counsellor Mrs. Mullens peeked her head inside the class. Her eyes caught mine, but I wasn't sure if it was a coincidence or if it was on purpose. My brain seemed to question every little detail now a days.

"Sorry to bother you Mr. Gibbs but I need to see Charlie in my office as soon as possible. She will need to bring her books and stuff with her as she won't be returning to class today." Mrs. Mullens whispered to Mr. Gibbs trying not to disturb anyone else in the classroom.

Mr. Gibbs turned to me sitting at the back of the classroom and nodded his head at me and waved his hand as in telling me to leave class. I knew that brief eye contact Mrs. Mullens made to me was directed at me but my mind was on edge because I didn't know what this was about. The rest of my classmates turned and looked at me. I could feel all their judging faces peering at me while I gathered my things, they were probably only wanting to know what was going on just like me, but because of the circumstances at home, I seemed to assume the worst in the people around me. Mrs. Mullens waited patiently outside the classroom for me in the hallway while I gathered my stuff off my desk. As I walked out I gave a quick brief wave to Mr. Gibbs with an annoyed look on my face, I was in biology class which was my favourite class, but I was anxious to find out what was going on. Couldn't they have waited until Math or Religion class, those were the two subjects I knew I would never use in life and wouldn't mind missing for a day. Math was a pain in my head and I knew I would avoid any job that made me calculate pointless calculations or finding the "x" of the triangle. And at this point in my life I had lost a lot of faith in any possibility of a God. I almost felt as if I hated whatever concept of a God. How could a God sit back and watch while dad tormented me every night? Maybe because it was normal or this so called God didn't seem to care, my circumstances made me lose whatever small faith I had previously. Biology was my favourite class, I enjoyed all the science classes. Evolution, dinosaurs, space, plant cells and human cells were all so fascinating to me and I didn't really want to miss anything in this class because once you fell a little bit behind you were basically screwed for the rest of the week.

I shut the classroom door behind me and looked nervously at Mrs. Mullens. Feeling a little awkward, I managed to get the courage to say hello to her and she directed me towards her office. She was polite but I could tell she didn't want to talk to me in the hallway, I knew it must have been something serious then.

"Did I do something or am I in trouble?" I asked while we walked quietly down the hall.

It was surprising how fast she could strut down the hall with her office pump heels on, almost like the shoes didn't even phase her. She turned to look at me with a very concerned look on her face as we walked toward her office.

“No-no Charlie you aren’t in trouble. We will talk when we get to my office. These hallways seem to carry every conversation across the school so I think it’s best if we just talk in my office.” she replied.

We continued to walk to her office. The hallway was deserted and quiet, all the kids were in their classrooms with shut doors. The only thing that broke the awful silence was her heels hitting the floor with every step. She made a quick stop at my locker so I could drop all my stuff off as my locker was on the way to her office anyways. Having her stand next to me while I turned my lock on my locker was nerve-racking. It was as if I had forgotten my combination even though I’ve done it a hundred times before. After a few attempts with my quivering fingers, I managed to get the lock opened. I unloaded all my stuff and she flagged me to continue walking to her office, I shut the door and clicked my combination lock shut. Her office was just one classroom away from my locker, through the library. It was a small, dark, secluded room with dim lights and comfy chairs. She had pictures of her kids and family on her small wooden desk the school cheaply provided her.

“Charlie please have a seat in whatever chair you’d like” she said while directing her hand towards the two fluffy upholstered chairs sitting opposite from each other.

I anxiously sat down at the nearest chair and she was quick to follow into the second chair directly across from me. She turned in her seat and plopped her books and papers on her outdated wooden desk and turned back to face me.

"I'm sorry for the non-scheduled meeting and I just want to remind you that you are by no means in trouble. This is a very safe place and I want you to know anything you say here is just between me and you. Your teachers have noticed a significant change in you for the past few months and I was wondering if you could tell me if something is wrong?" she asked.

I immediately became as stiff as a rail, and sat awkwardly in my chair. Almost like the big fluffy chair was suddenly very uncomfortable. My throat got extremely dry and I felt my eyelids refusing to blink as I focused my eyes on a spot next to Mrs. Mullens. Something about making eye contact with her intimidated me all of sudden. What have my teachers been saying about me? Do people notice? What will happen if I say what is going on? Am I really mentally ready for this right now? I cleared my throat and found my voice underneath all the anxiety.

"No Mrs. Mullens. I'm good." I replied still not making eye contact.

"Please call me Melissa." she interrupted.

"Sorry, Melissa. No nothing has changed." I repeated still gazing at the ground next to her.

She looked at me unconvinced I was telling the truth. She was the last person I had ever thought about telling about dad. School was also the last place I would want to cry or break down risking anyone else to see or hear. Rumours spread fast in school, I didn't want to be another victim of the grape vine or telephone effect. Her face lowered slightly so her eyes were peeking out on top of her sagging glasses.

"Charlie, nothing you can tell me will hurt you or get anyone in trouble. A little over 3 months ago you were a straight A student, your average was between 85%-100%. Now you are barely passing some of your classes and your highest grade is 71% not counting biology which seems to be the only class you are still doing well in. Do you have anything going on at home?" she continued to question.

"Well I'm not sure, my dad acts weird sometimes but its all good." I replied trying to minimize anything I could still focused on the ground.

"Weird stuff-how?" she asked.

At that point she knew something was up at dad's house. I was stuck on the idea that she was the last person I wanted to tell. I wanted to wait and tell Grandma, maybe she would control her son and tell him to stop and we can go back to normal. I didn't want to tell mom because I knew she mentally couldn't go through hearing about this stuff again. She already struggled enough with knowing Liz's shit, I didn't want to add to her demons that she already couldn't handle. At that moment, I had my mind set; I was going to tell Grandma. I got a small rush of confidence, maybe it was because I figured out a type of solution to my situation without having to involve anyone just yet.

"Nothing he's just a weird old man." I replied trying to come up with something I could tell her to get her off my back. "He just.... He's embarrassing sometimes, but isn't every teenage girl embarrassed of her dad at some point"? I added while trying to chuckle and now looking directly at Mrs. Mullen's face.

She laughed and pushed her glasses higher onto her nose. "Yes teenage girls will be embarrassed sometimes! How's your mom?" she said.

"She's good, has a new boyfriend that likes to drink, but that's about it. I don't see her much at all, maybe once a month." I replied.

"Hmmm. Once a month? Maybe you should go see her a little bit more. Might do you some good to have a change of scenery, especially if your dad is embarrassing." She replied with a big smile on her face.

"Yep will do." I replied.

"Well Charlie that's all I needed for today. It's the end of the day with 10 minutes to spare, you can go hangout in the library until you catch your bus. And please remember that my office is always open if you need to come see me again." she replied while grabbing her books off her desk.

"Thanks so much Mrs. Mullens. Have a good day." I replied.

"Melissa." she corrected as she began to write in her papers.

I smiled as I walked out of her office, thankful that she let it go and I was able to distract her for now. I made my way to the library to finish off my school day and eventually get on the bus. I texted mom to see if maybe I could come over for dinner. Her reply came sooner than expected, normally she takes a few hours to answer me, sometimes she doesn't answer at all.

"Sure sweet heart, Ken is gone out for dinner with some friends and Liz is staying at her boyfriend's tonight. Want me to pick you up after you get home from school?" she texted back.

"Yeah I'll be home at 3:30 PM. See you then." I replied.

I waited around till the bell rang and everyone plunged out of their classes all at once like a volcano erupting in the hallway. I shuffled through everyone to make my way to get on my bus to go home. School was beginning to be a blur, almost like I was just a ghost passing through and I wasn't actually retaining anything because I was always so focused on what was going on at home.
The bus ride flew by, from me being passed out for a quick cat nap in my bench seat, the nap was much needed. I was the last kid to get off the bus, and I was thankful for the opportunity to make up some missed sleep. Once we pulled up to my house, mom was already patiently

waiting in the driveway for me. A big smile immediately went on my face as I pranced off the bus toward her.

"Hi peanut!" mom shouted.

She always seemed to find the weirdest nicknames for me, but I didn't mind.

"Hi mom! I'm going to go drop my stuff inside and I'll be right out." I replied.

I walked to the back door and went into the house. The house felt different just then, almost like I was above it mentally instead of buried alive inside here. The atmosphere was light almost, maybe because I didn't have to be here for a few hours. I plopped my backpack down in my room and changed my clothes to go to mom's house. I was excited that it was going to be only me and mom at dinner, seeing Liz would almost be an ugly reminder of how I treated her before I knew what dad was. I always felt a great deal of shame whenever I saw Liz now that I knew deep down that dad was abusing her as well long ago when me and Drew didn't believe her. Almost like I betrayed her and made her abuse worse by lashing out at her and protecting dad, the only person in her corner then was mom. The shame filled me every time I saw her face, her eyes. I was part of the problem for not believing her, Drew was too. Dad manipulated us against her to protect his own reputation and selfish needs, a typical move he learned from his own mother. I sped out of the house and hopped into mom's car. Dad wasn't home from work yet therefor I didn't need to worry about saying goodbye or watching his face get nervous whenever mom and I were alone together.

"I'm super excited for dinner today!" I expressed.

"Me too! Just us will be nice." mom replied.

"I should probably text dad and tell him I'm not making dinner for him tonight and he will have to fend for himself." I said.

"Charlie your father shouldn't even be relying on you to make dinner. You are his 15 year old daughter, not his mother or his wife. He's the adult and parent, so he should be the one making dinner." Mom explained.

"I get that, but I don't want to talk about it right now. I just want to have some fun with you and not worry about it right now." I snapped while opening my phone to text dad.

"I won't be home tonight to make dinner, I'm at moms. Don't know when I'll be home." I texted dad.

In that moment I thought to myself. Should I tell mom tonight about dad since it's just us two? Would she believe me, probably, but she also would probably greatly over react. Is there a way to not over react when your daughter tells you something so awful, probably not. I was so filled with doubt and shame. Nobody would believe me, I thought. Dad makes himself out to be amazing to everyone, and I've done a great deal of suppressing everything so deep that I've become numb - nobody could possibly suspect a thing. All this time I've had the mentality of; if you don't look while he's doing it, or you don't pay attention to it - then it isn't happening. Also, despite the bad things he did during the night, I did have a lot of good memories with dad when he was normal, so did I really want to give those up? *Should I really give up my own dad?* Would I feel better if I broke my walls down a little and told mom tonight? So many questions ran through my head, so many twists and turns, doors open, windows open, but which one should I take?

"We are going to have fun tonight Charlie. A much needed girls night!" mom said while clicking the car radio on extremely loud. "You want to listen to Shania Twain?" mom added.

"Oh gosh mom.." I said while face palming as the famous Let's Go Girls song came on.

The entire car ride to her house I imagined ways in my head on how I was going to tell mom tonight, all while she rocked out to her favourite girl on the radio. I imagined what her face would look like when she heard the news; would it be angry or something a little more sad? I pictured the large glass of wine she would poor herself before I sat her down to tell her. Would she be able to handle it? I knew that large glass of wine wasn't to enjoy herself, she drank it to cope with what dad did to Liz. Would she fall to the floor crying? Would I cry? Would this be her final breaking point when she knew the abuse was happening to her other daughter as well? So many thoughts ran through my head loudly over top of the Shania Twain mom had blasting in the car. My head gazed out the window the entire drive, numb and not even in my body. I snapped when I felt the change of us going from the concrete road to the gravel driveway and I knew we were finally at mom's house. Weird, I didn't even really remember most of the drive because I was so deep inside my own head thinking of all the different outcomes that could potentially happen depending on how I proceeded with this.

"We are ordering in tonight, so why don't you think of where you want to eat while we walk inside together?" mom said.

"Sounds good!" I replied while shutting the car door behind me.

Mom's house wouldn't be so bad if I had to move here, I thought. I would be able to be a teenager and not a house wife. Maybe I could get a part time job and actually have the mental energy for it? Maybe I could sleep at night and not have to hear dad playing with himself every night like a high school boy. Maybe I could be free..?

"Well did you decide what you want tonight?" mom asked.

For a moment I forgot what she was talking about because I was so deep in thought about what it would be like living at moms. It took me a split second to trace back our conversation to remember what we were talking about.

"Chinese." I blurted out.

That was the first thing that came to mind when mom snapped me out of my deep thoughts. Mom nodded, smiled, and pulled her phone out to call and order Chinese for us tonight. I went up to where my room used to be to have a peek at how much it changed and if I could even picture myself living here again. Everything was still in the same place; my old bed and my dresser still in the same place. Except there was a treadmill tucked away in the corner with some storage on top of it, but all in all, it was the same room as how I left it. Mom came up the stairs to join me after getting off the phone.

"Ken had to put some of his stuff in here since he moved in and we haven't found room for some of his junk he collects. Not even sure why he has a treadmill, he doesn't ever use it ever and it sits there collecting dust." mom said.

"It's fine mom, I don't mind. I don't ever sleep here anyways so no sense having it as my room." I replied.

"Chinese will be here in half hour, what do you want to do till then?" mom said looking around my old room.

"Not sure, we can just go down stairs and talk I guess." I replied.

I followed mom down the stairs and mentally prepared myself to break the news to her about what was happening at dad's house. My heart was thumping like a loud drum and I was beginning to feel slightly dizzy from being so anxious. Mom stopped in the kitchen to poor herself a big glass of wine before we sat down, I watched her from the doorway as she filled her glass. It was disappointing to see how she couldn't really function as a normal human without any wine in her now. She never used to be like that. When everything happened with Liz mom began to drink more often, much more often. Then when Ken came around it escalated even more, but I tried my best to ignore it because I had enough of my own issues to deal with. We made our way to the couch and she sat on one side while I the other. I gathered my thoughts and decided I would feel around the subject of dad to see how much mom could handle emotionally, I didn't want to overwhelm her or have a big drama blow up about this. My phone vibrated and I knew ahead of time it was dad that was texting me.

"Hope you have fun at your mother's house. I'm going out with a girl tonight so I won't be home till late." dad's text read.

I wasn't interested in answering him in that moment, my heart was still racing from the anticipation of what I was about to tell mom.

"So was it awkward after I left with Jackson for the wedding and it was just you and dad there?" I asked.

"Yeah it was fine-well not really...." she stuttered while looking down at her glass of wine and taking a huge sip almost finishing the glass.

"Why what happened?" I asked.

"Oh nothing, your father just makes me uncomfortable." She replied trying to shrug me off.

I knew she was trying to shrug me off, I could feel it. But because of everything happening at dad's house, I knew something had happened with dad and her that evening and I wanted to know what.

"How did he do that?" I pushed.

Mom looked up at me, I think she knew I was pushing for answers but her hesitation was great. She had every reason to be hesitant with me, a while ago I would have defended dad no matter what, until I started to experience what he was like behind closed doors. She looked back down at her glass of wine and took another big long swig, finishing the glass. Then she sat up and rubbed her face in exhaustion.

"I need another glass of wine if we are having this conversation." she replied while walking to the kitchen.

I waited patiently as I heard the cork pop out from a new bottle of wine and the swift brisk poor inside the same glass she just emptied. I knew this one was fuller than the last serving, I could tell by the sound and how long it was taking to fill. My senses seemed to be amped up since moving to dads, almost like I was in a constant state of survival and calculating everyone's moves all the time. Having to know ahead of time what your night was going to look like if dad took a tumbler off the shelf to fill with his evening whiskey or rum, small things like that make you constantly read into everything, unlike a normal person that wouldn't think twice about it. I had to be super vigilant and sensitive to sounds and feelings and knowing what kind of mood he was in so I knew ahead of time if I needed the dining room chair in my room that night. Every little detail began to stick out to me like a sore thumb, it began to spread to everyone and everything in my life and not just with dad. I began constantly calculating and reading people, and reading between every single line of everything that anyone said to me. Talk about mentally draining.

“You know what babe it’s really nothing you need to worry about.” she shrugged walking back to join me on the couch.

“No, please tell me.” I insisted.

She gulped a bit of her wine and then paused to look at me, her eyes and facial expression further confirming that I knew she was uncomfortable telling me this, but I needed to know. Maybe because I needed further evidence for myself of what dad was.. I’m not sure why I needed to know so badly. She sat uncomfortably looking at her wine glass fidgeting her other hand against her pants, then she took a deep breath in and began to talk.

“Well I seemed to have got insanely buzzed off that small glass of wine. Ken had to put me to bed after he picked me up from your dads. It was a little scary to be honest... It really wasn’t that much wine and normally I can drink almost an entire bottle before I feel buzzed, but for some reason, that half glass got me really drunk almost. That has only ever happened to me one time before in my life, it was years and years ago before you were even born. I went to a bar with your father after Drew was born, it was our first time out since giving birth so it was a big deal for us and me and your dad needed a night out. I was with your father all night long and occasionally left my drink with him to go dancing. I only had the one drink but again I got insanely drunk off of it. We ended up having to leave the bar early. Once we got home, Robert's sister actually called an ambulance because I was non-responsive. They did a blood test and I had the date-rape drug in my system. I was shocked because the only person that had my drink other than me was your dad, I don't know it's really weird. I didn't think anything of it at the time, until it happened again. I'm sorry hunny. I just don't know what to think about that visit with him at your house the other day." she explained.

"Yeah that is really weird. I know dad's wine is very strong but I wouldn't say it would intoxicate someone after only drinking half a tiny glass. Do you think dad wasn't paying attention to your drink years ago and someone spiked it?" I replied.

"I'm honestly not sure, maybe. Your dad hung out with the weirdest men, men that made me and my friends all very uncomfortable. Not sure why he always surrounded himself with people like that." she replied.

There was an awkward silence between us after that conversation. I could tell mom was bothered and upset. I could tell she immediately regretted telling me that information, but I knew she needed to get it off her chest.

"I'm sorry Charlie, I just can't help but think and wonder... And I hope you are okay over there is all..." She said while beginning to cry.

I knew in that moment she could not mentally handle what was happening to me. I knew I had to be strong for her, I didn't want her to lose herself mentally because of dad's sick brain. It also clicked that dad was out with a girl tonight, maybe this will turn into a girlfriend and he won't need to do the things he does anymore. Maybe dad getting a girlfriend was my easy way out of this situation because he will go back to normal.

"I'm okay mom. You don't have to worry." I replied while pulling her into my arms for a big hug.

She began to cry a little in my arms but I could tell it was taking every bit of her to hold it in to try to be strong. It was hard for me to not feel like the parent of my parents.

"He also asked if I wanted to do something fun like old times since we were alone. After you pulled out of the driveway I could feel his eyes all over me and he asked if I wanted to go into his bedroom. So wrong of him to ask that and it was really inappropriate.." she said while wiping her tears from her face.

I had no reply to her, I knew how she felt because that's how I usually felt in front of dad... *Eyes all over me..*

“Anyways.... I need to fix my face now before the food gets here.” she replied pulling away from me and wiping the dripping mascara from her eyes.

She stood up from the couch and hurried to the bathroom. What she told me didn’t shock me, I knew she wasn’t lying. After everything dad was doing to me at home, I knew mom had gone through things with him too. That’s the thing about constantly reading people, your gut begins to get extremely accurate. Maybe that’s why their marriage was so bad. Mom had been dealing with his sickness for fifteen years, I was only dealing with it for a little over a year or so and I was already empty and numb, I couldn’t imagine how empty she must feel inside. Maybe that’s why she drank so much, to numb out the pain instead of facing it. Maybe that’s why she had zero self confidence in herself, because dad constantly belittled her and made her feel worthless. I knew the drinking wasn’t okay and it was just a bandaid, but I understood why she did it. I remained seated on the couch, gathering my thoughts and processing who I could turn to or confide in; Grandma, I thought. I will just ask her to keep her son in line, then everything will go back to normal, I thought. Or I could wait to see how things go with this new girl of his, maybe she will get him in line.

The rest of the evening with mom went really well. We enjoyed each others company and chit-chatted all through our Chinese food dinner. Mom was so much better to be around when Ken wasn’t here, she payed more attention to me and seemed to actually care about my interests. When Ken was over he demanded her attention all the time and would start arguments if mom ever put her kids first. I hated that man. He was an alcoholic, and was always pushing my mom to drink all the time. She accepted it, and often, the alcohol helped her brain cope with who she was married to before, my father. If I moved here I would have to accept the fact Ken lives here too, and I knew he would be put first in this house because that's how mom was with Ken. The drive home from mom's house was short, I kept asking her to take the long way or the scenic route, but there is only so many scenic routes you can take before you arrive at your destination. At least dad wasn't going to be home till late tonight and I could enjoy my Friday evening alone as I knew Drew would likely be gone as usual. The house was dark but I didn't care, at least dad was gone tonight. I reached over to give mom a hug before I got out.

"I love you mom, so much." I said.

"I love you too peanut, so much. Sorry about me crying tonight, I needed to tell someone other than Ken because he just got angry and handled it like an immature child." she replied.

"It's okay mom, goodnight." I said while hopping out of the car.

"Bye Charlie!" mom shouted out the window as she began to back out of the driveway.

I knew the first thing I wanted to do once I went inside while nobody was home, I wanted to check dad's room for anything sketchy since he's gone and I knew I wouldn't get caught. I swung the door open and flew inside clicking every light on as I ran through the house.

"Hello?!" I called out to ensure nobody was there and I was indeed alone.

No reply.

I crept into dad's room and began shuffling through his stuff to find anything that might prove what mom was saying was true. I wasn't sure what I was looking for, but something was telling me that something was there, again that strong intuition I developed. Perhaps it was my subconscious telling me I needed reassurance that I wasn't crazy about thinking dad was messed up, maybe I needed something tangible to confirm what I was saying or to confirm what mom said. If I had some sort of physical proof of him doing shitty things, maybe people would believe me easier. I looked everywhere in his room; under his bed, in his closet, in his tall dresser. Nothing out of the ordinary, unless you consider the mountain of porn on his desk to be ordinary. I clicked his computer screen on and began to search his pictures and google history. Besides the mound of random naked women that filled his computer, I couldn't see anything else that stood out to me, right away that is... I dug deeper into his nasty pictures, looked at hundreds of women in nasty, degrading poses till I found one that looked familiar. Well not completely familiar but almost, only the faces were recognizable. It was Liz, me and mom. Except it wasn't exactly us. He had cropped our faces onto other naked women in awful poses. Women that were either tied up, or spreading their private parts open to a camera, that's what he cropped our faces to. Fucking disgusting, I thought. My body trembled in shock. My gut twisted inside itself and I grew more and more nauseous every second I stared at that computer. I swallowed whatever horrid I was feeling and kept looking, I needed to take advantage of being here alone. His google history this time, I thought, I looked deep into his long list of google searches. Some very ordinary, pictures of other countries or the news, some were very dark; how to seduce your daughter, how to have sex with a woman without her knowing, and best places to hide cameras in a bedroom. My body froze at that bundle of words. Was I really reading this on my dad's computer. Was my own biological father googling this stuff? I turned away from the computer in disgust, looking around his room to try to relax my mind a bit. As I stood there trying to gather my thoughts, something else caught my eye. His nightstand which I had forgotten to look inside. It was a two drawer high mini night stand beside his bed. On top of it was more lotion and a couple of porn magazines. I pulled the first drawer open and saw socks and underwear. I pushed the socks out of the way to see if anything was hidden underneath, but nothing was there. I pulled the second drawer out and found where most of his porn was stashed. He had VHS's, DVD's USB sticks, magazines and pictures all porn related or girls in awful degrading poses. It was clear to me that he had no respect for women, that he thought women were just sex objects for men's pleasure. How can someone raise a baby girl from birth all the way till she's a teenager then be sexually attracted to her? A monster that's who, I thought to myself. I shuffled through the porn and found a bag full of different women's underwear, almost like his trophies. A pair of my underwear were inside, he must have went through my underwear drawer and took them, I haven't seen that pair in months. Behind the bag of underwear I found, there was a little zip-lock bag of little white pills. I picked the bag up to get a closer look, the name on the bag written in green Sharpie pen said "Roofies". I knew in that moment two things; my mother was telling the truth, even though not a shred of doubt ever crossed my mind that she was lying, and the other thing I knew was that I was in danger with him. I dropped the back of pills and underwear back in the drawer and closed up his room like normal, that way he wouldn't know I was onto him.

I went into my room and sat on my bed feeling defeated. What the hell was I going to do about him, he needed mental help. He needed therapy, he needed rehab, he needed something but I didn't know what to do. I rubbed my face and covered my eyes while my elbows sank deeply into my knees. Smokey our dog came in my room and put his head on my thigh and stared at me. I fell into him crying and my entire body was limp. He sat there accepting my meltdown like it was his job to comfort me. At least someone knew what was happening to me, and what I was dealing with. Even though Smokey couldn't speak, his comfort was far better than any words. I'm going to tell Grandma tomorrow, I thought to myself. It's a done deal, I'm going to tell her. I can't wait to see if things go well with this new girlfriend of his, this is only going to get worse if I don't tell anyone. I went into the dining room and grabbed my usual chair and propped it behind my door that way dad couldn't get in tonight. I didn't think he was going to bother me anyways since he was with a girl already tonight and probably got his fill from her. I laid in bed thinking about what I was going to say to Grandma tomorrow. The events of tonight replayed in my mind like a broken record. After hours of tossing and turning, I fell asleep.

I woke up to someone walking around outside my room. I peeked my head up towards my door knob and I could see it slowly and quietly turning back and forth. They tried to open the door but the chair was in the way. Dad is trying to get in, I thought to myself, and he was indeed trying to be really quiet. Or am I dreaming again and the man in black is trying to get in here to terrorize me once again? After a few unsuccessful attempts the door knob stopped twisting back and forth and it was silent. I laid my head back down in satisfaction that I had out-smarted whoever was out there, when I heard footsteps quietly walking through the house again, pacing almost. I laid there quietly listening, trying to figure out if this was another one of my dreams or was this real. I heard the front door open into the front screened room and the footsteps lead into there. I assumed maybe dad was about to have a smoke or something, until I saw his shadow coming towards my side of the patio room where my window was. That's odd, I thought, his smoking chair is on the other side. I kept my head down and didn't move a muscle, I wanted him to think I was sleeping so I could see what he was up too, or to see if this was the man in black. Maybe dad had a hidden camera somewhere and he was retrieving it to upload images, I thought, so I'll keep a close eye to see what he's doing. Or Maybe he has another peep hole, at least I will know where it is now if I lay silently and pretend to be sleeping. I laid quietly with my eyes only open a tiny crack so I could look at my window. Dad's face peeked around the wall and he began to look into my room towards my bed at me. He stood there staring at me, my room would have been too dark for him to see the chair on the other side of the room against the door, but my bed was near the window and he would be able to see me clear as day. I was still frozen pretending to sleep, looking at him through the crack of my eyes. He stood there for what felt like ten minutes, he was almost not even blinking. He slowly undid his robe and I could see his erect penis. I clenched my eyes shut in terror at what I saw. What the fuck was he doing! I thought to myself. I kept my eyes shut because I could still feel his presence in the window watching me. After a few minutes of laying there frozen and trying to deal with the unbearable feeling I was feeling, I cracked my eyes open and saw him masturbating to my sleeping body through the window. His eyes glaring at my butt and legs while he pumped himself over and over again. I clenched my eyes once again in horror for what I just saw. My feet and fingers were beginning to go numb because I was clenching so hard and holding my breath. Some would ask why I didn't just get up and yell at him, but at the time I thought avoiding that situation was easiest in the moment. Because if I would have opened my eyes and yelled at him, what would happen next? I would lose my father entirely once I knew he wouldn't be able to give me a logical explanation as to what he was doing outside my window. I knew I would lose all of him, even the small parts that were good. I knew I wouldn't have a dad anymore, I knew I would be thrown back into mom's house and I'd have to deal with two selfish drunks that didn't care about me. Life can be hard when you are trying to calculate which living condition would be worse to be in, especially when you are choosing between two parents that you are biologically programmed to love no matter what. After a few more minutes, which felt like hours, I peeked my eyes open again and he was gone. I knew he got his fix and I was safe for the rest of the night. I laid in bed for the rest of the night feeling dirty, disgusting, uncomfortable and alone. I felt stupid for ever leaving moms. Maybe this was the universe's way of punishing me for leaving moms house. Maybe I should have listened to Liz. But I knew if I stayed at mom's things would be bad there too with how much mom and Ken drink. Why the hell was the universe letting this happen, why was this happening to me. Then I would feel selfish for hating my life, I would think about the people in sex trafficking or the little kids that get dumped in dumpsters and I felt shame and guilt for hating my life because they have it worse than me. My life was bad, but not even close to what horrors some people live everyday. I tossed and turned in my bed every time the pillow would get too soaked from my tears on one side, I would roll over to let it dry while I cried on the other side. I felt alone in my life, *it was indeed the darkest place I had ever imagined my soul would be.*

It felt like it took forever for morning to come. I walked out of my room and put the dining room chair back before dad got up, even though I already knew he was aware I put the chair there at night, I went back in my room to get dressed and start the day. The feeling of exhaustion and numbness filled my body while I walked around the house. Almost like I was accepting this is the way my life is, this is the way it has to be if I want a roof over my head. I heard dad getting up and my body cringed, tension ran through my entire spine and all the emotion immediately left my face. I had become a walking puppet of my life, I was just flowing with the daily routine to get by. I became much like the man in black, puppet-like. Dad's bedroom door swung open and he came storming out with a big smile on his face and in a jolly mood.

"Good morning Char!" He said with a big smile on his face.

"Morning." I replied avoiding eye contact.

"What are your plans today?" he asked.

“Nothing during the day yet but I was planning on going to Grandma’s for supper. I haven’t asked her if I can yet though.” I replied fiddling on my phone.

“It’s Grandma you don’t have to ask, you just go.” dad joked.

Dad actually seemed normal today. The way he was looking at me was as if I was his daughter. Normally he looked at me like a wolf staring at a raw piece of meat. This is the good part of my father I would be losing if I spoke up about how he is sometimes. Why was he normal sometimes, and other times he was a terrible human?

“Drew might as well just live with Alexis, he’s never home. I’m going to give his room to you pretty soon.” dad added.

My brain froze and I peeked up at him and put my phone down. If I had Drew’s room there wouldn’t be a way for dad to watch me sleep. The only windows up there go out to the roof and the door to come up is at the bottom of the stairs and has a lock. Maybe once I talk to Grandma and she puts dad in his place and things go back to normal again, then I can have Drew’s room and things would be great again and normal and all the drama will be avoided and I can have my normal dad back.

“Yeah that would be cool if I could have Drew’s room.” I replied.

“Want to go apple picking today? It’s cooler out but still sunny. I thought maybe you can make some apple pies tomorrow with Grandma or something.” dad asked.

It was very odd. Why was he being so nice to me? It felt like my normal dad was here, and the demon that possessed him was gone. Does he have a split personality, I thought. Maybe if I spoke to a counsellor about him it would help more than Grandma, maybe he had two different personalities or something. I wanted to go apple picking with him, I wanted to be around my normal dad. But at the same time I hated him for what he’s been doing to me, for what he did to Liz, and mom, for what he had in his bedroom, and for the awful secrets he kept from everyone. He made all the women in his life seem like crazy nut jobs when in reality he was the one abusing them all. My heart tore into two pieces, I loved my dad but I hated him. The terrible things I knew couldn’t just leave my mind.

“No thanks, I was going to maybe meet up with Jackson later, I’m not sure.” I responded.

“Alright, well I’m going to fix some of the wood panels in the garage today. Feel free to come help if you want.” he responded.

He walked into the kitchen and made himself a coffee to bring outside with him. It filled the house with the smell of fresh coffee, which was something I enjoyed. I still stood in the same place in the living room staring out the window. I heard the back door open and close and turned to see if he had left. I could see through the storm door he was outside walking towards the back garage and inspecting the wood walls. I went into the kitchen and made myself a toast and got a glass of orange juice. I ate in my room while I did my hair and makeup and made my bed. I looked around the house to see what needed to be cleaned, and I decided it was going to have to be the entire house. I couldn't control the environment I was living in, but at least I could control how dirty the house was, almost like the more things I cleaned, the less disgusting I felt about my life. I walked into the basement to get the vacuum and mop pail we stored down there. The basement reeked of mould and the damp swampy air filled your lungs the minute you stepped down on the bottom step. I rolled my eyes as I walked past the peep-hole in the basement looking up at the bathroom. It filled me with anger even though I know he couldn't see me anymore because I covered the vent with my clothes every time I took a shower. A person shouldn't have to live like that, hiding in their own home because they aren't safe from the one person who swore to protect you from birth. It made me feel irritated, annoyed at his selfishness. I knew once I told Grandma tonight that she would make him stop, she would scare him a little and put him back in his place, she would protect me. It will all be over and back to normal after tonight and it can be the way it was before, I thought.

I grabbed the vacuum and mop pale and carried them upstairs. Cleaning the house seemed to be the only stress relief I had, at least I had control over this. Except I moved so quickly and zoned into it like a robot that I managed to always have the house spotless within a couple hours. It was a few hours of meditation, of counselling, of relieving myself of feeling constantly powerless, two hours of forgetting who I was living with and what my situation was. I stood in the dining room looking over at my regular weekly accomplishment, I may be in a shitty situation, but

I sure can clean a damn house, I thought. Dad came in for a quick glass of water.

“Holy enough bleach?!” Dad shouted with a disgusted look on his face.

I looked at him in confusion because I was so deeply zoned out I wasn’t comprehending the chemical smells in here. His eyes squinting tightly as the bleach fumes burned them. He covered his mouth with his hand, as he crossed the kitchen to see me in the doorway.

“Jesus Charlie you need to open a window! You can’t be breathing this shit in you’ll get sick!” He said as he opened the dining room window.

“Sorry I didn’t notice.” I responded.

“Don’t use this much bleach next time please, it’s not good for the old wood floors. It’ll ruin the coating on them and make them dull. Then I have to sand them and coat them again.” dad said.

“Well if you are so particular about how the house gets cleaned, maybe you should fucking do it yourself like all the other parents do while their teenagers sit on their ass’ playing on their phones!” I snapped.

Dad stood in shock in the doorway and stared at me. His jaw was almost to the floor. I had never dared to say anything like that to him, it just sort of blurted out of my mouth without thinking.

"Excuse me? You don't get to speak to me like that I'm the parent here, not you!" Dad shouted back with his face red as a tomato and anger in his face.

"You can call yourself a parent when you start acting like one.' I said in the most calmest voice and with a straight face gazing into his eyes and not blinking.

"Go to your damn room right the hell now Charlie!" he shouted while pointing at my room door.

I threw the broom on the ground and marched to my room, slamming the door behind me. I didn't care, I couldn't hold it in anymore. He calls himself a parent, what a joke, I thought. I stayed in my room almost the entire rest of the day playing Call of Duty until it was time to head to Grandma's house. I heard him come in periodically and walking around, but I didn't bother to care what he was doing. I could hear his shoes were still on while he walked around, clearly he didn't care that I just spent a few hours cleaning the entire house just so he could walk all over them with dirty shoes on. I peeked my door open and saw that dad wasn't in the house anymore. I walked out of my room and looked into the kitchen at the back storm door and I could see dad lifting a piece of wood panelling and hammering it to the garage wall. I ain't going out that way, I thought, I don't want him to tell me I can't go to Grandma's house or yell at me again. I put my shoes on and left out of the front door towards Grandma's, it wasn't much of a walk because she lived roughly 10 doors down the road. My eyes squinted at the sunlight as it pierced through my sore eyelids from playing video games for the entire afternoon. My nose tainted with the smell of bleach and a stain on my shirt from spilling pine cleaner on it earlier while cleaning. I got to Grandma's house and walked up her long driveway to get to her house. Seems nobody else was there and it was just Grandma and Grandpa. Perfect, I thought, I will be alone with them tonight and I will be able to ask for Grandma's help or advice on what to do about my situation with dad.

"Hi Grandma and Grandpa!" I yelled while coming in the back door.

"Hi Charlie!" I heard Grandma yell from the back bedroom.

I heard golf playing on the TV and assumed Grandpa was sitting in his rocker watching Golf like he normally is. Grandma was walking up from the back hallway where the bedrooms are toward me in the kitchen. The kitchen smelt amazing as always, like a fresh baked pie, and the table was already set.

"Hi sweetie, how was your day today? You're here early." she said.

"Yeah I thought maybe we could go sit on the porch and talk a bit? It's a really nice day out, figured we could enjoy it. Maybe bird watch on all your feeders." I asked.

"Well sure! I'm sure Grandpa wants to sit on his rocker swing out there and enjoy the nice day. I already have most of dinner prepped its just a matter of putting it in the oven, so we certainly have some time to spare.

I also made a beautiful blue berry pie for dessert with some berries I picked today. I'll get Grandpa off his butt and meet you out there." Grandma said as she walked into the living room to get Grandpa.

I sat on the cast iron chair that was across from the old rocker swing where they both liked to sit. I gazed around her yard and admired her beautiful flower gardens and how it seemed like every bird in this little town lived here because of the plentiful food Grandma had well stocked in her many bird feeders. The honey bees swarming from flower to flower, which were also in abundance. The slightest breeze was making the flowers dance and wiggle in the air with no effort. Her wind chimes calmly knocking in the small breeze and they played the most subtle chime. Grandma and Grandpa came out of the back door and joined me on the porch, sitting across from me in their favourite porch swing. Grandpa's knees weren't the best so Grandma had to rock the swing herself back and forth.

"What a beautiful day it is, eh?" Grandpa said with a complete smile on his face.

"Yeah it is! Did you guys do much today or yesterday?" I asked.

"Well Grandpa went golfing yesterday, I picked up the kids to watch all day and we picked blueberries. Today we haven't done much though. How about you?" Grandma said.

It was hard to hide the sarcasm and annoyance on my face. My Aunt Patty always either left her bundle of kids at Grandma's house to tend to, or she would make Grandma drive all the way to the other end of the city, a good 35 minutes away to pick them up and watch them all day. It seemed the kids were at Grandma's house more than they were at their own house.

"That sounds like a nice weekend. I went to mom's yesterday for dinner, and today I did a deep clean to the house. It really needed it." I replied.

Grandma mimicked the same sarcastic look as I did a minute ago. She hated whenever I mentioned mom to her. She always hated mom, at least she would act like it and had no problem showing me that to my face. Her sarcastic jokes or remarks whenever she was over when mom and dad were still married was pretty much a straight give away of how she felt about mom, it's no wonder why mom was always so uncomfortable coming here before. She also made a point to not let my mom feel included in the family. Grandma's lips clenched tight together every time mom was brought up as if she was restraining herself from a bash fest of judgment about mom. I knew how she felt about mom, but she had a biased opinion so it wasn't really a valid one The porch went silent and Grandma and Grandpa kept looking around their yard admiring the birds.

"Can I ask you guys something?" I said while swallowing my breath.

"Sure Charlie." Grandma replied.

"What do you think is the real reason that Liz doesn't come over or see dad?" I added while holding my breath for their answer.

I was nervous that I just asked that, but this was the reason I came here today to begin with. They both froze and stared at me in shock that I had the guts to ask such a question. I wanted to feel around the subject to see where they stood before I told them what was happening to me. I knew they didn't like mom, but that is normal for in-laws to not like the daughter-in-law, but Liz was different, she was their grandchild. I didn't want to be even more rejected from Grandma then I already was, which is why I made the decision to feel around the subject before telling her what was going on. Grandma's leg stopped rocking the chair and Grandpa's face went white as a ghost and he turned to look at the ground. It's difficult to describe the vibe I got from Grandpa just then in that moment, he didn't look like he wanted to avoid the question. He appeared more intimidated to say anything in front of Grandma, almost like he knew the true answer but was too scared of Grandma to say it out loud, I felt the guilt and shame projecting onto me from him, I felt the thirst he had to speak the truth, but it's like he knew Grandma would over-power him. Almost as if he knew exactly where I was going with this type of question. Grandma on the other hand looked right at me with a red face in hatred and she looked annoyed that I even dared to question anything at all.

"Liz doesn't come over because your piece of work mother coached her into saying lies about your dad. It's your mother's fault, she forced Liz to say awful lies. And Liz just follows her every command like a lost puppy to get attention. Your mother and Liz just like drama. That's all they've ever liked is drama, drama, drama. Robert is a great father and provided a roof over your heads all your lives while your mother was being a lazy no good piece of work. Liz needs to be more appreciative and stop being a spoiled brat." Grandma blurted out.

I could feel her emotions growing stronger and stronger the more she talked. Grandpa's head still pointed to the ground saying nothing about this situation. I bit my tongue, I wanted more information on where she stood and I wanted to see what kind of a picture my dad painted to people about the Liz situation because I knew he would do the same type of painting if I ever came out about my abuse. Dad didn't provide the roof over our heads, mom did. I saw it, everyday. Mom always balanced the budget, mom always made sure all the bills were paid, mom worked all day and then made dinner and cleaned the house. Dad could barely hold a job down, and spent whatever money he had on crap we didn't need or something that made him look like some cool man to all his friends that secretly hated him, dad was a show-boat. I also knew Liz wasn't lying because the same crap was happening to me in the moment and I barely ever talked to mom, so is Grandma going to say mom coached me into saying these things when me and mom don't even have a relationship? I felt my jaw clenching shut, almost chewing a hole through my tongue while I sat and listened to Grandma talk about stuff she didn't know anything about.

"I don't mean to say these things about your mother, but that woman is a piece of work and has put Robert through so much drama!" Grandma added.

I couldn't help but laugh in my head. It was the opposite, dad was the one putting mom through all this drama. Dad was the one ruining peoples lives with his selfishness. He was the one doing it to himself. Maybe that's why dad continued to do these things... Because he had a mother that never made him accountable for anything in his life.

"Does Liz ever try to talk to you guys?" I asked.

"Nope, she hasn't ever tried to contact us. We've sent her gifts and she ignores us. Nothing we can do about that." Grandma replied.

I knew that was also a lie. Liz tried to reach out to them multiple times and Grandma either hangs up the phone on her or calls her a liar and a drama queen. The gift that was sent to Liz, was from Grandpa but Liz had no way of talking to him without Grandma controlling everything to do with the situation. Almost like Grandma was more concerned about keeping her perfect families reputation intact than to actually deal with problems and protect the young girls within her family. I knew once Grandma said all this that I couldn't tell her anything about my situation. She would find any way she could to twist it to be my fault instead of admitting she raised a sick man. Her pride and ego were too big for her to see out of her blinders, no wonder why dad was the way he was. Look who raised him. I turned to Grandpa and waited for him to speak up, I waited for some sort of protection or reassurance from him. Instead, he kept his face turned to the ground in guilt, he knew exactly what was happening to me and what happened to Liz. He was a retired police officer, he knew the signs, he knew how these things worked, he knew what his son was. But he also knew the fight was pointless to try to prove to his wife otherwise. And what "signs" are really there to be seen? Signs are extremely hard to spot in some circumstances, yet completely apparent in another. Some people carry stress and abuse extremely well and can cope depending on how numb they can become, other people are very obvious when they are being abused. So is there really a way to predict signs with every person and every single individual situation? *No.* She's the type of tyrant woman that you can smack her in the face with all the proof you want, and she will still stand her ground about being right.

The conversation ended as quickly as it began and Grandma changed the subject to her variety of birds in her yard. Grandpa remained silent the rest of the night when I was there, not even making eye contact with me. Maybe he was ashamed that he stood silently when I think he could tell what was happening to me. I was quiet too, I got what I came here for, information on where they stood. And I knew no matter what dad did to me every night, no matter how much worse it got, no matter what proof I possibly had, Grandma was going to protect him at all costs. I left their house quietly that night, feeling as alone as I ever was. The weight of the world and everyone else's decisions weighed onto my little shoulders, pushing me down into a grave that wasn't even dug yet for a body that wasn't dead yet. I didn't know what I was going to do. And I didn't anticipate on what waited for me that night when I got home. I was truly alone in this world. My brain on the walk home raced. My thoughts ran in all directions, and the ball in my throat permanently embedded itself pushing me to cry at any moment. I walked step after step in the dark on the side of the road towards my house. Although it wasn't scary here in the county at night, I still felt the need to constantly look over my shoulder. Almost as if my brain was in hyper drive or a constant sketched out state of mind. I reached the house and I could see dad sitting in the front porch room having a smoke. He waved as I walked up the driveway, I quivered my arm up to mimic the same waving motion back. The narrow look never left my face as I walked into the back door into the house.

“How was dinner Char?” asked dad.

“It was good.... We had pizza casserole.” I replied.

“I love when she makes that!” dad boasted.

He walked into the house from the porch room, and to my surprise, he was actually wearing clothes and not a robe, which was something that was slightly comforting considering he was always naked with that stupid robe on.

“I bought some chips and downloaded a movie, want to watch it with me tonight?” He asked.

I felt awkward. I didn’t know how to respond, and I felt confused. He was acting so normal right now? Maybe he was getting hints I was onto him? Or maybe his sick phase was done and I could have my normal dad back? The type of unpredictability with him was mentally draining, never knowing what to expect when I came home can really have an affect on how you look at people. You constantly think people are being fake or messing with you. And if they are nice to you, you constantly think its just to put on a show. This type of mentality can spread to all your relationships if you are around it long enough.

“What movie?” I replied.

“Rambo First Blood, your favourite. Or we could watch John Wick?” He replied.

“Okay, let’s watch John Wick because I just watched First Blood the other day.” I replied.

Dad nodded his head, he looked happy that I actually said yes. Things felt normal for this moment. Maybe my dad was normal now and this hell is over? Or maybe I needed to take advantage of the time my dad was normal so I could at least have somewhat of a memory of a normal dad. Maybe the universe heard my cries and rid him of his sick ways. Again, how unpredictable things were can really mess with your emotions, and make you feel up and down all the time. I went into my room and grabbed myself a blanket and came back into the living room.

“I call the loveseat.” I said.

“That’s fine, it's too small for me anyways.” he replied.

He sat on the other couch diagonal from me and we turned the movie on with our big bowls of chips. I felt my body relaxing, things felt completely normal right now and I wanted to take advantage of it. We talked during most of the movie and for once it wasn't anything inappropriate. He told me stories about when he was in high school, and he asked how me and Jackson were doing and how things were progressing with us two. For this moment I forgot how awful of a human being he actually is. Some say this would be impossible to forget these things, but when its your own messed up parent you come to appreciate when things are normal and wish they stayed like that permanently, you also try to hang on to that little tiny part of them that may still be a good person. The movie finished and I was feeling really beat after today and decided to go to bed. Dad got up and stretched and went into his room as well. I saw his light turn off and him get into his bed and I thought maybe I didn't need the chair tonight because he was already going to be passing out soon and he seemed relatively normal tonight. I shut my door and crawled into bed clicking the TV on in my room with a sleep timer on it, that way it would shut off in twenty-five minutes. I laid in my bed watching Mister Ed while I slowly drifted off to sleep.

I woke to something moving around in my bed, something small. I felt it hugging my right butt cheek, almost like fine-grit sandpaper or a piece of leather. When I lifted my head to see if I had a mouse or rat in my bed, dad was sitting on the edge of my bed looking at me. He pulled his hand out from under my blanket with a shocked look on his face. That's when I realized what was touching my butt, it was his overworked hand. I sat there in shock looking at him with my jaw down to the floor. He sat there with a devious look on his face staring right back at me with a beet red face. I couldn't believe what was happening and what had just been happening while I was sleeping.

“What the fuck are you doing?” I asked aggressively.

“I’m just sitting here.” He replied.

He dropped eye contact, his gaze moved to the floor and his face became expressionless. I tried to wrap my head around his answer to my question, how can he say he was just sitting there. Does he think I’m a complete oblivious idiot? Did he not realize I just caught him with his hand up my shorts while I slept?

“Then what the fuck was your hand doing under my blanket on me?” I said with hostility.

“It wasn’t.” he replied.

“I just fucking saw you pull it out from under my blanket and I felt your hand against me!” I shouted.

“No, you must of dreamt it.” he replied while getting up off my bed and tying his stupid robe back together.

“Get the fuck out of here, are you drunk or something?” I shouted at him as he scurried out of my room like a coward who couldn’t face the outcome of what he had done.

I got up and slammed my door shut behind him. The blood rushed into my face and my heart pounded like a baseball bat hitting me. I stood beside my bed, contemplating what the hell I was going to do. This is it, if I stay here and not say anything to anyone, he is going to rape me, or drug me. I have to tell someone, I need to tell someone as soon as possible. I picked up my blanket and pillow off my bed and got into my closet. My closet was deep enough that I could sleep in there for the rest of the night with the door shut, and because my head was so close to the closet door, I could feel it if it opened. I laid there in that dark old closet trying to sleep, but who could actually sleep after that? My mind was completely numb, the ups and downs of emotion from this evening were killing me. Dad felt so normal earlier tonight, then all of a sudden that just happened, it was so hard for my mind to process how dad could just turn into that within a couple hours. Every little sound in the house would immediately startle me thinking it was dad coming to finish what he started. I didn't sleep the rest of the night and instead sat alone in the dark closet looking at my phone. I went through my contacts to see who I could tell about this without them judging me or blaming me. Seeing how Grandma twisted Liz's situation on her made me terrified to tell anyone because I knew people would twist this on me too. That's when a light-bulb clicked on inside my head. Mom made all us kids go to a counsellor a few times when my parents were divorcing years ago, I will call him in the morning and request an appointment and tell him what has been going on, maybe he can help me.

# Chapter 8

The next morning I woke up to get ready for school, except I wasn't really going to school that day. Dad left for work before I got on the bus so he wouldn't ever know if I skipped. I got out of my room and he was already gone, I could tell Drew must of stopped here as well because he threw his dirty clothes in front of the basement door for me to wash. I checked around the house to make sure dad left and nobody was there, I was in the clear and nobody was here. I pulled my phone out and called my old counsellor I had when mom and dad originally got divorced, I still had his number saved as a contact in my phone. His name was Steven DeAngelous, he was a big giant scary looking guy, but he was for sure a gentle giant, he was easy to talk to and helped a lot during mom and dads separation. The receptionist picked up and I requested an appointment for today, I didn't have a plan on how I was going to get there, but I didn't care, I'd walk if I had to and I had all day that I could easily walk there, even though it was 36kms away.

"Unfortunately Steven doesn't have anything for today." The receptionist said.

“I really need to see him, its urgent. Do you think you can maybe ask him if he can squeeze me in?” I insisted, I was persistent and pushy.

I needed this appointment no matter what, I didn’t want to be here a minute longer and I knew tonight would bring more horrors to my bedroom, so this appointment had to happen today.

“Can you wait on hold, I’ll talk to Steven and see if there is anything we can do for you.” she replied as she put me on hold.

Within moments she was back on the line with good news.

“Well Charlie, we can get you in to see Steven at about 3 PM. Does that work?” she replied.

“Yes that’s perfect! Thank you!” I said with excitement.

I knew what I had to do, and I was going to do it today, no more chickening out. I immediately called my Meme and Pepe to see if one of them could drive me. Meme picked the phone up and she sounded confused as to why all of a sudden I was going to see Steven. She wasn’t impressed I wasn’t at school either, she was a retired teacher and had the mentality that you better be dead than to miss school. I explained I was simply feeling stressed and needed someone to talk to. She continued to question why I needed to talk to a counsellor, but I was equally pushing back. This was the last way on earth I wanted to tell someone, I had my mind made up that I wanted to tell Steven and nobody else. At least I could get it off my chest to him, and then I'd feel better knowing someone else knows what I'm dealing with. She agreed she could drive me there but couldn't pick me up, I replied to her that I would figure out a ride home myself and I was thankful she was driving me there to begin with and she finally gave up on asking me why I needed to go there. The day went by slow, I wandered around the house trying to find any other peep holes in my room I may of not known about. I needed to take advantage of this while dad was gone for the day and I needed to prepare myself mentally for what I was about to tell someone and their possible reaction to this situation. I knew after I told Steven about dad, that everything was going to go back to normal. Steve would talk to dad and straighten him out, put him in rehab or get him mental help. Then things would go back to normal and we can start being a normal family again. My stomach was filled with excitement and nervousness, I didn't know what to think, I just knew it was time to tell someone. It was eating me alive being the only person knowing about this situation. I rehearsed over and over again what I was going to say to Steven once I was in that room with him. I coached myself on how to explain dad's situation. I walked back into the basement to see the peep hole through the vent going into the bathroom where dad watched me. I went into his room and opened the drawer of his underwear trophies and date rape drugs he used on my own mother, possibly Tania, and maybe even more women, maybe even me. I looked at the stack of porn he had in his room and the piles he kept in our living room, I looked at the demeaning types of porn he had. This stuff was dark. I looked at his google history once again to refresh myself about the awful things I saw he was googling. I looked once again at the photo my dad cropped of me, Liz and mom onto other naked women. All the manipulative, grooming conversations he talked about with me played over and over in my head. I needed to look at this all over again to make sure it's all real, to make sure I don't forget anything. *To make sure I'm doing the right thing by telling on him.*

I jumped out of my own head when I heard the horn of Memes car in the driveway. It's already almost 3? I thought. I kissed Smokey goodbye and left the house. When I shut the door behind me I felt as though I was closing a chapter to my life, dad would now get help and be cured and we would be happy again. Drew might come around more if he knew his dad wasn't sick and twisted, things would be great again, my optimism was pushing through. I got in Memes car ready for this session with Steve.

"Hello Charlie! How are you? No school today?" Meme said as she backed out of the driveway.

Meme always questioned us a few times if we were missing school for any reason. Maybe back in her day school was a little more valuable, now a days they just cram pointless information down your throat that you will most likely never use in your adulthood, and they don't teach you the stuff you really need in life because it isn't in the curriculum. I think my brain would be fine missing one single day of pointless knowledge and forced memorization that I'll soon forget a few years after high school is over, but meme always felt different and we agreed to disagree.

“No I took today off because I need to see Steve.” I replied hoping she would sit quietly in the car ride, that way I could gather my thoughts as to how I was going to tell Steve.

“How come you are stressed? Why?” she questioned.

“I just don’t want to talk about it with anyone else but Steve. It’s no big deal, I swear. Just want to vent to him about stuff at school.” I replied.

“Well okay…… You’re planning on going to school tomorrow though right?” She asked.

A smile came upon my face, Meme was so funny with how adamant she was about not missing school. Plus I knew she had given up asking why I wanted to see Steve, now she was back on the missing school train which made me chuckle.

“Yes Mim I am planning on going to school tomorrow. I just needed a day. Everything is all good, I simply needed a day.” I replied chuckling

“Did you figure out how you are getting home? I’ll remind you I can’t pick you up because I have a hair appointment.” she replied.

“Yes Mim I know. I don’t know who is going to pick me up yet but I’ll figure it out after. It isn’t a big deal.” I replied.

"Well I'll call your mother while you are in there and see if she will pick you up." she responded.

"No Mim, it's fine. I'll see if Drew or Alexis can pick me up. I don't want to bother mom right now." I replied.

We carried on small conversation for the rest of the drive to my appointment. It was a decent drive to the city, a good 30-35 minutes away from my house. Once we pulled into the parking lot, I said goodbye and thanked her for taking the time to bring me before her hair appointment, and got out of the car. The walk to the inside of the building was a blur, almost like I wasn't really there and I was dreaming it. Floating around in my own life like a character instead of my own soul. My mind was racing, excited to finally tell someone, but extremely nervous I was going to tell someone. If I say something, it flips everyone's world upside-down. But if I stay silent, it slowly eats me from the inside out until there is nothing left. I thought to myself over and over again. I was tired of fooling myself anymore, tired of creating excuses for him, tired of trying to ignore and forget what he was doing to me every night, tired of having to pretend to be okay in front of friends and family members. *I was tired of it all.* It's a different kind of tired when it's your soul that is drained of energy, and not just your body physically.

I was welcomed with a friendly greeting from the receptionist. That's funny, I was so caught up in my own thought that I don't even remember opening the door and walking into this building, I don't remember going up the stairs and opening the second door to come into this complex, I can't stress enough the feeling of being on auto-pilot 24/7.

"Coffee, tea or water?" She asked while directing me to the private waiting room.

"No thanks I'm good." I replied.

"How about a hot chocolate?" She insisted.

"No thank you. I always carry my water bottle around with me." I replied politely while following her into the waiting room.

"No problem, Steven will only be a few minutes and he will come get you when he's ready." she said shutting the door behind her.

I sat waiting patiently in the lonely waiting room. I could hear the muffled conversation in the room next to me, but not enough to hear what they were saying. The muffled voices were the only sounds that filled the waiting room. The florescent lights above my head pushed onto me as if the sun itself was directly above me. Maybe it was just my nerves, or maybe I could feel the weight of the world crushing down on me. My phone vibrated and I pulled it out to see who it was. It was dad's friend Kevin calling me.

"Hello?" I said answering the phone.

“Hey Char, are you home?” He asked.

“No I’m out right now. What’s wrong?” I replied confused as to why he was calling me.

“Oh nothing, just need to stop in to drop some stuff off for your dad. Wanted to make sure someone was home first.” he explained.

“Nobody is home but the door is unlocked.” I replied.

“Alright thanks kiddo. Have a good day.” he replied.

“See ya Kev.” I said and hanging up.

I wonder if Kevin had any weird feelings from dad? I thought. Most of dad’s friends always stopped being friends with him after a year or two because dad would make comments about women in front of them or he would give them creepy vibes. Seems lots of people were aware of how dad was, but most people ignored it, or there was the few that followed my dad around like an idol. Kevin was one of those. I heard the muffled voices stop in the room next to me and a door near me open, I knew the session before me was now finished and it was almost my turn. A few minutes of silence went by then the door to the waiting room pushed open.

“Well hi Charlie! How are you!” Steven greeted me with a big smile on his face.

"Hi Steve, you are even taller than I remember!" I joked while getting up to follow him into the private room.

"Yeah I get that a lot! Come right into my office. I'm excited you're here, I hope you're doing okay? It's odd I have you here randomly like this after all these years, and with an emergency appointment to boot. I'm sensing things aren't so good with you." He said shutting the door after we entered his office.

"Well yeah I'm okay. I just need to talk to you about something. Or perhaps to describe what I need better for you, I need your advice on how to help someone." I replied while sitting myself in one of the chairs available.

Steve's facial expression became confused, and slightly concerned while he picked up his notes off his side table, he sat himself down and looked to me for an explanation. The way he looked at me was almost as if he could see right through me, like he knew what I was coming here to tell him before I even said anything out loud.

"Advice to help someone? Hmmm... What's up Charlie?" he questioned.

"Well I don't want you to do anything, per say. I just need some advice on how to help someone with a problem they are having." I replied.

“Well who do you feel you need to help? Why do you think they need help?” He questioned while positioning himself in a more comfortable position.

“I don’t want you to tell anyone or do anything about it. Okay?” I said.

“Well Char, I can’t promise that. But I’d like to help you if someone is hurting you.” he explained.

I looked at him and tears formed in my eyes, the words about what was happening couldn’t leave my mouth. I began to shake, and my eyes got red. Steve's face narrowed and became extremely serious. He put his papers back down onto his side table and leaned forward to get closer to me.

“Charlie is someone hurting you and you don’t want to tell me?” he pushed.

There was a brief pause of silence within the room. I turned to look away from him, I felt too much shame to look him in the eyes. I felt I was betraying my dad, but I wanted him to stop doing what he does to me every night. My brain was fighting in opposite directions, and my heart was being torn in half. But I knew this had to be done, or things were going to get much, much worse for me at dad’s house.

“Charlie, did someone do something to hurt you? Or something that made you uncomfortable?” He added.

My mind went blank. All that coaching I did for myself did nothing. I didn't know where to start, I didn't know what parts I should tell and what ones I shouldn't tell, I didn't know where to begin or where to end. My brain just turned off like a light switch. I broke down sobbing uncontrollably in the chair. Hugging myself to try to get any kind of comfort.

"Charlie, you can't help him. Did he touch you in any way?" he pushed once more.

I looked back at him, my mind caught what Steven said. I was right, Steven did know exactly why I was here, he said *he*, as if he knew this involved my dad. My body was breaking. I was going limp, this is one of the hardest things I've ever had to do. I could feel my heart ripping in half and it beating uncontrollably fast. The tips of my fingers and toes were beginning to go numb because I couldn't get any air in between each sob. I had never felt this much explosion of emotion before.

"I caught dad watching me in the shower." I blurted out.

My head fell into my hands. There it was, I was free. Someone knew now, even if it wasn't all the details I knew, even if it wasn't the worst part as some would say, at least something was out now. The shame filled my entire body like a demon possessing its host. Everything was black while I cried in my hands. I heard Steve talking to someone and I picked my head up to see who was there because I thought we were alone. Nobody was in the room with us, but he was talking on the phone that sat next to him on his side table where his paperwork was.

"A client just advised she's being sexually abused by her father. Please call the police and her mother. Do it right now please." Steven said to the receptionist on the other end of the line.

"Charlie, it's going to be okay. You can't help someone like that." He explained while staring at me, although he didn't look shocked, which is what kept stumping me.

Almost like it was a matter of time before this happened to me. His words folding onto one another and everything he said became a blur. Like I was floating outside of my body again. The uncontrollable sobbing continued and my head stayed pressing against my hands. Having my eyes shut and seeing the dark was easier than accepting what was happening right now, and what had happened. I was scared at the fact the receptionist called the police, and mom. I didn't know what was going to happen, having the routine broken and having the strongest feeling of not knowing what to expect was the one of the hardest things about this. I had gotten so comfortable in the routine because the routine was the only thing that kept my head on straight, that I had such a fear of the unknown. I heard the door to the office open and I looked up to see it was mom, I didn't expect her to drive here this fast. Her eyes were filled with tears and running thick black mascara down her cheeks. It looked as if hearing the news on the phone devastated her, you could see it in her eyes.

“Charlie why didn’t you tell me!” Mom cried as she fell to her knees in front of my chair between my legs, and she wrapped her arms around me sobbing.

Steven stood there looking at us feeling helpless as we both cried in each others arms. Her hug felt warm, safe and comforting. It was something I haven’t felt in a long time. We hugged each other for a while, sobbing uncontrollably with each other while we both held each other tightly. Steven walked back into the room and stood by the door.

“My fingers are numb.” I said pulling them away from my face, and still crying and trying to catch my breath.

My fingers were bending and lengthening in all sorts of directions from the lack of blood in them. Mom pulled her arms out from around me and put my hands into hers to examine them.

“You need to breathe sweetie.” mom said while rubbing my arms trying to force more blood into my hands, her eyes still full of tears.

“Sorry Christine, could I have a word?” Steven interrupted.

“Yeah.” mom replied wiping the running mascara off from under her eyes.

She got up and walked out of the room with him. I could tell they didn’t want me to hear what they were saying but the rooms were so small and close together I could hear every word.

“We’ve called the police, they will be arresting Robert at his house tonight. Charlie won’t be able to get her stuff out of his house until tomorrow.” Steven whispered to mom.

“Okay do I have to do anything?” mom replied.

“The officer will give you a call tomorrow for further instructions. If Charlie wants to press charges she can, but it’s her choice. Most of the time when it’s incest the child won’t press charges. If she does, she will have to be interviewed by many officers and it is a long lengthy process. But at this point we now know about two girls, Liz and Charlie, who knows if there are others out there. It would be better for woman in the future if Charlie presses charges, even if nothing comes of them.” Steve said.

“Okay I’ll leave it up to her, because things didn’t go so well when Liz tried to press charges. They ended up dropping the case due to lack of evidence.” mom replied.

They both walked back into the room and looked at me. Mom was still crying and trying to wipe her tears away. As much as this was horrible to go through, I felt so free. I didn’t have to carry that weight around anymore, or try to sit there and pretend everything is okay all the time. And I knew nobody was going to hurt me at mom’s house. I knew, the worst was over.

"Ready to leave Charlie?" mom asked.

"Yeah." I replied while getting up shakily and grabbing my things.

"No charge for today Christine, I hope things work out for her. I suggest she continues to come see me weekly." Steve said.

"I'll call you." Mom replied.

Steve gave me a big hug before we walked out. As we were walking up the driveway I pulled my phone out of my pocket to six missed calls from dad. I knew the cops weren't there yet, he must have been confused why I wasn't home and why I wasn't answering him. I turned my phone to show mom the multiple texts and calls from dad asking where I am.

"Ignore that sick fuck…. Sorry Charlie I just hate that man!" mom said angrily.

I didn't reply, I couldn't find the words I wanted to say, nor did I have the mental compacity to be able to form sentences about this anymore. I just wanted to go to bed and to be done with this day. My brain was overwhelmed and exhausted, I couldn't think straight. We got into mom's car and began to drive to her house. I guess you could say it was my house too now. It was a quiet ride home, neither of us had any mental energy for conversation to break the silence, also how do you have small talk after going through what just happened and knowing the things you now know. The only occasional sounds were sniffles from crying so much. Mom made a turn into a parking lot on our way home.

“Where are we going?” I asked confused.

“I need wine. I can’t think straight.” Mom said while getting out of the car toward the liquor store.

I sat in the car alone trying not to let the silence consume me, while she shopped for her alcohol. A brush of slight anger came onto me. She needs a drink because she can’t think? How the hell does she think I feel right now? I thought to myself. Maybe I’m overreacting or being sensitive, this was probably a lot to process for her. I had two years of regular exposure of dad’s crap, I had time to process it all, she didn’t. I needed to cut her some slack, I thought. This type of mentality seemed to be a repeating pattern of mine, making excuses for people. Mom came back into the car and put her wine in the back seat. We continued the drive back to her house in silence. We eventually got to her house and I could see through the big front window that Ken was standing there waiting for us in the living room. When we pulled in he came out to meet us in the driveway. He looked uncomfortable, not uncomfortable with me, more so the situation. We both got out of the car, still no words coming from our mouths, I walked towards the door Ken stood in front of and he stretched his arms out for a hug. I walked into his arms and mom came in from behind me and hugged both of us. I had never hugged Ken before, nor were we ever close in any way, but the hug felt nice. We stood there awkwardly on the front deck hugging and we will didn’t break the silence, until Ken decided to speak up.

"It'll be okay Char." Ken said patting me on the back.

I had no reply. The pat on the back felt awkward, I could tell he wasn't used to comforting anyone, but he was trying. Mom walked back to the car to grab her bottle of wine from behind her seat and we all went inside. Ken sat on the couch alone, I could tell he was feeling the room and didn't know how to react or what to do. He had been living here for years, but now I think he felt like a stranger in his home given the situation at hand. Mom put her wine on the counter and turned to look at me standing in the doorway.

"I think we will all feel better if we go and get your room ready together." she suggested.

I wasn't up for conversing or saying any words, I simply nodded my head at her and stood up. We walked upstairs to my old room and began to empty Ken's stuff that was in there. Box after box, suitcase after suitcase, we moved it all into her room.

"We can take care of this stuff later, right Ken? And Char we will make your room how ever you want it. We will also take the double bed out of the spare room and give it to you, and put this single bed in the spare room. That way you can have the bigger bed and be a little more comfortable." mom said.

“Thanks mom. I want my stuff from dad’s house. I don’t want him having the free roam to my underwear and stuff while I’m not there.” I replied.

“I know but we can’t get it until tomorrow. You can wear some of my pjs tonight and I’ll give you some clothes for tomorrow. It’ll be nice we can share clothes again since we are both the same size!” she replied faking a smile on her face.

I could tell she was trying to be positive and optimistic for me. It was working, I was ready for the new start, this new chapter in my life. It was all very new to me and I knew I would have way less responsibilities here and I could actually figure myself out a little bit, figure out who I am and where I fit into this world.

“I want you to be a teenager here, not a house wife like at your dad’s house. Got it?” she instructed.

“Alright.... Ill try my best, it will be an adjustment though so please cut me some slack. I’m used to being the mother of the house, that now it’ll be difficult to try to get a teenager mentality again.” I replied.

This was hard enough, I felt she was expecting me to act different, but I didn’t know how to and I didn’t know exactly what she wanted from me. I didn’t even know who I was at this point. I was just the extension of what dad created, I didn’t really know my interests or personality because I was just this numb ghost on auto pilot who occasionally played video games. Ken came upstairs and helped mom switch the beds. I looked at my phone to see more missed calls from dad and more texts.

“He’s still calling me...” I said hesitating.

Mom and Ken looked at each other with this concerned and annoyed look on their faces, and then they turned back to look at me.

‘Just put your phone away.” mom said.

“Yeah Char, don’t even bother with your phone tonight.” Ken agreed.

“Do you have an Android charger? My phone is going to die and I’d like to talk to Jackson tonight and tell him what’s going on if that’s alright.” I asked.

“No we don’t have any Android chargers. We both use iPhones. Jackson will understand I’m sure. I also don’t think you should be worried about Jackson right now.” mom replied.

I wasn’t worried about him, I just wanted to talk to him. I pretty much went MIA all day today because I was anticipating about what was going to happen at the appointment with Steven. I assumed he must have been slightly worried because I got a few texts from him. Plus words and rumours get around quickly in Woodfellow that I wanted to be the first person to say something to Jackson about this instead of some twisted version that he would hear from the people in that small town. I snuck in the bathroom and texted Jackson quickly before my phone died.

“Hey I’m not going to be able to text until tomorrow. It’s a really long story but my phone is going to die and I have no charger until tomorrow. I’m living at my mom’s house now. Night xox” I texted.

I tossed my phone onto the freshly made bed and kept hauling Ken’s boxes out of my new room. I enjoyed having to do something to keep me busy. If I didn’t have to move these boxes and clean this room out, I’d probably just be sitting there feeling sorry for myself, crying, or replaying everything that just happened. Ken moved the treadmill out of the room and brought it in the basement. The room now consisted of a double bed, blinds and nothing else. It was empty and echoed, the walls were bare and the closet was hollow.

“Is this going to be okay until we get your stuff from your dad’s house tomorrow?” mom asked.

“Yeah it’s fine. I’m all set.” I replied.

“Don’t worry about going to school this week. I’ll be emailing your teachers tomorrow. Let’s spend this week getting you all set up and dealing with the cops and how you’d like to proceed about this situation.” She said.

I nodded as I looked around my new room. I was thankful I didn't have to deal with school this week. With the way I was feeling, the last thing on this planet I wanted to do was go to school and have to fake a smile some more in front of people. I was tired of faking that smile.

"Maybe you should go take a shower, you might feel better after." mom suggested.

I agreed and she went into her room to get me some pjs for the night. It felt weird to think I was going to shower in a bathroom where I didn't feel eyes on me, it was a privacy feeling I hadn't felt in a long time. It was also a little triggering when someone suggested for me to take a shower, because dad used to push for me to shower, then I found out why. Mom walked with me to the bathroom to show me how the new shower head works and where her shampoo and conditioner was.

"Ken hooked the taps up incorrectly on accident. So hot is cold and cold is hot… You going to be okay?" mom kept asking.

I think it was because I remained emotionless and expressionless, I had no more mental energy.

"Yes." I replied with a narrow face.

I didn't know how else to answer her. I felt like I should be more sad about this, but I wasn't. I didn't feel good about it, but I wouldn't say I felt sad. I always knew in the back of my mind since my abuse started that this day would hopefully, eventually come. And if this day didn't come, that would mean I was a dead soul walking around in a piece of flesh, being nothing but a slave to a sick man. Mom's house wasn't a place I particularly wanted to move, but maybe things changed over the years since Liz moved on her own now, and it would be good here now since me and Liz clashed together so much. Maybe we wouldn't clash anymore because we both went through this with the same man? I held the pjs in my hand looking around on the floor. Wait….. I thought to myself. There isn't a vent here to put my clothes on so nobody can see me. I'm safe here. I coached myself. Nobody would be watching me here, dad doesn't live here remember, I repeated in my head. I plopped the pjs on the bathroom vanity and began to undress. The bathroom was already filling with steam from the hot water. I got into the shower and plunged my head under the burning water, washing away all the dried up salty tears from the day. The shower felt so uncomfortable, almost like I carried that anxiety from dads house to here. I felt eyes on me even though nobody was watching. The thought I had earlier about the possibility of not feeling eyes on me, seemed to be unrealistic at this point, almost like it was permanently embedded in my head now no matter where I go. I sat on the shower floor for a while with my eyes shut, letting the water fall down on me and wash away all my thoughts. I wonder if the cops went there yet. I wonder what dad is thinking right now. I wonder if he's going through my underwear drawer since I'm not there. I wonder if Drew knows. I heard a knock on the bathroom door which snapped me out of my brain.

"Charlie are you okay? You've been in there for over fourty-fire minutes. Are you okay?" mom said frantically.

“I’m good. Just getting out.” I replied, picking myself up off the shower floor and turning the water off.

I put the pjs on and opened the door of the bathroom. A rush of steam left the bathroom behind me, almost like I was exiting a space shuttle. The bathroom door opened up to the living room. Liz was here, sitting on the couch with a pale look on her face looking at me. Ken sat across from her with mom.

“Hi Char. You okay?” Liz asked.

“Yeah I’m good.” I replied.

It’s almost like those three words were the only ones I knew now, or the only ones I was capable of saying. My brain was too exhausted to come up with another bundle of letters and words to phrase together to make anything else come out of my mouth. All three of their eyes beaming at me as I stood awkwardly wondering what I should say.

“Mom told me what happened and I came here as soon as I got off the phone with her.” Liz said.

“Yeah.” I replied while looking at the ground and making my way to the couch to sit next to her. “I......I believe you now...” I stuttered while breaking down again crying.

Liz hugged me tightly. All the anger I ever felt toward her just melted away. I knew she went through what I went through, who knows what else. I was angry at myself for ever doubting her, I felt stupid and blind. It made me realize how someone like dad can manipulate people so easily, how they can use small things to paint a picture of something they want everyone to see. I wondered for a brief moment what dad was going to say to manipulate people once the news about me moving out escaped. The night went on for a while, we all sat on the couch talking about what was coming our way in the near future with court and everything. I knew I wanted to press charges, I didn't want him to repeat this to anyone else. Even if nothing came of it, at least if he was charged, people would have a better idea of who he is.

"Tomorrow we will have to go to the cop station and discuss this. The cop called me while you were showering Charlie and said they arrested Robert and he's being put in a holding cell until tomorrow. They are also re-opening Liz's case as now there isn't a doubt she was lying years ago and this has now happened again. They also warned me that sometimes more girls will come forward once they see one girl is strong enough to press charges, so don't be surprised if that happens." mom explained.

I didn't say much, the occasional yes, no or nod. The words didn't come to me like they normally did, and Liz seemed to be more prepared for what was about to come. Maybe she was a little excited to finally have her chance at making dad liable for something in his life, maybe she was just happy she wasn't shut up anymore by people about her story. Maybe it was the fact she knew she wasn't alone now, she had someone to share the trauma with, or maybe it wasn't as hard because it wasn't her biological dad, but that was unlikely because my dad pretty much raised her.

"Maybe once you get settled here you can come over to my house and we can talk about what happened to me. Only if you're comfortable with that." Liz offered.

My head lifted to look at her. I wanted to know, I was anxious to find out how similar things between us were or if they were completely different. Maybe dad abused me in a different way because I was his actual biological daughter? I nodded to her and we continued to talk for what felt like deep into the night.

"We will talk also about what he did to me during our marriage... Liz already knows, but I always hid this from you Char because he was your dad and I didn't want you to hate him." mom said.

"Why did you even let me live there without telling me?" I snapped.

"The officers told me not to tell you because they figured it was highly unlikely he would abuse you because you're his blood related daughter. Liz was a step daughter, they figured Liz's circumstances were different from yours because you're his actual daughter. It was extremely hard for me to sit here and let you boast about how awesome your father was, and me and Liz had to sit here and chew holes through our tongues. I worried about you every night while you lived there Char..." mom responded while tearing up again.

It was baffling to me how much one man could affect so many lives negatively, and still be out and about living his best life. Hopefully me coming out will be the end of the sick career he had going on behind the scenes. Mom let me have a glass of wine that night, she wasn't as cool with me having a drink underage, than dad was. Although I knew now why dad wanted me and my friends to drink, because we were easier to target then. Mom and Ken drank a little too much and I could see the grogginess in their eyes and the slow blinks. Liz eventually left to go back to her house and mom followed me upstairs to go to bed. I got into my new bed and she tucked me in like I was five years old again. She pushed the blankets under me all around my legs and torso, till I was wrapped up tightly like a mummy. It felt nice to have this moment with her, as we never really did have any type of bonding during my adolescent years because we either didn't get along, or I was living at dad's house. I appreciated the glass of wine which made me feel pretty sleepy, it helped me fall asleep faster instead of me sitting in my head thinking about everything over and over again, and worrying about the future when I wasn't even sure how it was going to go. I needed the sleep after the day I had, and I figured tomorrow wasn't going to be any easier, a good nights rest was needed.

The next morning I woke up feeling hung over, not from the small glass of wine but from life itself and the events that took place yesterday. I jumped out of bed and made my way downstairs to see mom and Ken in the kitchen. Ken was making a coffee with his face plunged into his phone. I could smell a familiar smell but I couldn't make out what is was, something from when I was younger.

“Morning Charlie! I hope you slept okay. I’m making you some waffles like I used to. I wasn’t sure what your preferences are now but hopefully these will do.” mom said.

“I knew I could smell something good! I like them still, thanks for making me breakfast. I slept good actually, the big bed is nice. Weird with an empty room though.” I replied feeling slightly enthusiastic about the day because I knew I was getting my stuff from dad’s house today.

“Mornin’ Char!” Ken said after taking a gulp from his coffee.

“Are you working today Ken or are you coming with us to the cop station?” I asked.

“I’m working, it’s just you and your mom today.” he replied while stepping out of the kitchen.

“We are going to get ready then we will leave.” mom said.

“I need some clothes.” I said chuckling.

“Oh shit I forgot you didn't have anything here!” Mom said while putting her coffee down and rushing upstairs.

A few moments later she came back down with some jeans and a t-shirt for me. I quickly got dressed and ate my breakfast. This time mom sat and ate with me, which was weird because she never did that in the past. I could tell her and Ken drank more after I went to bed, she seemed a bit rough today, perhaps it was a mix of stress and excessive alcohol.

"Are you ready for today?" mom asked trying to feel around the situation.

"I think so, maybe it will suck when I'm actually there. But for right now I feel decent actually. Maybe my brain just hasn't registered what I need to do there." I replied.

"I'm glad you are strong enough to do this Charlie, not many girls are." mom said.

"I know mom. It's something that needs to be done." I replied.

I quickly finished my breakfast and headed out the door with mom. I was excited to get done at the cop station, that way I could go get my stuff out of dad's house. It made me feel even more violated than I already was that he had free access into my room with all my stuff while I was gone. I kept picturing him going into my dirty clothes and smelling my underwear and it made me cringe. Mom kept my mind off everything the entire ride to the cop station where my interview was going to take place. Part of me felt like this was nothing, I could do this no problem, especially after talking about it with Steven already. Then the other half of me felt like nobody was going to believe me and I should just not talk about it and forget it ever happened. Every time that thought ran into my head I would remind myself that I'm doing this for a reason, that it doesn't happen to any other girl after me. I was going to be his last one that he would ever hurt, no girl would ever feel that empty and numb from his selfishness ever again.

We got to the cop station and I could feel myself holding my breath as we walked into it. Cops always made me nervous to begin with, dad never had nice things to say about them while we were growing up, for that reason, it was drilled in my head to not like or trust them. It was going to be hard for me to ward out that stuff dad implanted in my brain, I underestimated how lengthy that process actually was of retraining your brain to think a certain way instead of the old way.

"Charlie, stop holding your breath!" mom said as we entered the building.

"Sorry, I'm trying. How could you even tell?" I said while letting a big gust of air out.

"Because I can tell." she responded.

A big tall man in uniform greeted us as we walked in. I mean, this guy was absolutely huge. He stood straight up and beamed at me looking at me directly in the eyes. He stood what looked like almost seven feet tall, I'm not very good at estimating, but he was the tallest man I had ever seen in real life. His face was serious and narrow as he looked at me with paperwork in his hands.

“Are you Charlie? We have a room ready for you.” He said holding his pen and paper.

‘Yes I’m Charlie.” I hesitated to reply, I felt extremely intimidated all of a sudden by this entire process.

“Follow me, Christine please go see the receptionist. You have some things you need to sign and someone will need to give you some directions about how this works.” he replied.

“Okay.” mom said while making her way to the reception desk.

She turned and looked back at me while I followed the beast of a police officer into the back interview rooms. I didn’t want to leave her, I wanted her to come with me, but I knew she couldn’t and I had to go alone. This cop seemed to be annoyed with his job today and it made me feel like I was a hassle, like I was burdening him by reporting my abuse. Seems most of my life I’ve had this feeling, *a burden.*

“You’ll be okay hunny. I love you. Good luck.” mom whispered to me.

“Love you too.” I replied while turning back to the monster officer.

He looked impatient, he looked annoyed with me that I wanted to talk with my mom first. This wasn't the best way to start this interview, I hoped this wasn't the person that was going to be questioning me because I would surely just give up and leave. I followed the police officer into a small questioning room. The lights were dim in there and once the door was shut you couldn't hear anything outside of the room, nor could you open it from the inside.

"Please wait in here and a constable will be with you soon." he said while leaving me in the room alone.

It was awkward. A plain white metal table was on the left hand side of the room with a crappy plastic chair in front of it. I sat on the other side of the table on another crappy plastic chair. A black small video camera hung from the right side ceiling pointing directly at me. A small red light was flashing on the side of it, and I knew it was on, recording me, a feeling I was already used to from dad's house. The latch of the door opened slowly and a thick blond woman came in with a smile on her face. She wasn't wearing a uniform or anything, just business attire. She seemed pleasant and vibrant which made me feel better about this process. Although it was still difficult for me to get comfortable when I felt like a criminal sitting inside this room. I assumed this is where they interview the robbers, killers or other witnesses, this for sure wasn't the ideal room to interview a victim.

"Hi Charlie. My name is Constable Caron, I'm going to be asking you some questions about what happened with Robert. I assume Robert is your father? Is that okay?" she said.

"Hi... Yes he's my dad.." I replied nervously.

"Your mom has given us permission to speak to you about your father, is that alright? Is it okay if I refer to him as your dad instead of Robert? If at any point you need a break or you don't want to talk anymore, that's completely fine, we can stop, and if you don't know the answer to something, just say so." she said.

"Okay, yes that's all alright." I hesitated.

"Also if you haven't noticed this will be done under video surveillance. Everything that is said here today can be used in court. I need you to reply loudly and clearly if your answer is yes or no to that. And please look at the camera when you answer." she added.

"Yes that's okay." I replied looking at the camera.

*Am I a criminal?* The thought ran through my head. Is this how they interview all abuse victims? If so this is terrible, it's no wonder why everybody backs out of doing this. Her questions began slow. What's my name, my age. What school do I go to. Where was dad's house located, what was it like there at first. After some time the questions slowly began to get more detailed. She would ask things like what dad was doing around the house that made me uncomfortable. What was he saying to me… What was he doing to me... As the questions progressed I could feel the feelings of yesterday coming back up. I tried to hold it together through the interview and I managed to for most of it up until the end. It felt like I was in there all day but it was only a couple hours. Although a couple hours in a windowless room with minimal light and not seeing anyone but the same person can seem like it was longer than it was. The questions continued to progress more and more. What colour was his robe, how do you know he was masturbating, do you know what masturbating is, how do you know it was his hand on your butt.... They continued to get more and more deeper. Some I didn't even know how to answer without sounding completely sarcastic and angry.

"I understand these questions might seem odd, but a lot of these details are forgotten over time. That's why if this goes to court, we need as much detail as possible for the judge while it's all fresh." she explained. "We're almost done though." she added.

The questions began to get more dark. When he would walk around naked, was he erect or aroused? How would you know if he was erect? Did he ever ask you to touch him? What colour and type of pjs were you wearing the night he touched you? My body was clenching tighter and tighter with every gross question, my brain was brought back to being at dad's house. Having to rethink about all these little details was killing me. I wasn't concerned about what colour my pjs were when I caught my own father's hand in my pants, why were these questions even relevant? I began to get angry, my tears dried up and I was no longer upset with the situation, more so angry at these questions. It's also hard to remember things when you've spent a great deal of time trying to suppress them. After she realized I couldn't really remember these small details, Constable Caron stood up from her metal chair and nodded with a small wave to the camera.

“That’s all we need for today, you can join your mom and we will call your mom with updates once we have them. Stay strong girly.” she said while flagging me to the door.

I cleaned the tears off my face and left the interview room and joined my mom in the waiting room. I felt judged and criminalized after being here, I knew that wasn’t their intent and they have a process to follow, but man was this brutal. Mom gave me a big hug and then we walked out of the cop station. A part of me felt as if I lost thirty pounds and finally it was done, but I was also filled with contemplating thoughts. Did I say everything that I remembered? What if I missed a small detail that maybe was valuable? Did I leave anything out? I also had some more guilt from reporting my own father, it’s mentally hard to accept that your own parent sexually abused you. Then I would be filled with shame that I even felt guilty about it, I didn’t abuse me, dad did, he did this to himself. Reporting an abuser doesn’t ruin their reputation, it makes it more accurate, at the time my brain could barely register that concept. Nobody ever talks about the aftermath of these kinds of situations, nobody talks about having to grieve someone who seriously hurt you, someone who raised you. You love them but hate them at the same time, it’s the most complex fight inside your head that you can’t explain to people without it either coming out wrong or it confusing people, confusing people who haven’t dealt with a narcissistic parent before. I loved my dad, the good part of him. I missed him, and felt extremely guilty for reporting him. But the other half of me knew he did something really wrong, and he did something that really hurt me, and this wasn’t a one time thing, this was a regular repeated occurrence that he does this. It is no longer a mistake at that point, it's pathological and will continue to happen again and again. Dad was a liar, and has gotten away with it before. People like him don't ever stop sexually abusing people, they just get better at hiding it in order to avoid getting caught again. Was he even sorry he did this to me? Did he not think it would affect me in any way? Did he feel guilt when he did it, or did it to Liz? Would he feel bad about doing it to another girl? *No, he wouldn't.* That's why this has been repeated, because his own needs are more important than another persons life. He would tell me when I lived there that women who are raped are their own problems because they allow something that was maybe five minutes of pain, affect their entire lives. Spoken from a true sociopath. Meanwhile he has no concept that that five minutes of trauma rewires how your brain thinks for the rest of your life. He never will have any care for others, even though he likes to think he does. This constant battle is something that stays inside you for a long time, and it's a very nasty fight in the beginning. All these thoughts passed through my head on the way home as I gazed outside the window watching the fields and trees as we drove by. My phone started ringing and I turned the screen to see who it was, part of me felt like it was dad but I knew he wasn't allowed to call me anymore.

"Aren't you going to get that?" mom asked.

"It's an unknown number." I replied.

"Answer it, maybe it's the police station and they need something else from us. Better answer before we are almost home." mom said.

“Hello?” I said answering the phone.

“Charlie?” a girl’s voice said.

It sounded familiar but I couldn't think of where I heard this voice from. It had for sure been a long time since I’ve heard it, and she knew my name?

“Who is this?” I questioned.

“It’s Tania……. I know you don’t want to talk to me but I heard what happened with your dad… Are you okay?” she replied.

I was confused as to why she was calling me, and how she heard about this already and where she may have heard it from. Also why would she even care about me or what happened after all these years? I debated in my head whether or not I should just hang up the phone on her, or if I should hear her out.

“Yeah I’m good.” I replied hesitantly.

“Are you driving right now? Can you call me when you have some time to talk? It’s very important.” She asked.

“Yeah I’m in the car with my mom on my way home from the cop station. I’ll be home in like twenty minutes, I can call you then.” I replied.

“Okay I’ll have my phone next to me waiting for you. Talk to you soon!” Tania replied hanging up the phone.

“Well that’s extremely weird.... It was Tania... Not sure if you even remember her...” I said to mom.

“Really? Yes I remember you and her use to hang out. What did she want?” mom questioned to me with a confused look on her face.

“I’m not sure, she wants to talk or something. She heard about this situation somehow...” I replied.

“That’s really odd. I’m anxious to hear what she has to say about it or what she would even have to do with it.” mom replied.

The car was silent for the rest of the ride home. I felt anxious that Tania called, it was so random to me. How did she know something happened with dad? Who would of told her this fast? Maybe she heard it at school because all my teachers knew and maybe one of them slipped up and said something. My mind wandered around in circles with the possibilities. Once, we got home I raced upstairs to call her back.

“Hey Tania?” I asked.

“Yeah Charlie. I want to talk to you if that’s okay?” She replied.

“Yeah that’s fine, it’s nice to hear from you. How have you been?” I replied.

“I’ve been okay I guess. Been a little mind fucked since I heard about what happened to you. Do you remember the last night I ever slept at your house?” she asked.

“Yes I do...” I replied confused.

“Well your dad did some stuff to me that night…” She replied.

That’s when my head immediately put all the puzzle pieces together about that night. Dad has always had his eye on Tania every time she came over. That’s why she never wanted to come over again after that night. My heart raced, I wanted to know exactly what happened that night. It now made sense why she was calling me.

“What happened?” I asked while mentally preparing myself for more awful news about my sick dad.

Steven and the cops were right, more women were going to come forward now that I came forward about his abuse.

“Well I heard you went to the cops, and it sort of encouraged me that maybe I should go too… But I wanted to talk to you first before I went to make sure you are okay with all of it.” she replied.

"Yes I'm pressing charges. What did he do?" I questioned again.

"Well this is sort of hard for me to talk about. I've only ever told my boyfriend about this, my parents don't even know....The last night I spent there was a very bad one. I was always comfortable with your dad because he was always so nice to me, almost like a friend. And it was nice because you know I was never close with my parents. Well after you went to bed me and him sat on the front porch talking for hours, just about random stuff, like my parents and his parents and stuff like that. I told him about my ex-boyfriends and how they were mean to me and I felt like I could talk to him about everything because he seemed to understand and listen so well. Well after you came out and saw us and went back to bed, he sort of... Made a move on me." She explained.

"A move? What do you mean by that?" I questioned.

"Well you went back to bed and passed back out. He asked if he could show me some family pictures of you guys on vacation in Pemtrail and I agreed because he already told me all the cool sight-seeing you guys did every year when you went up there. So we went into his bedroom and he was sitting at his desk showing me the pictures of you guys on vacation, I was sitting on the edge of his bed looking at the pictures on the computer as best I could. And everything was fine in that moment, then he turned his head to me and gave me this awful stare. I immediately felt really uncomfortable, I knew he was drinking because I could smell the whiskey on his breath and clothes. He stood up and sat next to me on his bed. I told him I was pretty tired and stood up off the bed to leave and go to bed. I felt his hand grab mine as I was trying to walk away. He pulled me back on the bed and told me he wanted to talk to me more about my ex-boyfriends..” she said.

“Alright.... Is that all that happened?” I asked.

“Not quite, no. I asked him what he wanted to know about my ex’s. He asked if I had fucked all of them. I told him I didn't’ want to talk about that stuff and I wanted to go to bed. He put his hand on my thigh and pushed his head into my neck. I pulled away as best I could but his hand gripped my thigh so tightly it sort of hurt. My body felt frozen, I was so scared and confused, it was so weird because it was your dad and I wasn’t expecting that at all. He caught me completely off guard.” Tania said as she began to cry.

“Its okay Tania. You can take a break if you need to.” I said.

“No I need to get this out. I haven’t talked about this and it needs to come out right now! Keeping it in is killing me more and more every day!” Tania yelled.

I understood how she felt, I knew the feeling of needing to release the burden on your mind before it either completely numbs you or kills you. I felt for her. I didn’t think dad would of had the guts to do anything to any of my friends. But she was so detailed I knew she wasn’t lying. I knew the kind of things dad did from my experience and Liz’s. I sat in silence on the other end of the phone and let her get it out, even if it was between cries.

“He put his other hand around my neck and pushed me on his bed. The other hand that was still on my thigh, he undid my jean button and he forced his hand in my pants... Like within seconds... I began to cry laying there and he told me it was okay. It didn’t feel okay, I felt awful and too scared to do anything. His fingers went inside me and I still laid there frozen. He told me to open my legs more but I didn’t, I was too shocked and disgusted. My fingers went numb from holding my breath. I didn’t know what to do or how to process what was happening. I told him that I didn’t like this and I wanted to leave but he didn’t listen. His hands were forceful and aggressive, my vagina was hurting from him forcing his fingers in and out. I didn’t know how else to get him off of me. I made up a lie and told him I heard you waking up. Instantly he took his hands off me and jumped off the bed. I got up and came and sat on the couch next to you. I was so scared but I didn't know what to do. I wanted to wake you up and I was scared you would hate me. I didn’t expect what happened at all and I was just so frozen in shock.” She said.

She was crying heavily, having a hard time catching her breath. I knew what she meant by thinking I would hate her. I knew the feeling. I didn’t know what my extended family would think, I was hoping to call them but I needed to process my mind first, I needed to process what as happening and what happened to Tania. People think they know you, family members think they know you. But do we really know what goes on inside someone’s head? Do we really know the details about their lives? People can be very good at hiding things, very good. The fact Tania had the guts to say something to me the next day about dad after what happened to her the night before, it was admiring how much strength she had. Just because someone appears to be okay and good, doesn't mean they are. For some people, it is almost impossible to tell they are being abused. I didn't know how to reply to her. I was disgusted dad did that to her when I was right there and could have stopped it, I felt sorry for her and angry at myself. I felt anger towards dad, I felt stupid for sleeping away peacefully while she was getting assaulted in my own home by my own father.

"Tania I'm so sorry, fuck!" I said beginning to cry.

She didn't say anything else, she just continued to cry hysterically. She could barely catch her breath between cries. I knew that feeling too, I had felt it during my appointment with Steven.

"I think you should tell the cops and I'll support you through all of it. I can also understand if you don't want to, it was a hard process." I replied.

"Thanks Char. I think I will go to the cops. I feel so much better that I got it all out to you..." She said sniffling.

"I cant believe he did that man... My brain is just fucked now.." I said.

"I know, and I felt so alone after because you hated me… What did he do to you?" she replied.

"He kept jacking off in front of me, I would pretend I was sleeping because it was just awful to witness. He was watching me shower.. I would wake up during the night and he would be sitting in my bed watching me sleep, and a couple times I woke up with his hand on my butt.... Just fucked up..." I said.

"Wow…. That's so messed. He's sick." she replied.

"Yeah I always tried to ignore it or bury it because he's my dad, ya know? But that seemed to only make things worse for me." I explained.

The conversation seemed to go on for hours about all the little things about dad we had noticed now looking back, knowing what we know now. Small little red flags or hints. Things you don't notice when it happens as a red flag, then after something big like this happens, all those red flags pop out at you like a stick in the mud. Dad's attempts at grooming were so obvious now, he for sure has been doing this for most of his life because he seemed to be an expert at it.

"I have to get going, I'm supposed to go to my sister's for dinner tonight. Glad we talked. Let me know how it goes with the cops." I said.

"I'll call you right after I'm done with them. We should get together soon, I really miss you and think we need a girls day or something." Tania said.

"Thanks Tania, I miss you too. Good luck with the cops.. And a girls day would be awesome!" I said putting the phone down.

I gathered my things and got ready to go to Liz's house for dinner. I was excited to talk to her about everything but at the same time I felt anxious about hearing her version of things because I never ever knew her version of what happened, I had only heard dad's manipulated and screwed versions that changed every time I asked. At least now I will finally after all these years be able to know what happened to her. Mom drove me to Liz's house, it wasn't a far drive, maybe five minutes up the road. She was waiting for me on her front porch, I could tell she was anxious to talk to me about everything as well because it was odd she was waiting outside for me. I opened the car door and mom stopped me before getting out.

"Do you think, only if you're up for it, that me and you could talk tonight?" mom said nervously.

"Yeah we can. I'd like that mom. I'm feeling strong today I think." I replied smiling back at her.

Comfort rushed over her face as I stared back at her before getting out of the car to join Liz on the porch. Despite everything that happened to me, and now hearing about Tania, and soon to be hearing about Liz's stuff, I felt extremely strong. Almost like the years of being numbed at dad's house prepared me to be rock solid. We waved to mom as she pulled out of the driveway and Liz turned to me.

"You ready to talk about this?" She said nervously.

"Sure am!" I replied.

We both walked into her house and walked into the kitchen. Her house was beautiful, her and her soon to be husband made a good choice. It was a ranch style house with lots of extra bedrooms and a beautiful back porch, and it was really close to mom, and Meme and Pepe. Liz took out a big bottle of red wine and poured each of us a tall glass.

"You're almost of age so I don't care if you drink. I also know you drank at dad's house too so you're probably already used to this. And I think we will need it before this conversation." Liz said jokingly.

I nodded to her while picking up the glass to have a big sip. Wine wasn't my favourite, but it's what was offered so I wasn't going to complain.

"You want to start?" Liz asked.

I wanted to get my story out first anyways. I was more interested in knowing her story and I felt the spotlight has been on me the last few days and it was getting to be a little bit draining. I rambled on about my story with dad and all the things he would do in front of me, basically repeating what I had told Tania. Liz's facial expression didn't seem too change at all, almost like she wasn't puzzled or surprised. When I finished my story, she lifted her glass and took a big gulp and put her glass back down on the counter top.

"Whelp, I guess its my turn now...." She said while taking a deep breath.

My body was anxious to finally learn what happened to Liz. It had been many years that I've been wondering what happened to her. What was it that truly caused the divorce, what was it that made mom hate dad so much. I lifted the glass of wine to my lips and gave it a small chug. The dry wine made my throat queasy, or maybe it was how nervous I was.

"He did a lot of the same stuff that you mentioned he did to you. That's why I wasn't too shocked at all, it felt like you were repeating all the things that happened to me. It began really slow but as time went on it slowly got worse and worse. It started at our old house in St Jameville. He would lay on the couch with his robe undone and he would be all exposed. He only did it when mom was gone and it was just him and I. He would ask me to sit on his lap and stuff, I was maybe 8 or 9 at the time. He would try to rub my thighs while we watched movies if mom wasn't around, he did it in front of Drew once when he was too young to even understand what was happening. I remember I pulled my leg away and he made me feel like the worst daughter ever for pulling away. He would ask if I even loved him, and he would say that this is how all daddys treat their daughters. As I got older he would slap my bum when I walked by him, or he would make comments about what I was wearing and ask me to do a twirl so he could check me out, if I said no he kept threatening he would let our hunting dog loose and it would eat my friends. When I was a teenager he had so many rules for me, I wasn't allowed out and he would go over my cellphone all the time, he was so controlling over me. That's why I started sneaking out and stuff like that because he never let me leave the house, almost like I was his possession. Sorry I feel like I'm all over the place and I'm not sure where to start because it was all so subtle and slow in the beginning." Liz explained.

"That's alright Liz.. Just say whatever you want to..." I responded.

"Some of my friends stopped coming over because he would make comments about their bodies. He told my one friend that he could see her pussy through her pants, he told her he wanted to rub her twat. That was the last time she ever came over or spoke to me. I didn't know what to do because I never saw my real dad, so I thought this is just how dads were with their daughters, especially since he had been telling me that from a young age. He used to take my one friend for long drives whenever she came over because he said he was trying to help her through her parents divorce. Looking back there isn't a doubt in my mind he was abusing her as well because she randomly dropped me as a friend too. I was always so filled with self doubt.. And I would question reality or create excuses for him about why he was doing what he was doing.." she explained.

"I thought the same thing. I also felt that if I ignored it then it wasn't truly happening or it would go away. Almost like my brain didn't want to process how uncomfortable it made me, it just suppressed it for years." I replied.

"Yeah same thing with me. I would wake up in the middle of the night and he would be standing in the doorway of my bedroom just staring at me. The look on his face would make me cringe so hard, it felt so uncomfortable. It was like he was undressing me with his eyes all the time." she replied.

"That's how I felt as well. Sometimes he was normal, other times he was dark." I said.

"See maybe that's because you're his biological daughter. But with me he was never normal. The way he would touch me always made me feel uncomfortable. The tight grips on my shoulders or thighs, or he would slide his hand across my waist when he would walk by. It made all my brain signals blow up with a fight or flight response. It terrified me. It escalated from watching me in my doorway to sitting on my bed. Same as you. I would wake up with his hand on my butt, just like you. Then one night I woke up and his hand was up my pjs shorts in my butt crack and vaginal area. Like he was trying to get to my butt hole. I turned over and threw his hand away from me and asked what he was doing. He said he was drunk and checking on me, he claimed I was having a nightmare..." she said.

"Oh my gosh, he said the same shit to me. When I would catch him in my room he said he was checking on me cause I was crying in my sleep!" I said.

"Yeah and his face gets completely red right? Or white as a ghost sometimes?" She asked.

"Yep!" I replied.

We both smiled at each other, not because it was funny by any means, but it was nice to have someone that understood us for once. We didn't feel so alone, we had someone who experienced the same things. The same red flags. *We weren't alone.*

"Well after he almost went in my butt hole I knew I had to do something because it was going to keep getting worse for me. When nobody was around I went on the computer to google what options I had or to see if there was a forum of what other people may have done in this same situation. I googled a bunch of stuff and spent some time researching, I knew I had to delete the history because I didn't want dad to know I was planning something or catching onto him. When I went into the history I was shocked at what was on there. He was watching all kinds of porn, porn as in like step daughter and step father sex. It was messed. He was googling things like how to seduce your step daughter and things like that. I knew he was going to eventually rape me. I took a picture of the history on my phone and showed mom when she got home. That's when she packed all his stuff up in plastic grocery bags and put them on our porch, do you remember that? The police officers didn't seem to care much because not only were you and Drew on his side, but the cops didn't see much wrong with it because I'm not his biological daughter. How fucked is that!" she explained.

The guilt came back over me. Liz had to deal with all that, and then her brother and sister hated her. She must of felt so alone when everything was happening.

"I'm sorry Liz that I didn't believe you. Why didn't you and mom tell me before I went and moved there?" I asked.

"Well you were a little young, and Dad had you and Drew so brain washed that you would of pushed us away even more. That man would of made a good lawyer by how good he can manipulate and brainwash people, instead he chose to be a pedophile instead. We also were being told by the cops that he only did those things to me because I wasn't his real daughter. So we thought he wouldn't do it to you because you are his actual blood. But nope he's just that fucked up... When I was growing up he had a way of always twisting things to be mom's fault, not sure if you remember their arguments much, but no matter what it somehow was always mom's fault. We figured if we fought too hard about my case, then somehow it would be twisted to be mom's fault, but it didn't really matter because your dad's family made it mom's fault regardless." she explained.

The room went a little silent. We both finished our 3rd glass of wine and stood in silence when Liz broke it after a few minutes. We needed the time to gather our thoughts.

"I ended up hearing from a few of my older friends that dad slapped their butts and made little gross comments to them too. Fucking pedophile man... He would give me more freedoms as a teenager if I would comply with his abuse, he's so manipulative, he literally wouldn't let me leave the house if I would challenge him about his abuse. I felt like he had possession over me, like I was a piece of furniture and not a human being." she said shaking her head.

“Yeah I heard from Tania today. Dad forced himself onto her too. Put his fingers in her and stuff. So gross man, I hate hearing this shit..” I explained.

Liz looked at me puzzled and shocked.

“She probably had it the worst out of everyone then… Wow... I hope he goes away for a long time. Statistics show that most girls don’t even come forward. So if me, you and Tania are all coming forward, imagine how many girls he’s abused that are too scared to come forward. Shocking isn’t it?” She said.

I stood there puzzled looking out the kitchen window.

“What a joke...” I said while pouring us another glass of wine.

“He’s probably going to be in jail for a long time. And people in jail don’t like pedophiles… He will probably get beat up repeatedly in jail..” Liz explained.

The night seemed to go on for a while, us talking back and forth about all the things we noticed and similarities. We talked about what our expectations were of court and how it would go. Mom came in the door and joined us at the end of the night for a glass of wine too before we left together to go back to her house.

"Well are you ready to head out?" mom said finishing her glass.

"Yeah I am. Thanks Liz for the night. Glad I know the truth now after all these years, my brain is a little overwhelmed now but I feel relieved knowing I now know the truth." I said.

"You'll remember stuff years later too. Your mind has been suppressing things deep in you, and one day those things will need to come out. Something will trigger you and you will have a memory of him doing something. They are so random, and sometimes you will have years in between them, but just know that it's normal..." Liz explained.

"I'm sure I remember everything..." I said.

"I thought I did too Char, then I remembered random little things whenever I would look back on everything. I'm sure it'll happen to you too, give it time." she explained.

We got in mom's car and began to make our way home. Mom kept glancing over at me, I could see her in my peripheral vision constantly looking at me. I wasn't sure if she was nervous to tell me what had happened to her, or if she was concerned I was overwhelmed after what Liz had just told me.

"You okay?" She asked breaking the silence.

"Oh yeah I'm good. I honestly feel better as horrible as that is to say right now... But it's nice knowing I'm not alone and it was so similar between me and Liz.. Like our stories were so similar. And I feel better finally knowing what actually happened that caused you guys to get divorced.. Dad's story changed like seven times in the time I lived there and it was getting frustrating." I explained.

"Are you still good to talk to me tonight or are you fried?" mom asked nervously.

"Yeah I'm good. If we don't talk I'll be really curious and overthink everything which will make me sleep like shit." I replied looking at her and smiling.

I could tell she was nervous to talk to me about it all. She looked shaky and anxious, and her foot was heavy on the gas petal while we drove. We got home and she put her arm around me as we walked inside the house.

"You can go in my top drawer and get some new pjs. I'll be waiting for you down here" mom said.

I rushed to go pick out some pjs and put them on and made my way downstairs and sat on the couch. Mom handed me a glass of wine and we both sat across from each other. I was anxious to hear about how dad was with her, even though I already had a pretty good idea of how things were. I remember them constantly fighting when we were kids, no matter what dad was never happy with anything mom did. When you are young you think that's just how parents are, again there I go making excuses. As I grew up and look back, I realize how awful dad treated her.

"By the way, the police station called and you won't be able to get your stuff for another three days because your dad is making it difficult for them. And unfortunately because he hasn't been proven guilty, there isn't much we can do.." mom said.

"Are you fucking kidding me?" I snapped.

This was bullshit, and the remark just blurted out of my mouth, I couldn't help myself. I didn't even have underwear here, and now it was going to take three days? Why was dad making it difficult, that's MY stuff, not his. I'm the victim of this situation and I can't even get my own belongings. I felt angry, I hated the idea of dad having such open access to all my things for so long, and I hated the fact this is how people are treated in these circumstances, there should be no reason at all why I couldn't get my stuff.

"I know you're angry but it is what it is, let's try not to focus on it too much before we have this conversation. Is that alright?" mom added.

"I know it's just annoying wearing clothes that aren't mine for three days and not having any of my stuff while I'm trying to adjust to a new place. It makes things harder than they already are for me." I replied.

"I get it baby, but it is what it is." she said.

Something about that saying seemed to trigger me. Almost like it was a way for people to diminish or demote how someone was feeling. Or it was a way to push someone else's feelings to the side. I understand not focusing on problems that are out of your control, but that doesn't mean how I'm feeling isn't valid or shouldn't be expressed. I turned to look out the window after mom said that, I didn't really have any response for her, it was easy for her to say that because she wasn't the one using her mothers clothes for three days.

"So I want to tell you some of the things your dad was doing during our marriage. If you are comfortable with that? I feel like I didn't really get the chance to explain to you how it was like being married to him all those years ago, and I think now that this has happened maybe I can get this all off my chest?" She asked.

"Yeah I want to know everything please. I'm so tired of everything being left in the dark or swept under the rug." I said turning back to look at her.

"Well.. Where to begin..." She said.

"That's a little funny, pretty sure Liz started hers out the exact same way." I said trying to make a light joke to ease into things.

"That's funny.... well to begin he always had a way of making me feel like crap about myself. He would always make little comments about his friend's wives, the attractive ones.. It always made me feel like awful about myself. But I think that was his goal maybe, to destroy any self worth I had, that way maybe it would be easier to control me." she explained.

"Yeah he always talked really poorly about women when I was there. He would mention that girls vaginas are destroyed after having a baby and become useless and unattractive to their husbands.." I responded.

"What a fucking loser. Sorry hunny I know that's your dad but he's a fucking loser. He used to say awful things to me like that as well. It always made me look at myself in the mirror and only see flaws." she said.

"I know how dad is, you don't have to apologize.. And he made me feel like that too, the little remarks he would make here and there about other girls bodies, it always made me reevaluate my own." I replied.

"He used to make me pretend to be his friends wives in bed, like the better looking wives. It killed me on the inside, it felt like he never just wanted me, instead he always wanted me to pretend to be someone else. And one time he asked me pretend to be my own cousin, who was seventeen at the time. And when I would say no or show that I was uncomfortable, he would tell me that all his friends wives do this and it's all very normal and I'm being too sensitive. He would guilt me by telling me all his friend's wives are super cool with doing those sorts of things for their husbands, and I was a piece of shit because I wasn't comfortable doing it. It killed my confidence and made me constantly beat down on myself." She said.

I sat in silence and listed to her. I wanted to hear what happened in their marriage, I wanted to know why it was so shit and what was going on behind closed doors. My mom hid so much from us to protect us, it's baffling she held herself together so well during all that. Everything she was saying made total sense now that I'm older. I remembered the fights when I was young, I remember the way mom acted and the way dad acted. Mom was always walking around like a submissive woman in constant emotional pain. Dad walked around like he was owed something. It made sense why mom had zero confidence despite how stunning she was, it made sense why she constantly second guessed herself. Because of how he treated her.

"After I had Drew and he was only three weeks old, your father pointed at my stomach and asked how long it was going to take me to lose all that fat, because he said I looked awful. I was so embarrassed. He said it in front of his own sister too, she even stood up for me which was surprising because they all hated me because I had Liz before your dad and I started dating." she added.

"His mother was a demon to me, your Grandma. She would tell Robert that I was a skank and he should leave me because I was an embarrassment. She thought I was a slut because I had Liz before I was married, which was not okay in her books. She would purposely exclude me from family things or make me sit on the outside of family pictures. Grandma's sister even noticed it and would ask your grandma why she was so mean to me. She would tell Robert that my parents must be ashamed of me for having a baby so young. Every time I went there she would talk trash about me the minute I left the room. She did it to all her other kid's husbands or wives. Shes just a nasty woman, and when me and Robert got divorced she twisted everything to be my fault. She would say I was cheating on your dad, when it was actually the opposite. Your father would have women here when I was away on business trips back when I used to sell medical equipment. I've heard the stories from the neighbours. He never wanted to watch you kids when I left for trips, that's why you all went to Meme and Pepes house for the weekend while I was gone. He didn't want you guys around so he could have other women over. That's why Fern our neighbour at the time, hated him, he would see these women come and go from our family home the minute I left for business." mom added.

"Yeah, I for sure knew that about Grandma, she has big favourites with the grand kids too. Aunt Deb's kids were the favourite even though both daughters were sleeping with half of Woodfellow. And Drew and I and Aunt Marie's kids were the least favourite and got treated as such with nasty passive aggressive comments all the time. Grandma made some nasty comments about you and Liz to me also, right before I told Steven about what dad was doing. I didn't think she would ever speak like that about something she knew so little about. I don't think Grandpa was like that though, I think he just kept his head down in fear of Grandma. He always had a weird look on his face whenever Liz was brought up, almost like a guilty face. I remember always going to Meme's whenever you were away, crazy looking back that it was because dad was a cheater, but it makes sense. I remember Fern always avoided him too, he helped you a lot when you guys got divorced." I explained.

"Yeah she hates your poor Aunt Marie, hates her. She used to say that she wished she was never born. I don't even know why she hated her so much but she did. Your Grandpa saw it too. Maybe it was a jealousy thing because your Aunt Marie was absolutely beautiful when she was younger. And your Grandpa for sure believed Liz when it all happened. I could feel it in my bones that he knew deep down." mom said.

"Yeah I saw a hole new side of Grandma the older I got. Its sickening. And Grandpa seems to ignore her behaviour though, whether he believed Liz or not, doing nothing is about it is just as bad…" I explained.

"Your Grandpa came here after everything happened with Liz. I don't think Robert or Grandma even knew about him coming here. But he came here and was trying to get me to drop the charges because he knew your dad was guilty but he was ashamed because that was his own son. He told me he always knew something was wrong with Robert growing up, but Grandma was always worried about their family image." mom explained.

"I was thinking about possibly calling Grandma and telling her. I think because now I'm the second grandchild to come forward, maybe she will believe us now because now this has been two girls that are in direct relation to her that have been affected." I said.

"Just be careful with that woman, she's nasty and manipulative. It's no wonder why your dad is the way he is." mom said.

"I also remember dad telling me about a few of my cousins, too and how he had wet dreams about them and how he would have sex with them in his dreams. Was pretty messed because those are his nieces." I added.

"So gross... What's more messed up is how comfortable he was saying those things to you!" mom said drinking the rest of her glass of wine.

"I feel a lot better that I finally got to share my story with you. It's been bottled up for years and it killed me the day you moved there with him. I didn't think he would do anything to you because you were his own daughter, but it still hurt me badly when you moved there. And people would make me feel like shit about it asking me how as your mother I could ever let you go there, but I had no control over anything. He had you and Drew so brainwashed no matter what I would of said it would of got twisted back on me like everything else always has." she said beginning to cry.

I got up and gave her a big hug. I wrapped my arms around her tightly and we cried together. A part of me felt at piece finally knowing all the details about what happened, even though the truth was ugly, it was better to know the truth than to keep having that thought in the back of my head wondering what actually happened. It was getting late and I knew we needed to go to bed and the night was over. We both put our glasses in the sink and went upstairs to bed.

# Chapter 9

The day had finally arrived that I could pick my stuff up from dad's house, the police were here to escort me and mom while we were there. That three days felt more like twenty-five when you have zero belongings. There was two cop cars that drove in front of us on our way to dads. It was a little embarrassing, they even had their lights flashing but no sirens. Dad wasn't allowed to be there when I was getting my stuff, which made this process seem a little less uncomfortable, I would have felt enormous pressure if he was standing there watching me while I packed my stuff. I was only allowed thirty minutes to get my stuff out of there, and mom wasn't allowed to come inside the house to help me, that was one of dad's conditions. Dad made a deal with the police that I was the only one allowed to get my own stuff, I wasn't allowed any help, not even to carry my futon frame or dresser out, what a nice guy, I thought sarcastically. I figured dad felt this was the only way at trying to hurt me since I reported him. Drew was waiting at the door to help me grab my stuff. He looked cold and shut down, and he made a point to make no eye contact with me and mom, he looked like a walking zombie. Alexis was already in my room putting my clothes in garbage bags and carrying them outside to mom and Ken who were waiting by the front door loading stuff into Ken's truck. Drew walked out to the first police car and began talking with the police.

"Can you please turn the lights off. This is small town and me and my dad still have to live here after all this mess is cleared up." Drew said.

"Sorry son, we have to keep our lights on. It's policy." the cop replied.

"Please I'm going to ask again, can you please shut the lights off, people are already talking around here about this and we don't need more attention brought into this." Drew pleaded.

"Look I'm sorry you have to deal with all this but unfortunately we are required to keep our lights on. I don't know what to tell you son. It's already bad enough that poor girl only has thirty minutes to get all her stuff by herself after already dealing with everything that happened to her, and her own brother is sitting outside talking to me instead of helping his sister who is the victim here, not your dad. Maybe you should re-evaluate yourself a little." the cop snapped.

Drew's mouth slammed shut and his face went even more white than it was. He came back inside to help take apart my futon so I could fit it through the doorway. He was quiet and distant, almost like he was a stranger to me now. Alexis was more friendly to me than Drew was, and I felt more support from her than I did Drew during this time. Maybe it was just his way of processing what was happening, and maybe Alexis just felt awkward about this and was over compensating by being overly friendly. As my room started to look more and more empty, I could feel a lump in my throat beginning to form. This was the last time I was ever going to be here, and see this room. Even though I was leaving the abuse, I was also leaving the few good memories I had there and I was leaving behind the life I had been living for the past few years. Once Drew was done taking apart my futon he sat on the dining room chair and watched Alexis and I finish up the few garbage bags of clothes and belongings that were left. I could feel the hatred from him, I could feel the blame. Little did he know he was sitting on the same chair I had been using for months to keep my door locked to stop our dad from touching me at night. The same chair that was my only defence in stopping dad from masturbating next to me, the only thing stopping him from groping me as I laid in bed defenceless. I thought to myself, I wonder what kind of conjured up story dad used this time around? He managed to get his way out of blame for Liz, what did he say to con his way out of this one? It must of been a pretty good story to be able to now get out of blame for two separate girls, that or people are that stupid. I wonder if my brother heard about Tania going to the police? I wonder how many more girls it will take for Drew to see. Once we were finished and I did my final walk though I went out the front door to join mom and the police officers. Alexis was quick to give me a big hug, it felt warm and inviting, I think part of her felt awful about this and I think she knew silently how dad was.

“Hang in there Char.” Alexis said.

I turned to Drew, he was still not breaking his silence and he remained monotone and uncomfortable. He reached his arms open and gave me a hesitant hug. It didn't feel like he wanted to, it felt like he only did it because Alexis was there and she just gave me one, and he felt obligated to. He felt cold, distant and annoyed. I thought he hated me, which made me feel worse about what was going on. At this point in my life it was clear to me what Liz had to deal with and how she felt, this is the same treatment she received from Drew and I years ago. Losing your siblings love is something that is sure to tear you to pieces every night, especially because Drew and me were inseparable for many years, and now it felt like we were two strangers.

We got in the car and I looked back towards dad's house and looked over it for the last time. Relief rushed over me that I finally had my stuff, even though I already could tell some more of my underwear was missing. At least now he wasn't going to be able to look through my stuff, or physically hurt me anymore. My heart was in constant confusion, nobody ever talks about the confusion during these types of situations, I felt happy about leaving, but incredibly sad at the same time. I guess once you are emotionally abused for so long your brain is left with only pieces now that it's broken, but it's up to you to either put those pieces back together, or remain what you feel is broken. We followed the officers back to mom's house, my house now, where my new beginning was going to start. I was anxious to start organizing my stuff in mom's house and get my room all ready, plus I was excited about not having to wear mom's clothes anymore. We arrived to mom's quick enough and I began to unload all my stuff with Ken while mom was talking to the cops about what our next steps were. I didn't want to know what the next steps were because I don't think I was mentally ready for them, plus I was satisfied with having my stuff in my possession. I felt a lot better that I had all my stuff out of there and I didn't have to worry about dad sniffing my underwear or stealing my bras anymore. Ken brought up the garbage bags and few boxes while I was upstairs in my new room organizing everything and getting settled. Mom eventually came up to join me and helped out with organizing my room, she helped Ken bring my dresser and futon up the twisty stairs. With the three of us going at it like machines we were done within a few hours. It's crazy that within a few hours, things went from being packed up and thrown together in a truck quickly, to now it was all completely unpacked and organized in a new room, I think we were all as determined as ever to get me settled. It looked almost like I had been there for years with how clean and tidy it was.

"Is this going to work for you baby?" mom asked.

"Mom you have no idea how relieved I am that my stuff is here, as if he made it so hard to get my own things.." I replied.

"Looks really good in here kiddo, anything heavy you need me to lift before I go work in the shed?" Ken asked.

"I think everything is all good. I might move some things around here and there while I tinker, but all in all I think we are good. Thanks for your help today, I know it was probably weird for you to be at my dads." I said.

"Anytime Char!" Ken said with a big smile on his face while he went back downstairs.

Mom looked around the room and examined all my stuff. A could tell a few things caught her eye as she scanned the room.

“Is this skull from a real animal?” mom asked holding a refinished skull up closer to her.

“Yeah its a raccoon, I found it hunting a while ago. It was half decomposed so I brought it home and boiled the flesh off, and put clear coat on it so it’s a little decoration now.” I explained.

Her eyes opened wider with surprise, but not in a good way. She immediately put the skull back down and rubbed her hands along her pants. She moved on to other things in my room.

“What is this?” She asked.

“It’s a fifty caliber bullet casing that was fired for me when me and dad visited the army reserve in Pemtrail.” I explained.

“You like these things?” she asked.

“Yes I do.... Why?” I replied.

She didn’t say anything back, and continued to scan around my room. I could feel her judging my things and hobbies, she wasn’t used to having a daughter like me because Liz was always a princess. After a few minutes she turned back and looked at me.

"Is this an okay setup for you? You going to be okay?" she asked once again.

"Yes this is more than okay!" I replied smiling.

"Alright, I'll let you tinker around in your room... I'm going to go help Ken outside." she replied leaving to go downstairs.

I knew why she wanted to help Ken, it wasn't actually to help him, nor do I think Ken was ever working on anything. They hung out in the shed so they could drink together and be outside. I knew they would probably be drunk by tonight, but I didn't care because at least I had all my things out of dad's house.

The days began to blur together now that I was back to school and back into some sort of a new routine. Adjusting to living at moms felt easier some days than others. I knew Ken liked to drink but I never knew to what extent it was until now that I was living here. And because he was always drinking, naturally mom began to drink just as often as well. Whenever they drank it would usually end up in screaming matches or fights between them. Usually the fights would get to the point where Ken would take off somewhere in his truck, then mom would come and pick fights with me because she needed an outlet for her anger. Ken had his own personal demons, and mom had hers, together that with alcohol created tornadoes. They began to fuel each other and everything got really toxic really fast, or maybe it was always like this and I didn't see it because I was living at dad's house. I could tell mom was using alcohol to cope with what dad did to her and her two daughters. I think part of her felt as if it was her fault, even though it was dad who was doing it and not her. She carried the guilt my dad should of been carrying, but he wasn't carrying anything. It was almost like she lost the boundary of what is her responsibility and what was someone else's responsibility.

Drew was coming over tonight, which made me very excited because he didn't come over much anymore since I moved out of dad's house. The few times he was here, he was mostly quiet, you could tell he didn't really want to be here or be around any of us. Although I couldn't figure out if it was because of sadness for his sisters or lack of belief of his sisters. His mixed signals seemed to play with my mind every time I was with him, if even but a few times. I thought all day about what Drew and I were going to do when he came over, I was more-so just excited he was coming over in general. We were always so close and the only thing I wanted right now was to be with him and play video games or something. I needed to get my mind off things, off dad, off mom and Ken's drinking, off the fighting, I needed him, I needed the support from him during all this mess. It was hard for me to focus on coping from what happened with dad, when I was constantly trying to be a parent or mediator to my own mother and Ken.

I hung around downstairs waiting for Drew to come, time always seems to go by slower when you don't want it to, it didn't help that he was late, he seemed to always be late the few times he came here. I saw his truck pull in the driveway and he jumped out to come inside. From the window, he already looked uncomfortable and defeated, this was a familiar look he usually had when he came here. He was quiet and timid, ghost-like almost, the same look he had the day that I moved out.

His face stayed narrow the entire time he was over and Alexis never came with him anymore.

"I can't stay long, I have stuff to do..." Drew muttered before he even said hello.

I felt sad, I haven't seen him in a while and I felt he didn't want to be around me anymore. He blamed me, like we did to Liz before. Even without him telling me that directly, I could feel it clear as day within me. Dad must of cooked up a good story to bail himself out again this time. He was very hesitant with me, cold and unwelcome. I felt even more alone in this situation, especially since mom and Ken weren't a very good support system during all this. I didn't know how to interact with him anymore, when I would try to open a conversation he would shut me down, or if I offered to play video games he would say he isn't staying long. This was hurting me, I didn't do anything wrong and he's treating me like I murdered someone or I'm some sort of criminal. Maybe he was only coming here because dad wanted to know what I was doing here, I thought to myself. Or he was only coming here because maybe he felt obligated.

"I'm only staying for a little bit then I have to go. Charlie can I talk to you alone please?" Drew asked.

"Yeah sure.." I replied nervously.

For a moment I felt brief excitement. Maybe he was only holding back because mom was standing here the entire time when he came over.

Maybe he would open up a little more if it were just us two together. We walked upstairs into my room and I sat on the edge of my bed waiting to hear what he had to say. Drew shut the door behind him and he looked at me with a serious look on his face.

"I have a letter for you from dad.... I'm going to bring it next week to you for Christmas, but you can't say anything to mom because dad will get in even more trouble..." He explained.

I remained quiet, I wasn't sure how to respond to him. I wanted to know the contents of that letter so badly. But I also felt I should tell mom because it's the responsible thing to do. Was it an apology? Would an apology even make me feel better? Was it him owning up to his mistakes and wanted mental help from a professional? A small glimpse of hope coursed through me. Was it him trying to get into my head and manipulate me? My brain once again fighting with itself back and forth between all the possibilities. Anxious yet excited for that letter and to read what it's all about.

"Okay, I'm okay with that." I replied hesitantly.

Drew wiped a tear from his eye and pulled me in for a hug. It was the first time during this entire transition that I felt any love or any emotion from him. For a brief moment, he felt warm and supporting. I needed it more than he would ever understand. *Little did I know at the time that this was the last time I would ever physically see my brother again.*

A week went by and it was almost Christmas, this would be my first Christmas not at dad's house which was a little odd for me. I was always the one who set up all the decorations and put up the tree. I would even bake sugar cookies shaped like festive trees. Except this year was different, mom wasn't really into the crazy decorations, she only put up a tree. It was going to be weird not having Drew here also, but at least he was going to be coming by to see me, so I thought. I texted him and asked about the letter but he seemed to never respond to me. My calls and texts would go unanswered, I knew he didn't change his number because it still had his voicemail. Mom and Liz couldn't seem to get a hold of him either, he simply disappeared from our lives. I wondered if dad brainwashed him again, but no way Drew could be that stupid and naive to believe him after what happened to Liz, and now me, but at this point who knows. None of us could understand why he wasn't talking with any of us, but he still lived with dad. We usually gathered every Christmas Eve at Grandma's and I wondered if dad even told them what happened yet. I didn't hear from Grandma or Grandpa since before everything happened, and I decided maybe I would give them a call especially since it's Christmas and it would maybe be nice to see them. I felt anxious as I wasn't even sure if dad had said anything to them or not about what had happened.

"Hello?" Grandma said on the other line.

"Hi Grandma, its Charlie." I replied nervously.

"Hi Char! How are you doing?" She replied.

She sounded normal, not concerned or anything, not sad or uncomfortable. That's when I knew dad or Drew hadn't even mentioned a thing about me leaving or what was happening.

"I'm okay… Could be better… I won't be at your Christmas party this year though..." I said hesitantly.

"Well how come? Why won't you be at Christmas?" She asked.

The phone went silent on my end. I felt speechless, she didn't even know I moved out. Dad didn't say a word to her at all about anything, he would be able to hide the fact I moved out for a while because she rarely ever went to dad's house. I figured dad would of concocted some story to bail himself out, I never thought for a second he wouldn't say anything at all.

"What happened Char?" She asked again.

Her tone was beginning to be very serious and deep. I could feel my heart starting to beat faster than normal, I didn't know what her reaction would be if I told her the truth, but I was going to have to try. My brain was caught in a corner. I began to cry on the phone with her.

"Dad was watching me in the shower and doing other things... I moved to mom's now..." I blurted out between cries.

"Oh heavens." Grandma said while beginning to cry.

"What happened Edith?" Grandpa yelled in the background.

"...Robert was watching Charlie shower..." Grandma cried to Grandpa while trying to muffle the phone so I couldn't hear.

"What in the hell is wrong with that guy! Again he does this crap!" Grandpa yelled.

"I'm sorry Grandma." I cried.

"Char, its okay. You don't need to come to Christmas, we will plan another day after to have our own little Christmas. I need to go right now, I need to make some phone calls." Grandma said immediately handing up the phone on me.

The line went silent, she didn't even say goodbye, she just hug up. I laid the phone on the ground and sat hopelessly on my bed crying with myself. Mom came up and saw me and sat next to me with one arm around me.

"Was that Grandma?" She asked.

"Yeah, dad didn't tell her anything at all. But I just did. So she knows now." I replied.

"You did the right thing Char.." mom mumbled as she held me tightly.

Mom wrapped her other arm around me and we sat in silence for a good half hour while I gathered myself and cleaned the tears off my face. I took a deep breath and stood up off my bed feeling better after the good cry, when the phone suddenly rang in my hand.

"Hello?" I asked.

"Hi it's Drew....." he said.

"Drew!" I shouted happily, excited he had finally called.

"Do you mind not calling people and telling them what's going on... This is already hard enough on dad, we don't need it to be harder for him!" he snapped.

"Hard on dad?" I asked shockingly.

The phone line went silent. He hung up on me after saying that. I felt my heart shatter inside me, I felt my knees wobble with weakness and water clouded my vision. This was hard on dad? He was only concerned about it being hard on dad, and not me or Liz, the ones who were sexually abused by this man every single night for years. He didn't care about me or how this might be hard on me, dad made the choice to do these awful things to me, but Drew was only concerned about dad. My phone dropped from my weak brittle hands and landed on the floor with a bang. My eyes stared blankly at the ground and all sign of blood left my face.

"What's wrong Charlie? Who was that?" mom asked concerned standing up off the bed.

"....It...... it was Drew.....he.... he told me.... not to tell anyone else about dad..... then he......he just....hung up..." I stuttered.

Mom's face became just as white as mine was. Her soul was equally as crushed as mine. Her son, my brother, had chosen his path, and it was indeed the wrong one. Little did I know, *this was the last time I'd ever hear his voice again.*

The days went by, and it was still hard to adjust living at mom's house. I never could bring myself to call it my house, I always referred to it as mom's house. I didn't like it at mom's, but it was the lesser pain of the two evils if you know what I mean. It was still better here than it was at dad's house, but mom's drinking became a lot for a grieving mind to deal with. But still, I'd rather deal with two drunk adults arguing all the time, than deal with a sick man touching me in my sleep every night or finding new ways to spy on me while I showered or changed. It was hard for me to grieve losing the relationship with dad, and Drew, while I was taking care of two drunk people constantly fighting with each other in the house. It seemed whenever Ken and mom were drinking together, once they reached a certain point they would begin to throw fire at each other. Almost like they were both fishing for arguments all the time with each other. Then if it got real bad, Ken would get in his truck drunk as a skunk and speed off and mom would come storming in my room either hysterically crying about how much she hates her life, or she would be raging fire and blaming me for everything wrong in her life. I knew she blamed herself for what happened to Liz and I, and throwing things back in my face or making me feel inadequate was her way of making herself feel better about her life. I understood her, I didn't hate her, I loved her, I knew she was dealing with this in her own way. I knew she didn't actually mean the things she said to me, but I did resent her for it, almost like an ever-lasting scar that never heals.

It was a month or so after Christmas, I still hadn't heard from Drew or Grandma. Mom tried her best to make Christmas amazing for me, and I appreciated her putting in the effort despite the fighting with Ken. Liz and I began to get really close, which is something I've never experienced with her before, but I feel our similar trauma brought us together. Tania and I spoke often as well with each other, she seemed to use dad's abuse as an added crutch to her emotional outbursts, and she wasn't dealing with this entire process well at all. I decided I was going to call Grandma and ask when she wanted to get together because I missed her and Grandpa, and wanted to see them and maybe talk about everything with them.

"Hello?" Grandma said on the other line.

"Hi Grandma it's Charlie." I said.

The line was silent, but I knew she was still there because I could hear the TV in the background and I assumed she was sitting in her living room chair with Grandpa watching golf or something. Even though she was still there, she was silent.

"....So I thought maybe we could get together since we never did during the holidays.. It would be nice to see you guys." I offered.

Again silence on the line, but her TV was still going in the background.

"..Grandma?" I asked.

"Yeah Charlie I'm here... I don't think we will be getting together. And I'd appreciate if you didn't call here anymore." she replied.

"....But Grandma.. Why? What did I do?" I replied beginning to cry.

Silence on the line once again.

"Grandma I didn't do anything wrong! He did things to me but I have to pay for it all?" I yelled and pleaded.

"Well hun I don't believe that he did anything to you. I think you are trying to get attention and your mother is forcing you to say these things!" she replied.

My brain turned to mush. I couldn't catch my breath in the deep sobbing I was doing, and my fingers were beginning to go numb again similar to at my appointment with Steven. My throat felt completely shut and I began to hyperventilate. How can she possibly not believe me? Or Liz? Or Tania? How many girls is it going to take! And how can she think mom is making me say these things? I barely even talked to mom before all this nor were we close at all, and I sure as hell didn't want to live here after this!

"Please don't call here again." Grandma said hanging up the phone after.

I felt empty inside, completely empty. I was stunned those words came out of her mouth. A woman I've been around since a little baby, a woman that watched me grow up, and a woman that is supposed to protect me, decided I was nothing to her in a split second. I felt like I truly wasn't ever anything to her. Everyone in her family is this big expendable group of her followers in her little cult and if you don't maintain her image, she shuns you out. Whoever posed a threat to her perfect image she paints for people, are eliminated or shunned from the family. I was crushed. My dad rubbed his penis next to me, in front of me and around me, my dad peeped on me while I showered instead of being a father and keeping me safe. My dad was the one touching my friends and touching my butt while I tried to sleep in my bed. My dad made nasty comments about how awful women are and how we are objects. Yet I've lost everyone, and he has all the support in the world. I lost my brother, my grandparents, my aunts, uncles, cousins, I've lost friends, I've lost myself, and I lost the expectation that I would have a real father growing up. I was grieving the father I never had, the one that is supposed to protect you and keep you safe, raise you to be a healthy grown adult, plus I was dealing with everyone else abandoning me. It's already hard enough to mentally wrap your head around the fact that instead of having a father that is a protector, your father is a predator, preying on you at every moment of your life. That is a feeling my cousins or aunts would never understand. That is a feeling my Grandma will never understand. *To grieve someone that is still alive.* That is a feeling that despite all of them abandoning me, I hope they never have to have the hardships that I've had. I hope they are never deal the same hand they indelibly slapped me with. *At this moment, I became a warrior, a lone wolf.*

# Chapter 10

College applications were coming up soon as I'm finishing up grade 12. It was intimidating, everyone seemed to know what path they wanted to go or what they wanted to do, most people had a rough idea at least. I couldn't relate to this, I felt like I didn't know what my interests were and I didn't know what hobbies I had. The only thing I knew was how to be a housewife. I spent years in survival mode, it was hard for me to know how I was to begin my adulthood. Dealing with court and the repeated delays with the court dates, dealing with mom and Ken drinking and fighting all the time, it was extremely hard for me to focus on what I actually wanted to do for a job in my life and Meme and Pepe kept pressuring me to figure things out, but my brain couldn't process everything going on. Part of me felt it would be better if I paused on the college applications and maybe work in general labour, that way I could get my own apartment and not have to deal with mom's drinking anymore, but Meme and Pepe did not like this idea, they also didn't understand the extent of mom's drinking. They didn't understand what it was like to live with her everyday and the constant toxicity and drunken stupor. Again I was shut down by grandparents, it was a feeling

I was very familiar with. My teachers equally looked at me like I was a failure because I was planning on holding off on post secondary education.

We would get regular court dates scheduled for months away, and then the day before it would be pushed or cancelled and rescheduled for a further date. This kept happening because there would be new evidence that was brought up, or another girl would call anonymously to report an incident with dad, but these girls often wanted to remain anonymous and not press charges. Only one didn't care to be anonymous, it was a cousin's ex wife on dad's side of the family. Apparently dad had admitted to her about abusing his daughters in a bar one night when he was drunk. He also said some nasty vulgar stuff to her trying to get her to come to bed with him. At this point the stories I was hearing from people didn't surprise me, because they were so frequent. Even men were calling in and reporting how dad talked about women on job sites and side jobs. Tania and me would take the day off school, Liz and mom would take the day off work to be present for the court dates that would ultimately be cancelled. This often left us in disappointment as we would be sitting there waiting all day at the court house, just for the crown attorney to come in telling us it's been once again delayed. Every time we went they would make us wait in this tiny room without windows and bright florescent lights, filled with toys for toddlers or small children and a handful of really outdated magazines. Liz often brought a book to read or she would scan through the magazines. They had a small vintage TV in there with a Nintendo hooked up that you could only play Super Mario on. This was entertaining to me for a few hours, but after being in there for eight hours straight, three days in a row, it got boring fast. Tania only came for the few days that her case was pending, for some reason they couldn't group us all together in one case, they had to have a separate case for her. Liz and I's case seemed to be dragged on and on for months.

During the court process we found out about eight other girls who were affected by dad as well. *Eight.* Most of which I didn't know or only heard their names once of twice through a mutual friend, mom didn't know most of them either which completely threw the theory out the window that my mother was coaching people, as my Grandma would say. Some were some of Liz's old friends that she lost contact with years ago because they never wanted to come over to our house because of dad. Dad had made a few nasty vulgar comments towards them about their private areas. All eight didn't bother to press charges because they had no evidence or proof, they only called in because they heard what happened and thought they could help our case with the information they had. Tania's case was only being considered because I was a key witness to that night, if I wasn't there her case would of been rejected or dropped. Eight girls were affected by him, and he got away with it for all eight of those girls. It's baffling to me that a man can affect eight separate people, they all have their own individual stories that involve him, but nothing can be done about it in our justice system. Although this was discouraging, it also fuelled me even more to nail him to the wall for me and Liz's abuse. He needed to pay for at least one of us, he needed to be held accountable for at least something. If he was let go for everything, what would make him stop? What would scare him into not abusing more girls? *Nothing.*

Once the rumours about dad began to spread around the small towns that surrounded us, I received more and more messages from people,

people who were affected somehow by him. A few boys dad had working for him years back, some said they knew dad was a weirdo by the way he talked about women and the way he spoke about me while he worked. Another was someone in Jackson's family, apparently dad made vulgar comments about this man's wife's butt, he said he loved how her fat butt moved while she walked. I'm not sure if people thought they were helping me or making me feel better by telling me these things, but it began to shock me less and less, the more I heard from people. It also made me angry because the more stuff I found out, the more I began to hate Grandma and Drew. How could they not believe me or Liz when literally all these people know what dad is like? How can they be this ignorant? I knew none were lying because I've straight up heard dad speak that way about women regularly, Drew has heard him too yet still allows dad to run his life for him. Some were Drew's ex-girlfriends, or girls that he had over previously in the years. All the stories were so similar to one another, weird comments, sexual remarks or awful vile stares. Dad had affected so many people with his sexual urges it was sickening to come to terms with the fact *this was my father*. It was baffling to think someone like this is able to walk about their lives freely abusing people, hurting them, giving them PTSD or other mental illness's, and barely anything is done about it. The fact he could permanently alter multiple people's lives forever, and be walking around and supported like a good samaritan. It really makes you wonder how many monsters lurk in the shadows in secret preying on people. People worry about the monsters in the dark, but not all dark things happen at night, it is sometimes in broad daylight. The shadows that monsters use to prey on people are created by their supporters by sweeping things under the rug. They are equally as guilty.

Tania's court date arrived first, and we were all anxious to see how it was going to turn out, I think it was going to mentally prepare me to see the procedures because I assumed my court session would be the same way. Liz couldn't make it because she wasn't allowed anymore time off, and she needed the time off she had left for the court dates regarding our case. I sat with mom in the bench watching Tania give her statement in front of the court room. Dad's lawyer asked her questions, trying to confuse her or make her story slip or change. This was his second lawyer, his first lawyer dropped him as a client because he wasn't morally comfortable defending a child sexual predator and the evidence was quite substantial that the first lawyer knew dad was guilty. This new lawyer was obviously a newer one, she stuttered and seemed intimidated while in the courtroom with the spotlight on her, she seemed timid and that her body could blow away at the smallest breeze. Tania was appointed a crown by the courts, and this lady was a walking intimidation, she stood strong and aggressive. Her eyes blew fire with every stare, her voice soared through the courtroom like a voice of Gods. I could see the uncomfortable look in dad's eyes every time she threw a questions at him. I could see him quiver like a scared puppy every time she caught him in a contradiction, and she wasn't scared to ridicule him further once she caught him in a lie. Watching him scramble for what to say or how to say things, watching him lose all his sense of power that he painted for himself everyday, was empowering for me. Seeing how powerless he was, was the best revenge because that is how I felt for years living with him. Watching his facade and image he portrayed for everyone shatter into a million pieces on the floor as the stuttering and confusion poured from his twisted lips, watching him hunched over replying in a low scared voice made me feel like my voice was finally louder than his. He had the same look on his face as he did whenever Grandma belittled him in the past, this was a trigger for him, and a trigger I was glad he was reliving. His friend Kevin came with him to Tania's court, it's baffling how that man could be around dad. Kev had two daughters of his own, and allowed them regularly around dad. It really puts in perspective what kind of parent he is to allow his daughters around a man who is accused of sexually abusing and harassing eight little girls. Plus Kev was around a lot when I lived at dads, he saw how I was treated like a housewife, he saw all dad's porn laying around everywhere, he heard the weird comments slip from dad's mouth, how could he be so dumb? Maybe he was in on it too, I thought to myself.

"You know exactly what you did. You pushed her on the bed and you put your hand into her vagina!" The crown yelled at him, echoing across the courtroom.

He stood there, white as a ghost, guilty as ever. Grandma and Grandpa were nowhere to be found, Drew didn't show up to support him either, only Kevin was there. It was like everyone knew he was guilty deep down but didn't have the courage to admit it out loud. The crown returned back to her desk because she was done questioning him, she had all she needed. I was then notified they couldn't use me as a witness for Tania's case, because I had an active case opened against him and Tania and me were friends. This meant I was a conflict of interest and my testimony was irrelevant in her case, even though I was literally there that night. This created a big problem for her case, because now it was her word against his. We all had high hopes because Tania's story was straight as an arrow, dad changed his answers multiple times, stuttered or contradicted himself repeatedly. The favour was definitely on our side, so we thought. The judge pleaded not-guilty due to lack of evidence and the fact Tania had alcohol in her system. They said her memory may have been clouded by the small amount of alcohol. I sat there in the benches with my jaw dropped to the floor. This judge was condoning this assault, even if Tania was completely intoxicated, that apparently meant it was allowed. I was there, I saw how non-intoxicated she was when we went to bed. Maybe that's why dad gave us booze all the time, he probably researched and knew this was a loophole in the system. Tania's face fell into her hands as she sobbed in the courtroom. Her cries echoed throughout the large courtroom, and our crown stood angry at the front of the room. The judge didn't seem bothered by our reactions, for this is how our justice system works in this country. My body was raging with anger and hate. The look on my dad's face seemed to be this subtle small smirk, happy with himself that he got away with it and could continue his malicious acts.

The crown came to the back of the courtroom and sat next to me. She looked utterly baffled he got away with doing that to Tania. Her face was blank, I could tell maybe she had been through something similar in her life because of how emotionally involved she seemed.

"This is so wrong..... This is why victims don't ever speak up, this is why kids keep their mouths shut when an adult is abusing them or making them uncomfortable. We will get him on your case, you have tangible proof and it won't be he said she said bullshit." The crown attorney said.

I kept silent. I had nothing to say at this point and my body was just full of anger. Mom and I stood up and left the courtroom, we weren't going to wait around and watch him leave here freely after he sexually assaulted a young girl. The drive home was also silent, neither of us said a word to each other, we sat in shock. I knew mom could tell I was upset, it was clear she was upset as well at the outcome we just witnessed. I knew that we still had hope with me and Liz's case, plus we had hard core evidence that the cops confiscated from dad's house. When the police obtained a warrant to search his house, they confiscated his computer and all the porn CD's. They also found his "trophies" of underwear in his night stand, and his date rape pills. They also found a hunting game cam he had in my room hidden from me. I didn't even know it was there so it must have been hidden pretty well, plus those aren't the smallest things to try to hide. They located all his google searches and the cropped photos in his computer. They said they found some "sick shit" in there but wouldn't tell us what exactly it was as they knew it would only make us feel worse. All this was in the back of my mind when we were preparing for our court date for our case.

The next few weeks went on like the previous weeks. I watched as mom's drinking escalated day by day, and her and Ken's fighting got worse and worse. Dad not getting any punishment for Tania's case really hurt mom, and Ken had a great way of twisting things to make her feel even more guilty about it all. Mom was a good mom, I think the drinking was just her way of putting a bandaid over her demons, a coping mechanism. The thing with inner demons, is they get more angry when you try to smother them with a bandaid, it was a viscous cycle mom was caught in and Ken did nothing but fuel it more. You deprive yourself the opportunity to heal and grow within yourself as a person if you keep using coping mechanisms that aren't healthy, alcohol is a depressant, which made mom's depression worse.

Our court date was approaching and I could feel my anxiety growing more and more as the days got closer, I didn't know what to expect but I wanted him to be accountable somehow for what he had done. By the morning of the big day, my hands twitched with jitters as we arrived and walked into the building and checked through security. So many thoughts ran through my head, including thoughts telling myself to chill the hell out. Some were negative and whispering in my ear that nothing was going to come of this and dad was going to continue to seek out young girls. As we were going through security, dad was in the line about five people ahead of us, Grandpa was with him this time but nobody else. I wondered why Grandpa went with him this time but not the last time, did they even know about Tania's case? I wondered. I hadn't seen Grandpa in so long it was like seeing a ghost, I went from seeing him almost every Sunday to all of a sudden nothing for months. I missed him, but I was so incredibly mad at him for abandoning me, and taking the side of the man who abused me every single night.

"Do you want to wait outside until he's out of security?" mom asked.

"Nope, I don't give a shit anymore!" I replied with a determined look on my face.

It's true, I felt I didn't care even though deep down I did, but seeing dad tremble like a coward in Tania's trial sort of gave me a new confidence about myself. Maybe my anger was the more prominent emotion that I was feeling which is what mimicked the thought of not caring. I'm not sure but I didn't care too much to try to figure out all the thoughts in my head, nor did I have the tools right now to be able to sort out the mental damage I had in my head from dealing with so many toxic people in my life. We continued through security and finally we got up to the waiting area outside the court room. Dad sat there with Grandpa except he had a different look on his face this time. He looked defeated, he looked as if he knew he was caught and was going to have to deal with some consequences. He looked sickly and in pain. He knew we had the evidence with this case, and it wasn't a matter of he said she said, that's why he knew he was going to jail today, how long he was going to go for was the real question today.

"Come this way ladies, we have a separate room you can wait in so you guys aren't uncomfortable in the same room as him." A security guard said while showing us the way to the room.

It was the same windowless room as before. The bright florescent lights once again piercing down on us while we settled into our seats. I think we were all anticipating on being in this room all day and things would be postponed once again, it was all a bit routine by now. We were in that room for maybe twenty minutes when the crown came in and sat with us to explain what was going on. Maybe this is for real this time? I thought.

"Okay so we are proceeding today with no more delays. Elizabeth you will be speaking first, Charlie you will be going after Elizabeth. We have a screen we are able to put in front of Robert so you girls don't have to see him directly. He will unfortunately be able to see you through the glass but you won't be able to see him, it's similar to the glass we use in interrogation rooms. Legally he has to see you when you are giving your testimonies, but due to the situation, you ladies don't have to see him. Would you like the screen?" The crown explained.

"Honestly, he's not my real dad, so I'm unbothered. I had years to heal from his abuse. I think it should be up to Charlie because it's her real dad and her stuff is way more fresh than mine." Liz said.

"I don't give a shit. Leave it down, I want to see his face when I tell my story. I want to see if he has any guilt in his face." I said.

"Alright so we won't put the screen. Also I understand only Liz will be reading a victim impact statement. Is that correct?" the crown asked.

"Yes I wrote one.." Liz replied.

"Okay, so we are ready to go. We will come get Elizabeth in roughly half an hour and she will give her testimony in front of the courtroom. Remember to stay strong, his lawyer will try to twist what you say, if you stick to the truth then nothing can get twisted and if you don't know the answer to a question make sure you say loud and clear that you don't know and stick to that answer." the crown explained.

"Alright when does Elizabeth get to read her victim statement?" mom asked.

"She would read it at the end, after they've both testified and the judge is ready to give a sentence." the crown replied. "If there are no other questions, I will be on my way. I'll come back for Elizabeth when we are ready." she added.

All three of us waited in silence for Liz to be called first. Not a sound was in the room, our nervous energies circled around like scared ghosts. None of us were even making eye contact with each other. I was mentally preparing for what was about to come, what questions were they going to ask, was dad going to have that evil look on his face he gets when hes masturbating, will the judge be mean. So many thoughts were going through my head, and I think it's safe to assume those same thoughts were going through Liz's head too. I regretted not asking for the screen to cover dad's face. I didn't want to see him while I tried to answer the questions.

"I regret not asking for the screen." I said outloud.

"I think it's a little too late now Char." Liz said.

"Why don't you take your glasses off, that way you can't see him clear enough to be intimidated." mom suggested.

"Yeah that's probably a good idea." I replied taking my glasses off.

"I forgot how blind you are Char." Liz added.

"Before they come and get you Liz, I have a little something for you girls for support." mom said while looking through her purse.

She pulled out two little mini silver gift boxes tied with a beautiful white sparkly ribbon. Liz and I both lifted the lid at the same time, inside was a stunning metal angel wing laying on a small plush cushion. The details in this angel wing were impressive, and there was a quote engraved on the inside of the wing, "On Angels Wings" it wrote.

"It's just a little something to give you guys some protection while you're out there. I hate that I can't go with you." mom said while beginning to cry.

"Thanks mom, this is really beautiful." I said.

"Yeah mom, thank you." Liz added.

A sudden sound came through the room, it was the door knob opening and the crown made her way inside.

"We are ready for you now Elizabeth." she said looking directly at her.

Liz nervously looked toward mom and mom gave her a comforting nod in return.

"You got this baby!" mom said.

"Thanks." Liz replied.

She stood up nervously from her chair and put the angel wing in her back pocket, and she followed the crown into the court room. Me and mom had to wait in the same florescent light room while Liz gave her testimony.

"She will probably be out there for a while, you should play that little video game while you wait to try to calm your nerves a bit. I think your mind will just wander if you don't keep it distracted." mom suggested.

I agreed and clicked the game on after tucking my angel wing in my front pocket. The room was sound proof and we couldn't hear anything that was happening in the court room next to us, we couldn't even hear anybody walking by or faint mumbling. Mom seemed to be right about the game calming me down, I was still extremely nervous, but it stopped the constant questions running through my head and the never ending overthinking. It was like I didn't know how to settle down. This game gave you the option to pick a character out of all the Mario characters, I always seem to pick Yoshi. He was too darn cute, he's a little cartoon dinosaur that jumps over crates and cliffs, landing on mushrooms and eating enemies with his big tongue. I tried to focus on the game, it felt like hours, almost all day I had been playing this game, when in reality it was maybe an hour. When suddenly the door knob turned to open and Liz came walking back into the room. Liz came in and sat back down at the exact chair she was at prior to leaving. She looked different, in a good way. Shocked and shaken, but at the same time empowered and strong, thankful the hardest part was over for her. Maybe I'm wrong, but that was my impression I got from her face. The look she had, empowered, made me feel a little more brave for what I was about to do, but nervous that I was going next.

“We are all done with Elizabeth. Now we are going to have Charlie come in.” she said while looking at me.

“I’ll shut the game off, just go. Good luck, you’re strong baby.” mom said.

Suddenly all my nerves came back like a punch in the face. I stood up from the seat feeling a little dizzy and light headed from all the blood rushing to my head in that instant and my heart was beating a million miles an hour. I followed the crown out the door to the adjacent courtroom where everyone was waiting. We walked up the alley beside the rows of benches which sat empty. It was dead silent in here, not a cough or sniff from anyone. The judge was an older gentlemen, sitting up front facing everyone, a lady with glasses sitting below him gazing at me ready to begin typing the court session narrative. Dad was standing on the left side of the court room, he didn’t turn his head when I entered, he sat facing the front like a nervous dog. He lost weight, a ton of weight, his hair full of grey and his face had aged what seemed like twenty years. He looked awful. Part of me felt sorry, after all, that was my father. The other part of me was glad he was doing so poorly, he deserved it, he was probably tired from having to do all the cooking and cleaning that I always did for everyone. He probably never realized how much work it all was, or he did realize and simply didn’t care. Beside him, a well dressed nervous blond lady sorting through papers, it was the same lawyer from Tania’s case. She seemed more unorganized than last time, almost like this was her first case ever. I scanned everyone in the courtroom while still following the crown up to the witness stand. Waiting for me there was a tall glass of water and a box of tissues. Once I was in the stand, they made me swear on a bible before we could begin. I wondered, did my liar of a father swear on that same bible they are making me swear on? Does swearing on this bible really stop a liar from lying? No, it doesn't mean anything and is a very outdated practice. To some, that bible meant to the world, to others, it meant nothing.

I looked around the silent courtroom. Someone caught my eye that didn't before, someone in the audience. They weren't in there before, they must of came in while I was getting situated in the witness stand. It was Grandpa. When Liz was giving her testimony Grandpa didn't bother to go in the court room to listen to her. But all of a sudden for me he wanted to hear? He sat there alone, staring at me while I stood up in front of everyone. It was a different kind of stare, a sorry stare, I could tell he felt awful for what I was going through, you could see the disappointment in his eyes when he would briefly glance at his son, the man who was sexually abusing his grand-daughters and other girls. The first to speak was the judge, he asked me basic questions to break the ice and begin this process. My name, how old I was, where I lived, where I went to school. It was the same basic questions I was asked when I gave my report to the police officers so long ago. I answered in a loud firm voice and always finished my sentences with, your honour. The first to examine me was my crown attorney, her questions also seemed very straight forward, and direct. The questions slowly elaborated the years of abuse I dealt with at dad's, the constant masturbating he did, walking around naked, watching me shower, sexual comments about me and my friends. I had to bring it all up. As I spoke, I kept glancing over at dad to see if any kind of remorse came from his face. He remained expressionless, not like Tania's case where he kept a cocky smirk, this time he was completely emotionless. He didn't look at me, he faced the wall in front and avoided looking at me at all cost. I figured me having my glasses off would make it easier not to see his face, but that didn't work.

Then came the time his lawyer needed to cross examine me, my crown warned me that she would try to twist things, but she could try her luck. She was jittery and seemed more nervous about this case then me and Liz were, this made me feel more confident and strong, for she clearly would crumble like crushing stone if she had to endure what we did. She was frantic with her papers as she walked up to the stand in front of me to begin. Her questions were much different than my crown's were. She would ask the same question five times but in different words to see if I would trip my story, it never worked though because I wasn't lying, that's why these types of tricks worked on dad and not me, because I wasn't the one lying. She stuttered often, she would also begin a question and then take it back in error and restart her sentence again. I could understand why she was so nervous, she had to defend a child abuser after all, dad probably only picked her because she fit his typical description for an ideal woman. Blond, big hips with a small waist, I assumed that was the only reason dad hired her, that and maybe she was the only one that would take his case that he was sure to lose. And because a more experienced lawyer wouldn't take dad's case, like his first lawyer. Her questions were directly off of what my crown asked me, except she would try to get me to change my story. But my crown was right, it's hard for something to get twisted on you when you are telling the truth, which was very evident by how rock solid my story was and it never changed once, not like dad who changed his answers repeatedly in Tania's case. After each question, I felt more and more comfortable up there, I forgot less and less that dad was in the room and I focused more on what needed to be done here today.

After an hour, they were all done asking me questions and I was brought back to the florescent room where we waited again for another hour. Liz told me about her questioning and I told her about mine. She said she kept drinking water after dad's lawyer would ask a question, that way she could process what was being asked and answer properly. Liz and I thought it was done and we could go home, we didn't know what to expect or what was going to happen next, I think Liz had completely forgotten about her victim impact statement. The door opened again and our crown returned in the room with us.

"You are both invited to sit in the court room on one of the benches as we will now be questioning Robert." the crown said.

We all looked at each other confused because we didn't know he was going to be questioned, we thought it was only Liz and I. We all followed the crown through the door into the courtroom and sat in the middle, lateral to where Grandpa was still seated on the other side of the courtroom. He kept glancing over at me, almost like he wanted to say something to us or tell us something but he wasn't sure how to. The sad sorry look never left his face the entire time he was in there and looking at us. Part of me felt angry at him, after what Grandma said to me, he never stood up for me, but I did miss him deeply. The crown walked up to begin her questioning to dad, she was on fire and aggressive, almost like she was ready to rip him apart. The questions began the same as me and Liz's did, state your name, occupation, and place of residence. As the questions slowly moved on one by one, I could feel the intensity growing within the crown attorney. She began to get more and more aggressive with him and her voice became intimidating, and it was apparent it was triggering dad. She grew more intense the more she saw him cower in the stand.

"Would you agree with Charlie that Tania was over every other weekend?" The crown asked.

"No." dad answered directly.

"How often would you say Tania was over?" the crown questioned.

"Maybe twice a month." dad answered.

The crown chuckled and grinned. "So basically every other weekend as a month has four weekends and you say she was over twice per month, which would put her at every other weekend." the crown replied.

Dad's face remained silent as he knew the crown was not going to let him manipulate anyone here. The crown managed to catch him in quite a few lies and contradictions, every time this happened he was left silent and stumped wile he tried to lie and con his way out of it. Nothing seemed to be working for him.

“What were you doing the night you put your hand in Liz’s pants in her bedroom while she slept?” the crown asked.

“She was having a nightmare, so I thought I’d check on her.” dad replied.

“Right... And you generally check on someone who’s having a nightmare by sneaking your hands in her pjs and touching her vulva?” the crown pushed.

“No.” dad said.

“And explain again why you felt it was okay to masturbate with the door open in your place of residence?” the crown asked.

“I thought she was asleep.” dad replied.

“And you felt it was appropriate to masturbate with the door wide open to porn on your computer or living room TV while you have two children in your home who could have potential gotten up for a glass of water or go to the bathroom?” she questioned.

‘Yes because she was asleep.” dad replied.

“And what would of been your response if Charlie would of gotten up for a glass of water and saw you masturbating?” she questioned.

"No." dad replied.

"No isn't exactly an answer to my question, however it is noted... One more question if you don't mind Robert. As your lawyer is suggesting, you say you were extremely lonely and influenced by that same loneliness to lurk on your daughters.. Is that correct?"

"I was very lonely yes." he replied.

"It's funny you claim you were so lonely that you would molest both your daughters out of desperation for human contact, as you claim. Yet you've also claimed previously that you had an open door policy at your house, that everyone in the neighbourhood regularly dropped by for beers or other alcoholic beverages. That type of lifestyle sure doesn't sound lonely to me." she said.

Nothing but silence came from dad, he had no response for what she just said.

"That's all the questions I have your honour." she added while closing her questioning and returning to her desk.

The judge ordered a few hours of a court recess while they came up with a verdict. We were all anxious to get a bite to eat because we weren't allowed to eat all day. We were out at a sandwich shop when mom got a call that the recess was ending early and we had to return back to the court room within thirty minutes as a plea bargain was received. A plea? What did this mean? I thought to myself. We rushed back to the courtroom eating our food as we walked trying to suck in as much sunshine as we could before we went back to the court house to go back in our awful waiting room. After a few minutes they brought us into the courtroom again with the judge sitting at the front of the room once more.

"Please sit here. Things are going to go a bit differently now because Robert has pleaded guilty to all charges. He's going to get much less time because he pleaded guilty. His lawyer probably told him to to do this because you two girls rocked those questioning sessions and they know there is nothing that can save them." the crown whispered.

We looked at each other shocked, what did this mean then? We sat at the edge of our benches waiting for the judge to give the sentencing, we had hope he was going to pay for this since he got away with Tania's assault. The few moments it took the judge to speak felt more like hours. It was so silent in there you could almost hear my heart beating across the room, I could feel it pulsing through my body radiating outside my feet and throbbing into the floor.

"I'm going to begin by saying I'm very sorry this happened to you girls, and probably more women too for that matter. This is a very selfish and disgusting act for a father to do to his own daughters, including a biological daughter. Family incest is a very disgusting thing. I'm sentencing Robert to three months in jail, with three years probation. The sentencing most certainly does not fit the crime, and I know you girls will be angry at this. Robert took a plea deal and I have to honour that with a lower sentence. Just know he will remain on the sex offender list forever, and this is a bigger impact than it probably seems right now." the judge said.

Our faces froze as we sat silently on the bench. Three months echoed in my head. I'm affected and changed mentally forever because of him, and I endured years of abuse, Liz suffered years of abuse and aftermath, and he gets to suffer for three months. The least he should get is the same years in jail that we had being abused.

"That being said....." the judge added as he turned his head to face dad. "I hope you realize what you've done. The next time this happens, which with your track record I assume it will, the penalties will be extremely severe. And I hope you get the help you need.." the judge added.

This was not good enough. He should at least go to jail for the same amount of time he abused us for. We endured years of living inside his jail cell. And he only gets to see the inside of one for three months. Because we are in the country we are in he will likely not have to stay for three months either, likely a month and a half with good behaviour. My mind was blown, and judging by Liz's and mom's face they were equally as astonished and angry. The police officers put the cuffs on dad and took him out of the courtroom. The judge stood up and left shortly after, once he was gone, we could all leave the courtroom now. Liz, mom and me all stood at the bench grabbing our things preparing to leave when mom noticed Grandpa walking up to us from the other side of the court room. I could tell she felt uncomfortable and protective of us, but I think the flush of anger overrode her emotions in that moment and she was unable to really care anymore about what he had to say.

“I just want you guys to know I’m really sorry...” Grandpa said with tears in his face.

“Unfortunately that means nothing now.” mom snapped back with aggression.

You could see the regret and guilt all over his face. His eyes moistened heavily from holding back tears as he looked into my eyes. He knew deep down what his son was, he knew deep down for years there was something wrong with him, but he didn’t have the courage or dare to say it out loud. Mom looked at him in disgust and aggression, Liz didn't even acknowledge him as they made their way into the aisle to leave the court room. I glanced at him with anger, the apology wasn’t enough for me. I blamed him, I blamed a lot of people, including myself. But in that moment my anger flushed towards him in a focused, eerie stare flowing of hate. My mouth was silent, but I didn’t need to speak for him to feel the energy beaming off of me and the message was clear about how I felt about his apology. An apology meant nothing to me, *an apology without action means nothing*. I turned away from him and followed Liz and mom out of the courtroom. He stood for a few moments in the aisle of the courtroom, staring at where I just stood a few moments ago. I couldn't look back at him anymore, my life was moving forward and that’s where I needed to go. I was ready to return home, and be done with this day.

# Chapter 11

A year flew by so quickly, the days blended together. Days turned into weeks, weeks turned into months, and months turned into a year. Drew hadn't spoke to me or anyone this entire time, not a text or a call, almost like he vanished from our lives. Drew's absence hurt us all, Liz, my grandparents on mom's side, myself, but it especially took it's toll on mom. I couldn't image my adult son estranging me in exchange for a man that sexually abused his own daughters. Mom never could quite wrap her head around why he didn't talk to us, it drove her mad. Her drinking escalated quite a lot. It was almost impossible for her to cope with losing her son, mourning the death of a child that is still alive. I watched it destroy her everyday more and more, I think the hardest part for her was trying to understand why. Why did he abandon all of us, why did he choose his sick father, the wrong that caused this big rut in our family, mom didn't have the closure she needed, she also didn't understand that sometimes in life you don't get closure, it's your job to move on from that without it. None of us could understand Drew's logic, eventually we all accepted it and moved on, except mom that is. Drew began to be just a family member that was around at a time in our lives and now he had gone, almost like he had died. It was hard at first, and sometimes later on it has it's moments where it's hard again. But forgetting him gets easier and less heavy the more the days pass on. We remember the good memories, and forgave the bad ones and accepted Drew's choice for what it was, his choice. Drew didn't seem to care about any of us, it often crossed our minds that what if one of us got sick, or got into an accident? He would have to live with that regret, guilt and abandonment for the rest of his life... But again, *that was his decision.*

I had reached out to Grandma and Grandpa a few times, they never answered or responded. I would call or leave a letter in their mail box which would also be left unanswered. Every Christmas I would make a hand written card and leave in it their mailbox, only to receive no answer from them. They had erased me from their lives, I was no longer a grandchild of theirs. The years of them being by my side and seeing me grow up, meant nothing. I was the same as a dead relative, forgotten, and vanished. I would often look them up on social media, I'm not sure why as it always made me feel like crap every time I did it. I missed them, and I never understood how you can just carry on living your life like normal after estranging a member of your family. I would look at their profiles on social media too see if they even showed any signs of missing me, or missing my presence, and I would ultimately be left disappointed and feeling angry. I saw in one of Grandma's pictures they had stopped putting my Christmas stocking up, all the other grandchildren's stockings were there, but me and Liz's were taken down. Every year she would hang all her grand children's stockings on her stairs, but she no longer put Liz and I's up. I wondered if anyone ever mentioned me, if any of my cousins I was close with talk about good times with me playing in the back yard. These were the good memories I tried to hang onto, it was hard for them to not be clouded with anger and hate.

Things were escalating badly at mom's house. We often fought with each other. She was always under the influence of alcohol, and her and Ken were constantly fighting. I began to get the same feelings of anxiousness and unpredictability I had while I lived at dad's house. Ken was almost always drunk or highly intoxicated. He would be slurring his words often before lunch time, and he did nothing around the house but sit in the party shed and drink himself into a tyrant. He didn't have a job, and when he got one he often would quit after a few months and make up some lame excuse as to why he can't work there anymore. My mother had no concept of boundaries when it came to Ken, he owned her basically, even though my mom paid all the bills and took care of everything, he still thought somehow that he owned her. She seemed to repeat the cycle of being with a man she needed to be a mother too. He was the drunk moocher that made her drink with him, he sucked her down to his level. And she let it happen, she would let him take over her life and invade her boundaries and self respect with his manipulation and toxic abilities.

Night after night I would lay awake hearing them argue in a drunk stupor. I knew eventually Ken would get angry enough and he would take off in his truck and peel out of the driveway. Once he took off, I knew mom was going to come into my room crying because Ken hurt her. It didn't matter if I was asleep or not, or if I had a friend over or not, she would come in and sit on my bed balling her eyes out. She would be full on drunk and talking herself in circles. If I gave any kind of input about how I didn't want to deal with her and Ken's drama anymore, it would often turn into an argument and she would tell me I should be thankful that she put a roof over my head. And I should just deal with it all because it's better than dad's house. She was right, it was better than dad's house, so maybe I should just deal with the drunk stupor that's always going on around here. Maybe I'm being selfish, or unreasonable, or immature. I just wanted a normal comfortable place to live without all the drama and a drunk person trying to micromanage me every second. I knew most people my age didn't get along with their parents, and this added to my feelings of constantly questioning if I was being selfish or not. It was hard for me to relate to mom, because when she was sober she would have one set of rules I had to follow, then when she was drunk it was a completely different set of rules. It was hard to read the room or distinguish what kind of environment I was going to be living in that day in that house. I kept it to myself because the few times I tried to open up about it to my grandparents they either didn't believe me or told me to just deal with it. Sometimes it felt like I was reliving a lot of triggers that I went through at dad's but just a different type of abuse.

That night, I awoke to some commotion sounds coming from outside. I jumped out of bed to look out my bedroom window which faced the driveway. Someone was rubbaging through my Bronco parked in the driveway. I stared for a moment not realizing what I was actually seeing, I couldn't believe my eyes that there was an actual burglar out in these parts breaking into my truck!

I flew out of bed and ran down the stairs. I didn't even bother to wake mom and Ken up because all I could think about was my truck. I slammed the front door open and peered outside to the front yard.

“Hey there fucker! What the hell do you think you are doing!” I yelled while storming towards my truck.

The headlights were on and blasting into my eyes, I couldn’t see what was happening. My driver door was wide open and I didn’t see anyone run away, they must still be in there, I thought. I swung my body around the open driver door to see inside my truck and who was in it. I was ready for a fight. To my surprise, the truck was empty, nobody was inside and not a sound came from anywhere around me. My head turned all around in confusion trying to see what the hell I missed, because I swore I saw someone in my truck. I climbed into the truck and turned the keys and headlights off, and I looked around in my compartments to see what was stolen or missing. It was quiet, extremely dark and you couldn’t hear a thing out here besides the faint crickets singing to one another. As I was looking through my truck, still shocked that someone was in here trying to steal from me, I was also shocked that mom or Ken didn’t hear me yelling, I heard a deep voice coming from beside me.

“I got you now.” The voice said.

I turned in fright to where the voice was coming from, I couldn’t believe what I was seeing standing directly beside me on the outside of my opened driver door.

*It was the man in black.*

He stood there with his same puppet like body motions, staring at me with his big cartoon smile. My throat cleared and my heart froze, while

I sat there staring at him. He slowly began to raise his right hand to wave at me.

"Fuck you!" I screamed in a loud angry voice.

I lifted my arms and lunged out of my Bronco at him! I was going to end this man once and for all because I was tired of being his little toy he could unleash his horror pleasures upon. My hands gripped his throat and the anger poured out of me through my hands. That stupid cartoon smile left his face as I pushed him to the ground and began throwing repeated fists at his face. He never bled, or cried, and I didn't give him any opportunity to fight back. I screamed at him while my fists knocked dents into his cheek bones. His face got more pale than it already was, and all emotion left his face. I continued until he was motionless and not moving anything. His chest wasn't raising or lowering with any possible breath.

I stood up over him and looked at what I had done. My fists and body were covered in his blood, but he did not have a single drop on him. For years this man has been tormenting me in my dreams, and I was finally strong enough to fight back. I was breathing heavily still standing over top of his body laying directly beneath me. My fists were shaking and my legs trembled. *I was no longer afraid.*

It came to my realization that I was having another nightmare, except this time it wasn't a nightmare. *This time I won.* I heard a familiar voice from near me, a voice I hadn't heard in a long while. When I looked up on top of the man in black, Grandpa was standing there looking at me.

“You won kiddo.” he said smiling at me with a proud look on his face.

# Chapter 12

Years later I was a much different person, I never thought I would ever become the woman I am today. I never heard from anyone on dad's side of the family again, even when I had a baby later on. Drew hasn't met my son, and hasn't met Liz's two kids either. It angered me for many years in the past and I lived as a very miserable angry person, but feeling anger is better than being numb. You have to feel anger to be able to turn it into disappointment. Once you've reached disappointment, you have a higher level of understanding of the situation, this helps you heal and grow as a person. For years I blamed the world, I felt like the world or universe was picking on me, then one day I woke up and didn't want to live like that anymore. I didn't want to be constantly angry, I didn't want to continue carrying all that hate all the time, I wanted to be happy, I wanted to show my son happiness.

Liz was right about remembering stuff years later, it's crazy how much your brain tries to suppress things, and then some random smell or sound can trigger you to remember things. I had quite a few of these episodes. I remember when I was about six or seven years old, when my parents were still together and we were living in St Jamesville, I remember it was my first time ever having a shower as I always had baths before. I remember turning around and dad was smiling at me watching me in the shower with just his head poking through the curtain. Obviously at the time I didn't think anything of it, maybe he was just proud I was finally taking a shower instead of having the usual long baths which hogged the bathroom for almost an hour. He's always been a sick monster, we didn't turn him into that when we were in our teens, *he was always a monster himself.*

I also remember he had a friend in Pemtrail we used to visit, a fifty-six year old man who lived in a trailer park by himself. I remember he would make awful sexual comments about me and dad did nothing about it, he remained silent. Probably because he was trying to condition me to that kind of behaviour, *dad was grooming me.* I remember telling dad how uncomfortable I was around that guy, and dad didn't seem to care, he actually thought it was funny. Little did I comprehend at that time it was because dad himself was a pedophile just like him and that's why dad always surrounded himself with these types of men. Because it further fuelled his mental thinking of "all men are like this".

I had spoken with Alexis years later after her and Drew broke up. She told me how Drew knew dad was messed up and whenever Alexis slept there and Drew got up for work, he would always make her leave with him because he didn't want dad to do anything to her while she slept. He protected her, but he didn't protect Liz and I. That was the hardest thing for me to accept when it came to Drew. He knew what was going on the entire time, he would avoid being there, and he would not let his girlfriend stay there without him, *yet he left me there alone every night with dad.*

I ended up hearing from one of my younger cousins on dad's side years later. She was also alienated from the family because she heard dad making dirty comments about her butt to his friend at a family reunion. She felt awful for not believing me, and she felt gross about herself that her own uncle was talking about doing things to her butt. But the rest of the family still don't want to do anything about it, instead they support him. This was the hardest thing to wrap my head around in my healing process, and still to this day I sometimes catch myself thinking about it over and over again. And then I remind myself all that I've accomplished, all that I've been through, and I remind myself I am a warrior. I was forgotten completely from the rest of that family. Grandpa even came to the shop I worked at when I used to be a mechanic. He spoke to me for twenty minutes about how to get his old red truck to pass an emissions test and he had no clue who I was. The only thing that made him realize who I was, was when he was leaving and I said out loud that "It was nice to see you Grandpa!", I said with a sarcastic smile. He felt awful for not even recognizing his own granddaughter after twenty minutes. He tried to speak with me after but I simply walked away from him. I didn't care what he had to say. A couple years after that, he had passed away. I missed out of the last years of his life because of my dad sexually abusing me. I've missed out on everybody's lives for something that isn't my fault, but that was their choice, not mine. I attempted to go to Grandpa's funeral, but I was told I wasn't welcome there by Uncle Junior, dad's brother. I wasn't allowed to say goodbye to Grandpa before they put him in the ground, dad was allowed to go though. The closure I have to this day in my mind, is that Grandpa at least knew the truth now, he was watching everybody and shaking his head in disappointment. He knew now that I wasn't lying about what happened.

Mom continues to hurt from this, she became her demons, she was letting dad win by living the way she lives. She was our family rock, except our family rock was crumbling. I still carry the angel wing key chain mom got for Liz and I in court. Sometimes when I need a reminder of where I came from, I pull it out and admire it and I remember how mom gave us that for strength in a time of need. Life continued for me, I was living that comfortable life everyone else calls boring. I wanted boring, I wanted calmness and no drama. But calmness can only go on for so long before a little riff-raff comes along. I received a message one day from dad's friend Kevin from years ago. It was quite a shock for me and random to see his name on my phone.

"There is a conversation and healing that is long overdue. If you are interested in starting the dialogue to begin this please drop me a message. We need to talk." His message read.

"Can I ask what this is about?" I replied.

"We have all been down a path that cost everyone involved a great deal. I think there is an attempt to mend some bridges. Your father very specifically wants his daughter back and wants to be part of her life and I will assume his only biological grandson's life as well. You can say no and it's understood but I think you all have a great deal more to gain since you have already lost so much." his reply.

“Why can’t he message me himself instead of having his friend message me?” I snapped.

“He has been asking about you for over a year. He has been on me about it, And today we came to an agreement that it was probably time. They say that time heals all wounds.” he replied.

“It’s easy for him to say time heals all wounds when he’s not the one who was wounded?” I snapped back.

“Charlie I am not in a position to pass judgment. I am not in a position to argue. I am simply trying to open the dialogue to get you guys to talk. I will never know what all transpired. I can only go by stories told by prejudiced opinions. Your dad served his time in jail. I am not trying to justify any of his actions. He does not trust anybody or anything easily anymore.” He replied.

At this point his answers were almost comical. I would love to see him tell his own daughter to allow the man that sexually abused her back into her life. The nerve this idiot had.

“LOL, please forgive me for laughing. My dad is scared of people? He’s the one that caused all this. He’s the one who ruined his own life and ruined other people’s lives by his selfish actions. And you are put in this position because he told you to message me and you decided to do it. That puts you in this position. If he has anything to say to me he can say it to me himself and not have his friend message me like the coward that he is. Time heals all wounds he says, so is he going to reimburse me for the years of counselling I had to do? And as for you, if you don't want to be involved or put in this position, then stick within your boundaries and say no next time someone asks you to get involved in such a situation. Please don't reply to me or message me again." I replied.

I didn't hear from him or dad again. I knew I wasn't going to hear from dad because he is intimidated by strong women. He prefers ones he knows he can manipulate and take advantage of. Also, the thing about narcissists, is they have a hard time facing any kind of consequences for anything they do, They take zero accountability for hurting others, nor do they care when they do it. I carry on with my life with my little family, and Drew and everyone carry on with theirs. Men like dad don't change, they just get better at hiding it. If we only had all bad memories of the family that hurt us, letting them go would be easy. But the truth is that we give up a lot of good times and good memories when we choose ourselves over family. It doesn't feel right at first, it feels lonely, and selfish. It feels almost as if you'd rather endure the crappy environment instead of rock the boat. But each time you are in that environment you must pretend like you were never hurt because no one in that environment will allow you to speak. That is the cost of their love, it is not unconditional. The condition for their love is your *silence*.

As someone who has gone through this journey, *I beg you to speak. Speak loud, yell if you have to. Never ever remain silent or in darkness because other people can't handle reality.*

Trauma can be thought about like a giant hole in the ground in the middle of the woods. When it initially happens, it feels so huge, and it's ugly despite the beautiful woody landscape around it. At first that giant hole can be very intimidating and scary. What is the only way to get rid of the giant hole? Start filling it with dirt, for most people that is the hardest part. And that one shovel full of dirt you put into that giant empty void in the earth may seem like nothing, but it's getting filled slowly. It may take months, years, decades, depending on how big someone's hole is. And once the hole is filled, you can still see it. You can still see the disturbed dirt that lays where a giant void once was. You'll feel tired, exhausted after all the work you put into yourself and filling that void. Eventually, things will begin to grow on that disturbed dirt. It will eventually settle, grass will grow on it, trees and other plants will eventually cover it up. For a stranger, they may walk around in the woods and not even know it's there. But for you, you'll always know that at one period in time there was a giant empty hole there. You may be able to tell exactly where it is by a small dip in the ground, but if the wonders of the forest grow over that void, you'll realize beautiful things can come from trauma once you heal it.

Made in the USA
Middletown, DE
27 August 2021